# G CANYON

## DEN OF BIGFOOT

JEFF ENGLAND

outskirts press

Grey Canyon
Den of Bigfoot

v4.0



Outskirts Press, Inc.
http://www.outskirtspress.com

ISBN: 978-1-4787-3240-2



PRINTED IN THE UNITED STATES OF AMERICA

*I tell this nighttime story for Josh and Xander;*
*and with deepest gratitude for the help and inspiration*
*given by dear friends and family.*

# Chapter 1

## MISSION

**PUSHED BY THE** biting night's wind and the pounding rhythms in their headphones, Nicole and Ian pedaled their mountain bikes deeper into the forest. Runner's headlamps provided their light, as the moon's silvery beams rarely penetrated the dense evergreens that lined their path. The sharp Oregon, November cold added to their exhilaration, though it was not only the thrill of night trail riding shooting their adrenaline. It was the task at hand. Weeks of planning and training provided confidence they would complete their mission, and the righteous necessity of their actions drove them further into the Rogue River National Forest.

They rounded a corner seeing the same thing too late to stop, crossing into a wall of thick fog. Blindly they rode on, their headlamps glaring the damp, glistening mist swirling around their bikes and bodies. Suddenly breaking free of the fog back into the forest night, they looked at each other wide eyed and laughed at finding themselves still dead center on the trail. Rain that afternoon had packed their dirt and pine needle paths well, so they fairly flew under and past swaying branches. *The trees are waving, they're cheering for us; they know why we're here,* Nicole thought to herself, pumping her legs harder. They rode side by side whenever possible.

Ian's orange boxer shorts finally appeared, flapping on the bush he tied them to as a marker hours earlier. They braked, got off their bikes and took off their headphones, Green Day's, American Idiot blaring in sync. Nicole embraced her boyfriend as Ian looked down into her face, his headlamp exaggerating her wide smile. Squeezing Nicole tight before letting go, Ian strode to the side of the dirt trail and retrieved his boxers. She laughed when he pushed back the hood of his sweatshirt and set the Halloween undies on his head, turned and pointed dramatically into the trees.

Ian then pulled a US Forest Service trail map and a compass from his back pack, unfolding the sheet marked with handwritten notes and drawings. Checking the compass while shifting his feet and pointing at the map, Ian spoke in firm, deliberate tones, managing to project calm resolve despite the excitement of the moment, and held the rapt attention of Nicole.

"OK, the loggers crossed us up by making the logging road go this way, they seem headed to this ridge here. I'm not sure why, the trees thin as it gets higher there but this is where their road is going. When we re-conned here yesterday we saw all of 'em except the road crew leave after bringing the yarder and crane, so the targets are still sitting right here. The camp with the road crew is way over here; they won't be able to hear us. We can do close to a million in damage when we pown that yarder and log loader." Ian looked up from the map smiling. "That'll cost 'em and seriously piss those logger boys off. Our forest won't come free to those jackasses."

Taking off the boxers and ski cap Ian let his auburn, shoulder length hair fall down. Nicole had never seen this intensity in his dark brown eyes before. A single droplet of sweat hung on his narrow, hawkish nose and Nicole wanted to flick it away but Ian was far too serious now. She thought he had never looked so handsome as he started again. “This is ecotage, not vandalism and we are the warriors of this forest. Use our weapons the way we practiced and the FBI can kiss ass for taking down The Clan. When I tag AVENGE THE CLAN on that yarder, they’ll know the game isn’t over. I wish we could take out the bulldozer, that bitch has killed a lot of trees the last few days. The road crews’ still gonna have a sweet surprise in the morning.”

Looking into the forest, Ian went on. “We’ll hike about 150 yards on the same deer trail we used today, then stop at this berm and get the tools out. We circle the berm this way and attack. We stay together no matter what after we get off this OHV road, no screwing around. You stay with me and remember how we practiced when we get to the targets. After the yarder and crane are wasted, we hike back to here together and take the bikes to the car. Then we get our asses home. I know we’ll feel awesome about this but no talking to anyone, friends or family. We learned from The Clan it only takes one going weak to bust everyone. Too many good soldiers are doing prison time because of one gutless piece of crap. Any questions, baby? You look really hot by the way, muy caliente, mi senorita es bonita.”

Nicole smiled, then changed her expression as she pointed at the map. “Yeah, what if we get separated? We thought their stuff would be closer to the dozer crew’s camp here by the creek trail.”

“If we get separated,” Ian said, “use your compass, go south until you hit this OHV trail and work your way here. You know I won’t leave without you. You have the car keys, remember?”

He looked into her eyes, "I want us way out of these woods before first light when the road crew starts up. Just remember how we practiced."

Nicole nodded and hugged him again. "I love you, Ian, and thank you for my compass, it's a beautiful gift." Nicole said. "We have a great plan. I told you my horoscope this morning said a great adventure was near. We made it this far, forest spirits are with us. I feel it totally in these trees. They know we're here to help them."

"If you say so, baby." Ian smiled and shook his head. "You know I think horoscopes are balls. Stars and planets and personality traits, seriously?"

"Oh, Ian, embrace your Sagittarian sense of adventure, not my way or highway side. Tonight is the perfect night to get your happy-self open to the spirits. How many times do I have to say everything's connected, stars, the moon, planets, this planet, stuff on this planet like you and me and the trees we're here for. A logical progression you should appreciate. Ocean tides and moon, ta da! We're just part of all that same stuff, our electrified brains, same energy. God sending Jesus and angels watching out for us and the trees and stars knowing why we're here all makes sense if you just let it make sense. God works through everything, especially if you're open. Turn that brain off, fool. Or, make your choice like that Einstein poster in Cardwell's class says. 'You can live life as though everything's a miracle, or live as though nothing's a miracle.' I like thinking about miracles."

With a quick grin Ian said, "Spirits should be with us, Nicole. If there are spirits, if there is a Great Spirit, then this forest wasn't made just so some loser jerks could make money off it. You and me baby, let's do what we can to save our forest. The powers against us are strong; we know they can go get another crane and yarder, but if Gerring Timber has to pay a million for new tree killer machines to jack these woods, then fu-"

"Ian please, I know we're crazy excited, but try not to cuss, you've been cussing all night, you sound stupid like those football players when you cuss and I need you smart right now. Next thing you'll be going out for football."

"You know you'd love me in football pants."

"Not if you cussed all the time."

Ian wrapped his arms around her and held tight, then pulled himself from Nicole while looking into her eyes, his headlamp accentuating shadows that emphasized the Japanese rather than the Irish ancestral side of her exotically pretty face. Hugging her again, Ian let go. Turning north toward the deer trail, holding out the compass he said, "Let's go baby, let's jack Gerring Timber."

They stepped into the trees, the floor changing to damp pine needles, pine cones and tree roots, brush and ferns. Low hanging branches and brush had Ian walking with his hands out in front, Nicole following closely. They ducked and worked their way along the deer trail.

"We should have brought flashlights too," Nicole said. "It's so dark on the sides where our lights aren't. I know that sounds dork."

"No, I get you, baby. We're out here in it, for sure, more light would be cool. I just didn't want to haul more sh- I mean, stuff."

Despite the headlamps and the comfort of each other, hiking into the wilderness at night was scarier than either of them had anticipated. When taking night practice hikes in the woods near Medford they had always listened to music. Now, without their headphones the wind in the trees constant, eerie wail encouraged Nicole to move up closer behind Ian. She called into his ear, “That tree on your left, what is it?” Ian grinned, as they had played this game while scouting the logger’s location that afternoon. He walked under the huge conifer.

“Ah let’s see, this is a nice old one.” Ian cleared his throat and tried his best to imitate the gravelly and full of dramatic pauses delivery of Mr. Cardwell, their Environmental Sciences teacher. “She’s about a four foot diameter around the trunk here ... can’t see the top, might be up to 180 feet though, yes, the bark is grayish, rather scaled if you’ll just feel this, Miss Quinn... no, well... the needles of each twig are upright at rather a 45 degree angle... not unlike a little ski jumper in the air... or my morning wood, heh, heh, care to feel those, Miss Quinn? Mmmm, please note as we shine our light up, the needle’s undersides have a lovely, silvery glimmer. This, Miss Quinn... would be the Pacific Silver Fir.”

“Bravo, you might pass Cardwell’s mid-term,” Nicole cheered while clapping her gloved hands. Her face under the beanie rekindled that wondrous inner warmth Ian felt the moment he’d first seen Nicole’s face, the morning she walked into Spanish class their sophomore year at Central Point High School, the moment Ian knew that hers was the most uniquely beautiful face he had ever seen.

Nicole’s Japanese grandmother and Oregonian Irish-Catholic grandfather met when they were students at Cal Berkeley in 1967, married joyfully and forever during the ‘Drums and Space’ section of a Grateful Dead concert at Golden Gate Park. She’d inherited her mother’s deeply brown, Oriental eyes, so calming when sharing her serene smile, or the eyes of a tigress if flashing the Irish temper. Nicole’s soft, rounded cheekbones and full lips reflected the heavenly beauty of both Japanese and Irish women.

Now in their first year at Rogue Valley Junior College, they had been inseparable since Ian mustered the courage to ask her to the homecoming dance that 10th grade fall. Their small circle of friends, college bound stoners who partied occasionally with the football and cheerleader crowd but for the most part hung out on their own, were a familiar sight biking or skateboarding together around town. Making each other laugh by somehow mining gems of amusement from the interminable boredom that was life in Medford, Oregon, they planned their escape by studying hard enough to pull the grades for college. Nicole and Ian had especially set their sights high, applying to attend together at UC Berkeley. Both were accepted there, but painful financial realities were keeping them home at the JC for at least one year.

Two months before on a camping weekend along the upper Rogue River, Ian and Nicole decided to commit vandalism or ecotage, against the logging equipment of the Gerring Timber Company. Inspired when their Environmental Science class studied the spotted owl habitat cases, debating the in-court intersection of science and politics and with the old growth forest in play where Nicole and Ian biked, hiked and camped, they became keenly interested in the proceedings. Eco-terrorism came into their classroom during the spotted owl debates as well when a rag-tag group calling themselves The Clan made headlines for Molotov-cocktail torching a Hummer dealership, an upscale housing development near wetlands outside of Portland, and a Bank of America in Medford before getting arrested. Ian had become intrigued by their court case and cause as well.

On this chilly November night, with each step deeper into the woods, Ian and Nicole believed themselves eco-warriors marching, the wind in the trees no longer eerie but a sacred, roaring battle-call. They would keep this night their shared secret forever and Ian did wonder if Nicole was right, that their love and finding this mission was part of some greater plan.

They were almost to the berm, a raised mound covered in brush and ferns, not quite a hill but tall enough to hide the yarder and crane. "The equipment is right on the other side," Ian whispered.

"Listen," Nicole whispered back. "I hear something. Sounds like metal." A groaning metallic noise was discernible.

"Just the wind blowing the chains and cables, sounds freaky though," Ian answered.

A new yarder, the key machine of the logging industry for hauling cut timber out from ravines, mountainsides and the roughest wilderness would cost several hundred thousand dollars to replace. Without this mechanical beast combination of giant crane and steel pulley cables, loggers might still rely on mule teams, water flumes and rivers to move cut timber. And, the colossal log loader; crane and claws which stack cut logs and load them onto the trucks for hauling, would be a several hundred thousand dollar trophy. Ian raised his right hand, dropped his back pack and Nicole lowered hers carefully to the ground. They opened and retrieved their instruments of destruction. Nicole slowly removed a wrapped mason jar that she'd lifted from her chemistry class room. A label properly described it, 'sulfuric acid'. Ian reached into his backpack and checked a crowbar, mallet and 3-foot long sharpened metal spike, wire cutters, a spark plug socket and ratchet, and two cans of spray paint.

They had learned from the past mistakes of needlessly reckless eco-terrorists. Incendiary and explosive devices brought wonderful damage but also attracted attention before sufficient escape could be attained. They also caused collateral damage and Ian had realized, what could be stupider than starting a forest fire while committing ecotage? Their weapons would cripple the logger's machines quietly, the necessary damage would be done and they would make their escape.

"Take the acid jar, leave your pack here." Ian whispered, shouldering his pack. "Ready?"

Rounding the berm, the wind sound and steel moaning pitched louder as they neared the logger's road. The metallic groan suddenly stopped. "What happened to that noise?" Nicole asked, squeezing Ian's arm tighter.

"I don't know, that's weird, the wind's still blowing," he whispered back.

"I hear something," Nicole said. "Over there." They were quiet, listening. A rustling in the brush was not the least bit helpful.

"Must be raccoons," Ian said bravely.

His girlfriend was not as sure. "Sounds big in the dark," she added, trying hard to sound calm.

"You know the drill," Ian said. "I'll spike holes into the dashboards, you pour the acid in. I'll spike the radiators, then pop the hoods and pull a spark plug, cut wires and smash the motors. You pour the rest of the acid in the spark plug hole, on the motors and into the fuel tank. Add some dirt in the fuel tanks and our work is done. Then the fun, we take the spray paint and tag their asses."

"What's that smell?" Nicole asked. "Must be skunks over there. I don't want to get skunk sprayed."

"A small price to pay for the trees," Ian said eagerly. "Let's go."

Nicole still gripped Ian's sweatshirt sleeve on the upper arm, creeping until they reached the last of the brush at the edge of the berm. They held for a moment before moving into the open. About to step forward, Ian froze, suddenly feeling tiny needles dancing up his spine to his neck. But Nicole spoke first, a whispering panicked, "Ian, the hair on my neck is straight out, oh God this is too scary!"

"Look at mine," Ian answered, his eyes wide. He turned, lifted up his nape and in her headlamp she could see his every neck hair standing on end. As he turned back to her, Nicole saw the look of determination returning to his face. "We can do it, baby, we made it this far," Ian implored, grabbing her gloved hand and pulling while stepping out. She followed, together they walked then stopped, shining their lights at the yarder and crane.

"Oh my God," Nicole exclaimed first.

"No freaking way," Ian finally was able to gasp. The giant tractors were already demolished. Staring in stunned disbelief at the pummeled metal hulks smashed and broken, both driver cabs crushed, "who the hell already got here?" Ian asked incredulously. Several large rocks were scattered around, small boulders seemingly dropped like bombs from out of the sky.

"Look at the tower on the yarder!" Nicole said, pointing. The yarder's sky-line cable tower had somehow been pulled downwards, the seventy-foot steel rod bended impossibly toward the earth, a brontosaurus neck grazing. It quivered. Rustling in the brush again caused them to turn, "aah," Nicole screamed at the shining red glow of four sets of eyes shot back into their lamp lights. "Oh God, Ian what's that!?"

"Don't panic!" he commanded. "It's raccoons or owls, look how high in the tree..." Ian did not finish. The lowest set of red eyes moved and they were not flying from a branch, the eyes moved directly toward them and a dark face appeared. Immediately a black, hair covered hand reached through and yanked the face back into the trees. Nicole screamed again and dropped the acid jar. The red eyes turned, she and Ian saw dark, furry heads moving swiftly away. Ian dropped his pack and they both ran scrambling around the berm, then sprinting. Branches slapped and scraped as they fled in pure panic, Ian running ahead, battling to stay on the deer trail and setting the path for Nicole. He turned, saw her close behind so turned and ran, not stopping until he broke through the brush and dropped to his knees on the trail, breathing hard. Ian looked up, surprised at not seeing Nicole's light.

Running through the trees behind Ian, his head lamp her beacon, Nicole fought through the low branches and brush. But she tripped on a tree root and fell hard, then pulled herself up and his light had vanished. "Ian!" she yelled and only heard the wind. "Ian!" she screamed again. Working her way forward as fast as she could, Nicole stopped at an old fallen tree she had not crossed paths with before, confirming she was off their trail. Stepping over the deadfall sure she would soon find the OHV road, Nicole pushed aside panic, but after a time began doubting her path. Her compass was in the backpack at the logging equipment, so she searched for a clearing to locate the moon or the big dipper. They had practiced for this, but the woods only became denser the further she walked and Nicole could not find the night sky. Worse though, was knowing those hairy things were somewhere in the woods.

*They had to be Bigfoots,* Nicole thought. *I can't wait to tell mom I saw Bigfoots, she'll so wish she was here... I so wish mom was here...* A stark vision of the dark face coming through the branches came abruptly back to her and she remembered there had been something weirdly familiar about it. Something in the glimpse of the strange boyish face reverberated, the deep set, rounded eyes and Nicole asked herself, *am I dreaming this? Am I dreaming now... no, I wish I was just dreaming, those red eyes were coming for me, the hairy hand pulled it back...*

"Ian!" she yelled again. Her thoughts turned pleading, *Help me find the trail, God please, please send Ian to find me, please don't let him... no, no, Ian will never leave me...*

"Nicole!" It was Ian, somewhere near. "Nicole!" echoed through the trees again and she turned to his voice. Then, out of the darkness it came, flying through the air towards her. The rock hit from behind, glancing off her hood, Nicole crumpled limply to the ground.

The beast walked out from behind the trees and stood over her, looking curiously at the still face. Crouching and bending closer, it breathed in her sweet smell, blocking the irritating glare of the headlamp with one large, hairy hand while reaching a long, black furred finger on her hood first, then the ski cap, pushing them back. As Nicole's hair fell out from under the cap, the young Bigfoot considered his choices. He was afraid he had killed her and knew his mother would be very, very angry. Having no concept of deceit though, his deliberation was brief and besides, he knew his mother would discern that *something* had happened.

In the early season of his adolescence, standing just over six feet tall with long muscles strongly evident beneath the coming winter's undercoat and hair, raising up and lifting his head, "aaahhhrrrhooroohooo," he howled into the night sky.

Still excited after helping destroy the tree men's machines, he'd been swinging on the bended yarder sky line with his father when they saw the lights, smelled and heard the two humans coming and slipped behind the trees. But the young Bigfoot saw Nicole's face and forgot everything taught about human contact, making it two steps toward the girl before mother reached with her claws, yanked her son back roughly and barred her teeth in his face.

And yet after nodding he understood, the young one broke from her and hurried to pick up Nicole's trail. The juvenile Sasquatch did not mean to hurt the girl. Throwing the rock was impulsive as walking toward her at the berm had been, simply a way of saying hello. He bent closer again, sniffing near her face, watching for any movement, then turned toward the sound of his mother coming.

# Chapter 2

## HAPPY RETURNS

**THE MAN DRIVING** the minivan was grateful to see the forest open to the outskirts of Mazama Creek, Oregon. Michael Gardner rolled down the window and quieted his music for the wind's continuous *whoosh* in the trees. Already feeling nostalgic, he did not mind the rain hitting his face or that the first image to his left was the abandoned Mazama Lumber Mill. A chained gate and NO TRESPASSING sign framed the sight he slowed to take in. Rust had won the battle with the mill's mountainous smelter so long ago it seemed to Michael the trees would release the wind and blow the cone smokestack into reddish brown dust at a time of their own choosing. The giant cylinder loomed mute before the evergreens at the edge of the meadow, Michael pausing for their waltz in the windy rain and closing his eyes hearing the forest gale, a chorus witness to the mill's disintegration. The nostalgic feeling waned as he considered what the mill once meant to the good people of Mazama Creek.

Driving on, passing the city limits sign and State Highway 62 became Main Street. Seeing that Beckie's Café, the Union Creek Resort and the Travel Lodge with that same old sleepy bear sign were open, surely surviving on the summer tourist traffic to Crater Lake was encouraging, but further down Main was less cheerful. The Woolworths, a Farmers Insurance office and a real estate office appeared long closed. Edna's Grill and Roy's Shell Station were open but empty of customers. Michael smiled thinking about the night he and Eric had removed the word AT from the, EAT AT EDNA'S sign out front. He then made a mental note to fill up at Roy's rather than in Medford before heading home to California.

The van stopped at Main and Roosevelt. To the right stood the Crater Lake Natural History Museum, a bronze plaque in the brick facing declared, *Erected 1936*. Up a block and across from the museum, two stories of brick and windows housed Walden High School. Roman columns framed concrete steps at the entrance and at the base of those steps another plaque stated, *Erected 1938*.

Michael nearly pulled the van over again to fully appreciate the next view. Walden High was blessed to have a football field with covered wooden stands. These were scattered throughout the Pacific Northwest, charming like covered bridges and old barns. His mind drifted to an old, inspired notion never followed through while a college student in Eugene; wooden covered football stadiums would make an interesting photographic study.

Truly great news for Michael was posted on the 'Home of the Walden Wildcats' sign out front, the 2005 annual Vet's Day game versus rival Prospect High was tomorrow, Saturday. Perfect, what would be better than enjoying Walden battle Prospect from under those covered stands? He really hoped Eric would show up.

Now passing through the far end of town, Michael was relieved to see the Larssen Orchards Packing House still standing. With the lights on, a dozen or so cars in the lot and a delivery truck backed to the dock, the activity meant Eric's family still grew and shipped fruit from their orchards. Clearly the economic savior of Mazama Creek, the packing house looked tired, but there it was, up and running. Michael planned to visit the Larssens tomorrow.

The old fruit shed was the last building on Main Street and leaving town driving east, dense forest soon lined both sides of the two-lane highway again. The rain and wind blew harder and Michael strained to see for fear of passing his destination. He knew the Buckhorn was close. Emerging out of the mist and seeming to barrel right at him a log truck, whipping a sheet of water onto the van's windshield. Michael gripped the wheel and glanced up at the chained wall of bark passing close to his face. "Dammit," he breathed more than said. Had he missed the Buckhorn at the moment the truck went by? He remembered a tiny opening in the trees and thought, *damn, is it gone?* Trees and more trees, how far should he go before turning around? And then his forest oasis appeared, reassurance in the form of the Buckhorn Tavern and Grill. "Thank you, Lord," he said quietly, pulling into the gravel parking lot.

Parking alongside three distinctly Oregonian vehicles and getting out, Michael contrasted them with bemusement to his minivan. An actual 60s or early 70s Volkswagon bus, the back covered with stickers, sat next to his Plymouth Voyager. A faded Grateful Dead skull and Jerry bears danced in the back window, beneath them, ARREST BUSH-CHENEY, REAGAN LIES and, JESUS WAS A SOCIAL ACTIVIST LIBERAL. An old favorite, DON'T CALIFORNICATE OREGON, made Michael laugh. Quite naturally, at least to Michael, a nicely pounded Ford 250 pick-up sat parked in counter balance. It featured but one bumper sticker recommendation, SAVE A TREE, WIPE

YOUR ASS WITH A SPOTTED OWL. Michael smiled with the further reassurance the great Oregonian battle of the loggers and hippies raged on. The third vehicle, a muddy red and also well broken-in, seriously lifted with tires big enough to really 4-wheel rag-top Jeep, also sported but a single sticker statement on the back, GIRLS KICK ASS. *I wonder if that's Kelly's,* Michael thought, smiling to himself.

Walking into the Buckhorn after 21 years Michael immediately recognized the décor, the ancient wooden bar, and Kelly. Even the two locals sharing a pitcher were oddly familiar. The vaulted ceiling with its massive beams still gave it the feel of a mountain cabin and the tavern's namesake, the mounted elk and its stunning rack of antlers, lorded over the establishment from the wall behind the bar. The deer skin quill with feathered arrows and wood bow hanging jauntily from the antlers were still there too. Michael recalled Eric telling him the legend of the bow, arrows and quill confiscated from a rowdy Indian a hundred years ago and tossed up over the antlers, remaining there to this day. A CD juke box playing a new style country tune appeared to be the only addition since his last visit to the Buckhorn back in 1984.

Michael sat at a small wooden table and as the waitress walked over he stood and put out his hand. "Hi Kelly, I'm Michael. I'm an old friend of Eric Larssen. You and I met back when Eric and I were going to school in Eugene and when we came down to visit his folks."

She shook the hand and looked into his face. "Oh hell, I remember you. I met you in Eugene a couple of times. You partied up on the bluff with us and spent that summer here. Eric used to talk about you."

Michael nodded. "Oh yeah, we got a little crazy out there at the bluff. That was a lot fun. Many, many laughs with you guys at the bluff."

"Damn, Mike, that was a long time ago."

"It feels like a long time until you walk back in here. It's amazing that I can remember anything from those days. I did find the Buckhorn though, good thing I've tried to save one or two brain cells since then. A few beers is about as wild as I get anymore."

Kelly smiled and said, "I'm afraid saving brain cells still isn't much of a priority around here. Boy Mike, you still got your California good looks. You and Eric never seem to change. So what brings you up here? You still live in California?" Michael gave an embarrassed chuckle, the way he always took a compliment about his looks. It was true though, tall and still athletic looking, his dark brown hair only sprinkled with grey on the sides and still wavy, but not as thick and bushy as the old days. His hazel eyes were still sharp and engaging.

"Thanks, Kelly, you're looking great yourself. Yeah, I live in the bay area. I just needed to escape for a couple of days. My wife suggested I go somewhere, anywhere and I was going to bring my son up, but that didn't work out. Apparently I've been on the grumpy side lately. I was hoping to camp out at the bluff, is that still possible?"

"Well, you didn't pick a great time to camp. We're getting first decent rain all year but they say will let up later today, then rain again tomorrow. Yeah, you can still get to the bluff, they've actually fixed most of that road since they're starting to log out there again."

"I thought that whole area was banned from logging."

"It was, between saving owls and sending wood overseas they shut the mill down and screwed up everything around here. A couple of years ago they counted enough damned spotted owls so the feds rolled. Of course the tree huggers took it to court, but they lost this time. My nephew, Jason is actually on the logging crew that's out there. He might've been a baby when you were here."

"I remember that, Baby Jason, you called him. Weren't you helping your aunt and uncle raise him?"

"Well, I tried. He's a good kid, turned out to be a logger and he loves it. What can I get you, Mike?" Michael asked for a cheeseburger, fries and coffee.

"I see the Larssen's packing house is working. Do they still own it? How are Eric's folks?" She seemed to consider her answer, looking at him for a moment. "The Larssens are good, just working too hard in those orchards and at the packing shed. I'm sure they'd be glad to see you, especially since that dang Eric hardly gets down here anymore."

"I left messages to let him know I was coming. He may show up."

Kelly smiled. "Eric the hotshot Assistant D.A. doesn't come down off of his perch in Seattle too often. If he does show, we'll all have to head out to the bluff."

"Sounds great, Kelly, thanks, it's really good to see you." He meant that. Kelly was just good people, smart, funny, and also still looking great in a Buckhorn Tavern t-shirt and snug jeans. She was a natural beauty with sandy blonde hair and her blue eyes still as riveting as any Michael had ever seen.

"Oh, hell Mike, speaking of lost brain cells, these two jokers at the bar, you know them. CP, Dewey, I don't expect you'd remember anything back that far, but try if you can without hurting yourselves. This is Eric's buddy, Michael. He partied on the bluff with us a couple of lifetimes ago. Eric might show up this weekend."

CP and Dewey smiled, came over with their pitcher, shook hands and sat at the table. "Did I hear you're gonna camp at the bluff?" It was easy to recall which was CP and which was Dewey. CP asked the question. Clearly the owner of the VW, sporting a silver pony tail and faded Pearl Jam shirt, CP squinted through round wire frames.

"That's the plan," Michael said. "We'll see if the weather cooperates. I'll sleep in the van if the rain doesn't let up, that's easy. I need a couple of days in God's country and thought I'd come up here."

"Might not be as quiet as you were hoping for," Dewey said. "They're logging a few miles northeast of there." Dewey adjusted his camouflage baseball cap and briefly revealed a balding dome amply compensated by a bushy brown and grey beard. He wore a wool plaid shirt open and a black and orange Oregon State Beavers t-shirt underneath.

CP replied, "If they actually drop into the canyon to cut you likely won't hear them. Still can't believe they're logging Grey Canyon. It's all Kelly's nephew's fault, you know."

"Fault my ass," Dewey snorted. "They find that old growth he thinks is in there they'll make enough money to cover through the winter, maybe a bunch more winters. That's if they can get trees out of there."

"That's if they can get into Grey Canyon," CP said quietly. "We'll see what they find."

"Oh don't start on that again," Dewey groaned. "Spare me the UFO base in Crater Lake, evil Indian spirits and guardian skookums in the lava tubes all hidden by the U.S. government Conspiracy Paul bullshit for one day, please."

Kelly set Michael's coffee down.

"CP, Conspiracy Paul," Michael chuckled. "Sorry, but I have to tell you that's still about the funniest nickname I have ever heard."

Kelly shook her head. "He only gets worse with age. Just

don't bring up Bush if you want to get out of here before dark. Your burger will be right out, Mike." Kelly smiled and added, "You'll have to come back tomorrow for the Oregon-Oregon State football game, six o'clock tomorrow night."

"You're still a Duck?" CP asked hopefully. "If you're here, that'll make two of us and a Buckhorn full of meager Beavers."

"Once you're a Duck, CP, you're always a Duck. In that case I'll be here, few things in this world better than a tavern full of sad, quiet Beavers."

Dewey's response was immediate. "Ducks suck and you two can buy a roomful of happy Oregon State Beavers a round after it's over."

"Fair enough Dewey." Michael grinned at CP, "It should be over by half time."

"Typical Duck arrogance," Dewey said. "We'll see who's crying in their beer. You might remember getting your Duck asses kicked last year."

Michael answered, "Sometimes the Beavos get crazy on us in Corvallis, I do have to give you last year. It was ugly. By the way, nice shirt CP. I've seen Pearl Jam a couple of times, great band."

"They play with the old spirit, not many that still do. And Ed's a story teller. I don't get to concerts much since Jerry died." CP said wistfully.

"I hear ya on that CP, I really miss Dead shows, the music, the tribal community feeling, dancing like a happy fool," Michael said with a smile and dreamy sad eyes. "Oh well, all things do pass. Last year the wife and I took our kids to see The Chile Peppers, they were really fun."

"Pearl Jam and Chile Peppers, 90's bands," CP said. "Those are new bands in my musical time space continuum."

Michael laughed. "Yeah CP, I have a tough time dealing

with the stuff my kids listen to. Too harsh and painful screaming or too whiney, "emo" as they say. Or what I really can't take is that thunka chunka rap. We paid dearly a couple of years ago to take the kids to see the Stones. It was good for them to see a band that can actually play and throw their bodies into their instruments. And Mick is still the world's greatest dancing white man."

"The Rolling Stones," CP mused. "I saw them in Seattle in '72. Primal, just as get down to the bones as white boys playing Chuck Berry can get."

"You'd be happy to know they still kick ass," Michael added.

CP raised his glass and said, "To English white boys playing Chuck Berry." The three men clinked coffee cup and beer mugs.

"If you want to hear a decent guitar solo and real drums," Dewey said, "you should start listening to country. Try Brad Paisley, that's him playing right now."

"You might be right, Dewey," Michael said smiling, "that sounds more like Chuck Berry than what's considered rock these days. Didn't you guys have a band going way back when?"

CP grinned, "The Altered State Troopers, jeez I haven't thought about that for a long time. We played here when the mill was going, a few bars in Ashland and Medford. You should find your bass, Dewey, it would be fun to jam." Kelly walked out with burger and fries as the front door opened.

"Hey, Jake, nice you could make it," Dewey said to the older, round bellied man walking in. "No worry, Kelly took care of us, as usual."

"If you two actually worked at anything you might know what it was like to need some rest," the big man replied. Michael stood and extended his hand. "Hi Jake, I'm Michael. Glad to see you and the Buckhorn are both still here. I met you here a long time ago."

Jake grinned slightly. "Did you know he had California plates before you served him, Kell?"

"Of course Jake, he has no idea what's in that burger."

They all laughed, including Michael.

"You remember how to get to the bluff?" Kelly asked.

"I'll take a reminder, thanks. And great burger, whatever you put in here."

CP leaned toward Michael and whispered conspiratorially, "I have some killer green if you want to take a nice bud out to the bluff."

"Very tempting CP, but I'll pass today. I have some business I need to deal with out there and I'll start by working on it straight. I have beer of course, but reasonably straight. Thanks though, maybe for the Ducks game, for old time's sake."

"10-4 that Mike, good to see you."

All heads turned to the front window at the sound of someone pulling into the parking lot. "Would you look at that fancy crap," Dewey said. A black Toyota SUV pulling a mini trailer with two shiny all-terrain vehicles came to a stop. In a moment two men, one wearing an LA Lakers ball cap, the other a USC Trojans cap, strolled in and sat at a table.

"You got any decent beer here?" the USC guy asked. Kelly recognized bourbon on his breath.

"If you mean something other than Bud, Coors or Moonshine, I have a Deschutes Mirror Pond pale ale or a Widmer Brothers Heffenweizen. Both fine Oregon ales you might like."

"When in Rome, what the hell, a pitcher of Deshits, Deschutes, whatever, thanks babe," the USC cap said while stroking a narrow goatee. He pointed to the mounted elk head. "Damn, that's a big deer. Check that rack, Brian, almost as nice as hers."

"That's an elk," Dewey offered from his table, making little effort to hide contempt. "Elk season ended a couple of weeks ago."

"Can we get directions to the Deer Creek campground? We have permits to deer hunt out that way this weekend," Brian in the Lakers cap asked.

Before Kelly could answer, Dewey spoke up again. "I can get you there. I'll draw you a map, piece of cake. Kell, can I borrow your pen?"

"Thanks," Brian said.

"I gotta piss," announced the USC cap. "Where's the can?"

"Lucky for you we just installed indoor plumbing," Kelly said with a thin smile. "Go out the door and left around the building, you'll see it."

They went to the men's room together. When the front door closed behind them, Michael whispered to Dewey, "You gonna direct them to the middle of Crater Lake?"

Dewey grinned as his left hand fingers disappeared scratching into thick beard while drawing onto a napkin with his right. "Good idea, Mike, but not quite far enough. If they follow this correctly, those rump ranger LA boys should wake up all snuggly together in Idaho."

# Chapter 3

## STEPS

**MICHAEL ROLLED OVER** surrendering to the voice in his head, his mind not permitting sleep. Another beer might help, but he was warm in the sleeping bag. Still, another beer was worth a try. He opened his eyes to countless stars sparkling against black sky. Yes, another beer could actually help, one more maybe finally connecting him with the stars. He exhaled deliberately, watching the warm air become steam drifting up toward those stars wishing thoughts of work, the wife, their kids, continuous worries relentlessly worked through, sleep and stars be damned, might also drift away so easily. *I should have taken the weed from CP,* thought Michael while releasing another steam cloud. *Dammit, I just need to breathe, why can't I just shut up my brain?* Yes, he then decided, another beer and a few more cleansing breaths might quiet his persistent mind's voice. Michael pulled himself out of the sleeping bag and the cold night immediately reached beneath his sweatshirt and sweat pants. He pulled a beer from the ice chest, opened it and took a long pull, then adjusted his knit cap and snuggled back into the warm confine of the sleeping bag. Laying on his back, holding the beer in both hands on his chest, he tried just looking at the stars, looking without thinking. He breathed out again.

The sunset that evening had been spectacular, the rain stopping and the breaking storm clouds and setting sun giving the amazing sky he'd hoped for. Alone, with his feet over the edge of the bluff, the green valley and hills carpeted with trees rolling to a horizon of ethereal beauty and yet Michael was frustrated, his picture somehow incomplete.

Connecting the mountains and sky to the brain had been so much easier on his first visit to the bluff in 1981. Back then one simply awesome October afternoon, Michael sat in the same spot with Eric, watching the sundown join the sky. Blazing red, orange and yellow exploded from the setting sun and dissipated ever so gradually upward into green, yes, green sky, before fading into pale blue. He remembered how darkening blue shades then crossed a line to purple and looking back, purple had melted into the ebony night of the east. Watching black take that sky, only to give way to the brilliant stars, two great revelations arose from that autumn sunset in 1981. The first was the surety special colors were always there, the Oregon green bud and margaritas were not creating illusions, but merely helping to remove the blinders.

But here in 2005, Michael tried to really see those colors again and knew he had failed and believed it had little to do with the absence of pot and tequila. He also knew he longed for the old feeling, the knowing, that same surety, wanting to prove the colors at the bluff in 1981 were there always, something more than a hellacious pot and tequila buzz back in the day. Sitting on the bluff's edge today a vague awareness did grow though, that his restlessness itself prevented the state required to have some type of meaningful moment, be it seeing colors or any small or great epiphany. Now he searched the stars in the Oregon night sky.

"Damn," he muttered at the stars. "Damn," because Michael's second great revelation, a conclusion reached while looking, meditating and talking with his best friend Eric that distant first time here, he now considered a life changing moment. On that day, Michael Gardner decided and declared nothing less than there is in fact a living God who created the universe, the sufficient evidence the rainbow sky and forested hills laid out before himself and Eric.

"Man, I just don't see how this world can happen randomly," Michael said in that magical moment to his friend. "It's too perfect, too integrated and complex to be an accident. A world this amazing occurring randomly just makes no sense. And if it's created, a Creator created it and if so, it must be for a reason. What better reason than for a living soul to appreciate this, live and learn and try to get as close to this Creator as possible?"

"A logical progression if ever I heard one," Eric affirmed.

Many years later at a small group bible study, Michael would reference this as the transcendent moment he'd made his first leap of faith, though leaving out the weed and tequila part and feeling like a weenie for it. Another God through nature moment at the bluff these many years later had been more elusive than Michael expected. Finally sleepy, he finished the beer and set it aside. Perhaps a moment of pure knowing many years ago those colors were there *always* should be enough, that seeing those stars connected that night, however long ago were all that really mattered. His thoughts drifted, *just choose to be grateful for that day and night, however far past. Its ok, a truth of the past is still a truth, is it not?* He smiled at the stars and closed his eyes.

When Michael awoke it was still dark. It took but a moment

to realize the beer that had helped him cross to dreamless sleep now woke him to take a whiz. *Damn,* he thought. About to pull himself from the sleeping bag, he heard an odd sound. He yawned to get his bearings, looked around to confirm he was not dreaming… open space next to the forest by the old logger's road about 30 yards from the bluff edge, the van still sitting by the trees, the camp fire out. Rolling over he looked up at the crescent half-moon, the bright, cratered half-face showing with astonishing clarity. "Wow," Michael whispered, also noting the dark orb lurking behind the illuminated lunar half face. Awake enough now he asked himself, *what the hell is that?* It was the crunch, crunch, crunch, of steps. At first he thought they were coming from the forest and peered into the trees. Then it dawned on Michael they were coming from below the ridge. *Ah no, they can't be steps, what the hell is that?* He listened, and crunch, crunch, crunch, crunch, they were steps and yes, somehow louder, moving upward, somehow coming up the bluff toward him. *Mmmno, no, steps could not be coming up the bluff,* his mind repeated.

Sitting at the edge that day Michael had contemplated rappelling or sledding down the steep slope on his ass with a piece of cardboard, eventually deciding rappelling would be safer to get to the forest valley floor, so, *nothing could be walking up the bluff…just what the hell is that?…* and yet, crunch, crunch, crunch, *Jesus, something is walking up the bluff!* They were definitely steps, could not be anything else, one and then another over the broken granite and clearer, louder, closer, *what the hell could be coming up the damn face of the bluff?* Michael imagined elk or a bear and then stopped breathing to listen. *Oh shit is that two feet?!* One after the other they came, nearer with each crunching step. *Oh shit,* he suddenly realized, *whatever it is, it's really big!* And then he heard it breathe, breathing as it walked up the bluff, breathing followed by an exhale deep, seismically deep and *almost a voice in there, what the hell was walking up the cliff...* his mind said *run, just run into the forest, run to the van, just run...* but it was reaching the top, so instead he burrowed into the sleeping bag. It crested the edge, he heard it climb over grunting and then *stand on its feet.* He crawled deeper into the sleeping bag and curled up small when he heard the first grunt, a grunt of surprise and followed by another grunt *of deliberation,* Michael knowing it had seen his sleeping bag there on the ground. He heard the steps again, soft on the dirt but moving toward him, Michael trembled and curled up tighter, the steps nearing to the sleeping bag. He knew what it was, what it had to be. It stopped, sniffing the air, snorting loudly. *It smells me, oh God, oh God, oh God,* he prayed when from everywhere at once the smell hit Michael, a horrid, million rotting skunks at once stench he tasted in his mouth. And then it moved away, walking faster each step. It reached the edge of the clearing, shifting branches to enter the forest, quieter as it moved deeper into the trees.

Michael breathed and began to uncurl when he could no longer hear the steps. Edging toward the opening of the sleeping bag he dared to poke his head out. "Aahhroooooohooooo," it screamed suddenly from the woods, an eerie mostly animal, mountain lion or coyote pack howling that echoed wildly in the trees. Michael pissed his beer there in the sleeping bag.

# Chapter 4

## SEARCH

***WHERE ARE YOU,*** *it's taking too long*, Ian thought, sitting in the trail, his breathing finally slowing a bit. Standing up he knew he'd come out at a different place. *We veered east.*

"Nicole!" he yelled. Suddenly walking without thinking into the woods again, Ian stopped after a few strides to call to her and realized he was alone, utterly surrounded by darkness and the windswept forest. *Bigfoots, holy shit, we saw Bigfoot!* Breathing faster he pictured Nicole's face to summon his courage, then yelled, "Nicole!" He yelled again, listened for her, then called out once more. What came back to Ian, floating ghostly through the trees was the howl of the young Sasquatch calling to its mother. Ian crouched reflexively, low like a basketball player, closing his eyes and fighting the fear telling him to flee by forcing images of Nicole to his head.

Opening his eyes he peered into the headlamp's light and remembered instead they had left their packs and tools behind at the berm. *They'll blame us for the damage, I have to go back now. I'll find her along on the way,* Ian told himself. Coming up out of the crouch quietly saying, "I love you, Nicole," Ian pulled the compass from his pocket, set himself and started north once more, sweeping the headlamp back and forth, looking for her and calling out, and always with the creepy feeling of being watched.

Finally he stepped into a clearing and realized he was on the fresh road created by the loggers. Jogging west, the hulking, dark shapes of the yarder and crane appeared at the edge of his light, Ian sprinted toward them and stopped, once more taking in the incredible damage the Sasquatch had done. Ian lowered his light to the ground; there was the acid jar, thankfully unbroken. Walking toward the berm, finding the scattered tools and spray paint, he then rounded the little hill and tracked down their backpacks. Quickly he went back and retrieved the tools and picked up the acid jar, wrapping it carefully before putting everything into the satchels. Wearing both packs he stood and yelled, "Nicole!"

"Rrrrrrgggghhh," a low, deep growling came from the trees to his left and this time Ian broke and ran. Something big moved alongside him, shaking branches and thumping the ground but staying unseen a few yards away. Ian tried not to look, forcing his eyes straight ahead, but he could hear and see the rustling, feel the ground pounded beneath its feet, hear it breathing and grunting. And he could smell it, musty, unpleasant. When Ian staggered again onto the OHV road he stood motionless save his own hard breathing, expecting a monster to come out of the trees with him. None did.

Praying Nicole would be there Ian followed the trail but only found their two bikes waiting. He stared back into the woods sitting down next to the bikes and opened his backpack to check his cell phone, no signal. *Why didn't I think of radios, how could I be so stupid? How could I put Nicole in this situation?* Ian looked up between the tree tops to the starry strip of night sky. *God, please, please bring her back, please help me find her, I'll do anything, God, please, anything!* The wind blew cold through Ian's sweatshirt and t-shirts, but he pulled off his knit cap, clasped his fingers behind his head and finished the list of things he would quit or change if God would bring Nicole back to him, then said quietly, "Ok, please God and Jesus, Amen."

Calculating the time, Ian worked through everything and estimated it was 3:00 a.m. Standing up, he cupped his hands to his mouth and shouted, "Nicole!" A low, surly grunt followed by a large pinecone flying out of the trees sailed just over his head, Ian ducked and sat back down, his heart still pounding. *She must be hiding*, he told himself, *I'll find her at sunrise, I'll find her as soon as the suns up.* A wind gust shook the trees violently and Ian caught the smell again, the same dead, moldy stink he told Nicole belonged to skunks back at the log loader and yarder. Crawling next to the base of a big fir tree at the edge of the trail, the wind break immediately helped him feel warmer. Setting his back against the tree trunk Ian closed his eyes to imagine finding Nicole at dawn's first light, but another image came to him. Ian saw Nicole's bedroom, sitting at her computer while she does calculus homework on her bed. Knowing this was the day he decided to attack the logger's equipment, Ian groaned, yet did not resist the remembering.

"I'll find a way to save our trees and avenge the Clan," he heard himself say to Nicole, angry while reading of the arrests and convictions of what the Yahoo News described as, "an environmental terrorist group based in Eugene, Oregon." Ian told Nicole what a terrible joke it was, all of The Clan going to federal prison for trying to save the planet. The bought and paid for media, the bought and paid for government all needed to be shown the fight was not over, Ian said ruefully. Nicole did not look up from her calculus.

Their Natural Science class at the junior college discussed eco-terrorism one morning in September and Mr. Cardwell was quietly thrilled when the Clan member's trials sparked an actual debate in the class. The Clan, as they called themselves in rambling letters to the local media, were an oddly mixed group of college, high school students and unattached others living in Eugene, three hours up Interstate-5 from Medford. They found each other through Harold Yak, a painter and self-described, "old-time agitator." For a few months they enjoyed making headlines and the evening news by explaining their pyro vandalism through rambling letters fed to and happily shared by first local, then national media.

Following the Clan's exploits took Ian to explore eco-terrorism on the internet, where he was led to an inspired reading of Edward Abbey's, The Monkey Wrench Gang. When The Clan's members were arrested after one of their own ratted them out, choosing a nice reward and getting the FBI off of his ass, Ian felt distressed for the prison bound and deeper contempt for the government that cheated by paying an insider informant to catch them.

"I think the Clan are heroes," Ian said to the science teacher, Mr. Cardwell during class discussion. "Isn't it a war for the environment if the courts and the government are corrupt? Spikes in trees aren't cool, but stuff like Hummers destroying the ozone, why isn't that fair game if the earths' starting to go meltdown?" Mr. Cardwell had stoked their interest by showing Al Gore's, An Inconvenient Truth, a few days before.

"That's an excellent question, Ian. Anyone care to answer?"

Nicole raised her hand. "I think Ian is right about fighting for the environment, but what good is it if they put your stupid ass in jail? Oops, sorry, Mr. Cardwell." Mr. Cardwell liked the quiet pair. He saw Nicole and Ian show up together for class every day, take notes while sometimes looking torturously bored and routinely ace their homework, quizzes and tests. They seemed to keep to themselves and be reasonably ok with life at the junior college. He was happy to overlook a mild profanity to have Nicole contribute to the class discussion. Mr. Cardwell waited for anyone else wanting to speak. A hand in the back raised.

"What about people's jobs? How many loggers can't take care of their families and mills have to shut down before the tree huggers are happy?" The dissenter, a twenty-something named Keppler asked arms folded across his chest, staring at Ian as several students sat up and nodded their agreement.

"Balancing environment and jobs requires good government," Mr. Cardwell stated with pauses timed to enhance earnest conviction. "To your point Ian, the Bush administration you consider corrupt others look at as pro-business and pro jobs. Corrupt people and administrations you disagree with will come and go. We learn, we change, we forget and have to learn again. But working within the system is the way to fight the good fight. Think about being an environmental lawyer Ian, not an environmental terrorist which is just a common criminal. I have to agree with Nicole on that one, your butt in jail serves no good purpose. I hate to say it Ian, but I think The Clan are loser punks who might actually believe they were doing something noble, bigger than vandalism, but I'm afraid that's the best I can say for them. And they will do prison time, they will be made an example of."

Later that afternoon in Nicole's room Ian was not deterred, believing they could be the catalysts for a hundred Clans. "One great act of destruction, one safe but epic, symbolic act, what could we do? When they log The Rogue forest, that would be the time, baby."

"You better study for this calculus test, Ian." Nicole said, curled up on the bed behind him in her bedroom, notebook and book open in front of her, fingers tapping in bursts onto a calculator. He ignored her advice, staring at the computer screen.

"This article sucks," he responded.

In class, Mr. Cardwell made his case for the system after calling The Clan loser punks. He pointed to recent decade's legislation, court rulings and successful episodes such as the 'spotted owl strategy' to prove well-articulated science, dedicated grass roots lobbying and high paid lawyers can prevail against the darker forces of capitalism and politics. Ian was not swayed. Camping, biking and hiking the Oregon wilderness and snowboarding Mt. Ashland in the winter were Ian's loves before Nicole and now they shared those passions. Just east of Medford up Highway 62 along the Upper Rogue were the campgrounds and trails they loved the most. Together they had also followed the legal fight to open the forest there to logging again.

"Cardwell might let you do your final project on how the science data is used by both sides to make their points," Nicole suggested while pausing between calculations.

"Good idea, we've done the research, he'd go for that," Ian answered with a note of detachment Nicole found vaguely disconcerting. His infatuation with The Clan, his joy at their exploits and brazen public communications she now found less amusing, and shifting to annoying. But The Clan and the logging case sparked his interest in both. Researching on the web, reviewing old court rulings and finding obscure sites, Ian found on-line reports of how the Forest Service and Department of the Interior fired good, experienced managers and replaced them with industry hacks with no respect for prior public policy and the science that had guided it. Ian focused blame for the current president, George W. Bush. When the federal court in Eugene, the same court that would later try and convict The Clan ruled in favor of the loggers by agreeing new methods for counting spotted owls were valid despite independent and the government's own scientists testifying against it, Ian was sure the system was hopelessly corrupt.

Sitting at Nicole's desk, quietly reading the computer screen he mulled the headline, RADICAL ENVIRONMENTALISTS GO OUT WITH A WHIMPER. He shook his head and said to Nicole, "See how the media wants to make them out to be losers? Bullshit on you liberal media, this isn't just Fox, they're all jumping on The Clan." Yahoo News detailed how nearly all of the defendants had begged the court's forgiveness by proclaiming the error of their ways, repudiating their acts as senseless vandalism.

"I apologize a million times over," said one. "I am grateful for the opportunity to reconcile my destructive and reckless actions," another Clan member said through her tears to the judge. An odd emptiness settled inside Ian. They confessed and begged for mercy and got sentences at or near the maximum allowed for their convictions anyway. As he read the article that fateful afternoon, Ian came to the one exception in the defendant's pre-sentencing statements, The Clan's founder, Harold Yak.

"They buried Yak's statement," he complained to Nicole. "He's the leader, but they put all the cry-babies first. They just want The Clan to look like total losers, liberal media, my ass. Listen to what Harold Yak told the judge." Ian looked to see if Nicole was listening. She reluctantly raised her eyes. "There was a time I accepted Nelson Mandela's belief that the use of non-violence is not only a moral principle but it is good strategy," Ian read. "Sadly, I must submit the failure of these very courts to uphold established environmental law prioritizing dollars over our planet, the gutting of enforcement agencies of good and wise people by the Bush administration and the mockery of justice this trial is, leave me no choice except to say there can be no moral goodness in a failed strategy. Vandalism or ecotage, criminals or warriors, call us what you want, those are just words. I only regret we didn't do more." The judge then gave Harold Yak the maximum 14 years in federal prison. The article concluded with a quote from a U.S. Forest Service spokesman declaring the death of the radical environmentalist movement.

Ian leaned back in the desk chair. "We have to avenge The Clan, Nicole." She did not look up from her math homework. A light tap at the door was followed by the door opening and Nicole's mom calling in, "Ian, your mom called, is your phone off, buster?"

"Come in, mom," Nicole said, and as she walked in and smiled, Ian was reminded where his girlfriend's cross-cultural beauty passed from.

"Ian, your mom needs you to make tracks now so you can beat your dad home and get the dog poop cleaned up. Evidently certain promises were made, yes?"

Ian groaned and Nicole laughed and said, "See you tomorrow, dog doo boy. And don't message me until you get the calculus done."

"Dog crap and calculus, there's something to get excited about going home for."

"That's why you need to work at your homework Ian," Nicole's mom added. "I don't imagine you'll have dog poop to shovel in Berkeley, but you need to take care of business or you'll be dog-doo and junior college boy right here in Medford the next year too."

The next Saturday morning Ian and Nicole headed toward a favorite destination, a campground along the Upper Rogue. With no RV hook-ups and spartan, state maintained no showers bathrooms the extent of the facilities, minimal intrusion by other humans in late September was assured. Ian sat at their site's picnic table, gazing at the river while Nicole lounged on an air mattress next to their tent, content watching fluffy clouds passing through the robin blue space between the tree tops. The joint they smoked earlier had put an end to thoughts of hiking, which would now wait for tomorrow.

He closed *The Monkey Wrench Gang*, one of the books he had brought, setting it in front, looking at the cover, then at the Rogue. Aware of his melancholy and not minding, Ian expected the Sunday hike with Nicole would mend his spirit. "I want to be George Hayduke. I just read again where he drives a big tractor over a cliff. Action, real action, Nicole," Ian said suddenly. "Arguing with Mr. Cardwell in class is one thing, actually doing something... we'd have our chance when they start logging right here in a few weeks." Nicole rose up onto her elbows and Ian appreciated again how pretty she looked without make-up.

"I was just thinking about your discussion in class last week with Cardwell," she said.

"You mean the one about The Clan? Cardwell wants to use The Clan going to prison to show the errors of anti-authority behavior."

"Clearly, he would, baby. You held your own though. You did a good job of making your points and supporting with facts, especially when you brought up the way the government changed the way spotted owls are counted so they could open the Rogue to logging again. Cardwell didn't have much of an answer for that."

"Bush and those assholes are real cocky now that the Clan is going to jail," Ian said bitterly. "Cardwell is just wrong. If the system is corrupt, what choice is there except to fight? One act against the loggers right here could move others. I don't want to make the mistakes the Clan made. Just a one time, something that gets the media's attention to inspire others, that's all I want to do, Nicole."

She looked at him and frowned, "First, please don't cuss like that, you know I don't like it. Think about getting caught, Ian, fool, we could kiss going to school in Berkeley good-bye, you know they'd lock us up, just like those Clan fools."

"We have to be smart, we can't get caught, Nicole, I agree." Ian looked around at their forest. "But how can we not do anything?"

Nicole sighed. "No Ian, I love you baby, but no. They'd find us."

"How? We have no records. We just have to be smart. We'll blow up a yarder, ok, not blow up, too noisy, too visible, something quiet, yet destructive."

"Quiet, yet destructive," Nicole said dreamily, putting her head back down.

"Quiet, yet destructive. Look at our forest, Nicole, look at the trees and think about chainsaws attacking them. This guy Abbey, who wrote *Monkey Wrench Gang* said, "Sentiment without action is the ruin of the soul."

"Sentiment without action is the ruin of the soul," Nicole repeated, then added, "that is a challenging statement, isn't it?"

"We'd have to plan this together, Nicole, I agree," Ian said getting up and walking to her.

"I love your Sagittarian sense of adventure Ian, but this is really serious."

"Now there's a stupid concept," Ian sneered, "personality traits based on astronomy."

"Ian," Nicole countered, "You fit the Sagittarian profile totally. Be grateful for Jupiter, your positive, adventurous attitude is why I love you. How do you know the universe and the stars and planets and us human folk aren't all part of God's big system? If the moon can pull the ocean tides back and forth, then why can't the moon and planets have a pull on us? How much of your body is liquid?"

"Ahh, adult body is up to 60% water, your heart and brain 73% water." Ian settled on his back next to Nicole, watching the same rolling clouds.

"Surprised you remember that, nice. So, doesn't that make sense, the moon or planets shifting your DNA around to give you certain traits? You need to get sub-atomic, dude. It's there."

"So, it's in the stars I'm such a jackass?"

"I'm not going that far. The universe leaves room for growth and change, in some fool's cases, a lot of room."

"I'm feeling some growth right now."

"Ian, I thought you were going to read today. I am kind of horny though."

Curled tight against the tree trunk, arms wrapped around his knees, a wind gust shook the branches above, bringing Ian back from remembering, back to being alone in cold dark woods. Looking up, he saw their bikes side by side, then cried and prayed for Nicole to be safe, until finally he slept. *Sunrise,* he said to himself drifting off, *I'll find her at sunrise.*

# Chapter 5

## AFTER

**TOO SCARED OF** entering the trees to drive out, Michael sat in the front seat of the van, staring into the darkness to his right. Dissipating moonlight and the windswept night forest created black shapes moving within blacker shadows, and his heart still raced. Forcing himself to break from the mesmerizing woods to systematically check left back to the edge of the bluff, thoughts ran wildly, *my Bigfoot buddy might have friends, followers...* Working to manage his inner voice, incrementally slowing himself down despite visions of giant, hairy monsters walking up to the van from the trees or climbing over the cliff, rambling thoughts, *a Bigfoot, oh God, oh shit, oh man a Bigfoot...a Bigfoot...*had eventually slowed and he'd shifted toward thinking more rationally, *ok, easy now Michael, settle your ass down now Michael, settle your ass down... ok, do we stay or drive, stay or drive... what time is it... go to the Larssen's or to the hotel... they're solitary creatures, right? He won't come back, really don't want to drive through the woods... right, you smelled a Sasquatch, do I tell the kids I pissed my sweatpants?* It would take some time, but finally, exhaustion overtook the mind and Michael fell asleep.

# Chapter 6

## FIRST LIGHT

**JASON IBSEN POKED** his head inside the dark tent. "C'mon Sam, wake up, daylights wasting."

"Daylight, my ass." Sam Kloss rolled over, rubbed his eyes and scratched his scruffy beard. "You're dressed already? Damn, give me a minute." When Sam stepped out, he noted only a thin pink strip of false dawn in the east. Jason stood by the truck, waiting and smiling.

"Let me grab some food, Jeez."

"It's in the truck, so's all the gear."

"Coffee?"

"Of course."

Sam finished pulling red suspenders over his plaid wool shirt and thick, rounded shoulders, checked the truck bed and saw packs, rappelling gear, canteens, two chainsaws and two axes all set in very organized fashion. He looked over at Jason, only 22 years old but already a skilled logger and respected by the crew. Also dressed for work in jeans, boots, plaid shirt and vest, Jason tugged on the bill of a yellow and green John Deere tractor ball cap and showed Sam the spark in his blue eyes that he'd noticed since they'd first arrived in the Rogue

National Forest. "You look like my dog thinking he's going for a ride," Sam said.

"I guess my tail's wagging a bit this morning. We're gonna make history today, Sammy," Jason answered. Sam couldn't help but grin at the earnestness the kid exuded, reminding him of Jason at 18, his first year with the crew. Four hard earned years later, another fifteen pounds of muscle stretched easily over Jason's 6' 1' frame. A no shave for days look sharpened high cheekbones framing sky colored eyes. Hank Gerring's words introducing Jason to the crew came to Sam just then.

"This kid's the grandson of Jason Ibsen, goes by Jason named for his granddad. You've heard me speak of the Ibsen brothers, so you boys know logging's in his bones. Take care of him, I'm accountable to his grandmother." Taking care of him did not mean baby him, Jason found out quickly. Working in the woods apparently was passed on though, as hard day by hard day he earned his logger's stripes.

"How far do you think we'll be climbing down?" Sam asked. "Remember we gotta climb back up, or was that a consideration?"

"You can ride a tree out on the sky line Tuesday if it's too far, Sam."

"Great, what if we get down there and it's just lava rock?"

"No way, Sam, that permanent fog in Grey Canyon is there because a rain forest is down there, rain forest untouched by human hands. The climb out might be a mother but we'll make serious bucks on the old growth wood down there."

"Did I hear old wood and making bucks?" Jason and Sam turned to see a beaming Hank Gerring step out of his tent. A few days before his 70th birthday, Hank's barrel chest, muscular arms and shoulders filled his night shirt. A protuberance of morning wood unashamedly filled his long johns. "I knew you couldn't wait," the boss said. "I'll get the dozer going. Sorry we didn't get the road done yesterday. I should be to the ridge by early afternoon. Try the radios from down there and keep me posted. Once you know a path for the sky line is workable or if helicopter really makes sense let me know, then take a few trees down to get us ahead while you're there. I want to experiment with getting trees out of there as soon as possible. That is if there's anything down there bigger than ferns."

Jason ignored the crack about ferns and answered, "I'll mark the trail to the tunnel I found, its right where you'll need to blast. The avalanche chute should make for a decent climb in and out, Sam can slide down on his ass if he wants."

"I might slide down on my ass just to get it over with," Sam said yawning.

"We'll blast Tuesday," Hank said, "Just get down there safe, check it out, cut a few trees and get back up way before dark, say 3:00 pm. It feels like the rains' gonna hold off for a while. Oh, and check the fuel on the yarder and crane. Hopefully, the boys weren't in too big a hurry to get their weekend going and remembered to refuel. I don't want a surprise on Tuesday morning since the fuel truck won't be here yet."

"You got it Hank," they said in unison.

"Jason?"

"Yeah, Hank?"

"What dumbass woodpeckers live in these woods that start knocking on trees late at night? They were knocking wood going back and forth, three or four sounded like, then they all stopped."

"I'll have to ask my Aunt Kelly, if it moves or flies around here, she'll know it. You ready, Sammy?" They drove the 4-wheel drive truck over the rough but passable road that Jason, Sam and Hank's bulldozer had carved. Jason's knowledge of the area, using official and unofficial all-terrain vehicle roads and deer trails to shorten the distance to the canyon rim had saved days. It had not rained since the prior afternoon and the mud was not too bad. Sam slurped coffee and munched a banana in between bumps and pulled the sun visor down as they headed north and east.

"That was pretty cool of Hank to give the rest of the boys the Vets Day weekend off after they dropped the equipment," Jason noted.

"Hank is one smart boss," Sam answered. "He knew what a pain in the ass it would be to move from the last operation to here. He got three days-worth of shutting down and moving into two because they were motivated to get it done and have a long weekend. Hank gets that happy miners mine more trees. I know I'd be in a better mood coming back Tuesday if I was seeing the old lady this weekend. Three days is just about right, then time to head back to the woods. Oh well, she'll be happy enough with the O.T. I pull on the next paycheck. Just make history exploring the mysterious Grey Canyon and put up with your ass this weekend for a nice fat pay day."

Jason thought he'd be taking one of the younger crew members into the Grey Canyon because of the climb, but Hank had decided otherwise. "There isn't much Sam hasn't seen or done in the woods, he'll be ok," Hank told Jason, not mentioning his reasoning also included Sam's good nature and sense of humor. Keeping Jason loose might be helpful, as Hank had learned how the young man's mood could sometimes go south.

The road curved into the turn-out and Jason stopped the truck, stunned. Their devastated yarder and crane illuminated in the headlights. "What the hell?" Sam croaked, surveying the scattered small boulders, crushed and dented machines.

"Holy shit, Sammy." They got out of the truck, stood

speechless before walking slowly, trying to grasp the damage.

"Watch your ass, Jason, they might still be around."

"Who?"

"Punk-ass environmental terrorists, Jason. Damn tree hugger pieces of shit."

"You got that right, Sam. This is crazy though, just how in the hell did they throw these rocks? How did they bend down the yarder tower like that?"

"I don't know. They had some kind of tools, I guess. Who knows what liberal asshole funds these punks. I'm surprised we didn't hear 'em."

Jason shook his head. "Dammit, we better get Hank on the radio, we're gonna have to tell him."

Sam found the radio in his pack and spoke into it. "Hank, do you copy Hank, copy?"

Hank's voice crackled back. "I copy. Did those fatheads forget to refuel? I'll be calling somebody in off their weekend, over."

"No Hank, worse. We got vandalized. Bad. Some environmental terrorist bullshit I'd say, the crane and yarder are totaled Hank, over."

"Totaled?! What in hell do you mean totaled? Over."

"Really big rocks smashed the hell out of the crane and yarder, do not know how. Just know they are smashed up and big rocks all over the place that were not here yesterday. I'm sure it's some of those punk asshole hugger terrorists. But these guys have some serious tools or something to chuck rocks like this. Maybe from a helicopter, don't know Hank, over"

"Be careful, dammit, these assholes are capable of anything. Over."

"10-4 that, Hank. Hey, we're gonna have to call the cops, you want us to come back? Over."

The radio was silent until Hank's voice, very angry, came back.

"I can't get a signal to call out and the radio won't pick up anyone but us. Listen up, I'm sure the pieces of shit are long gone and it would take me an hour to get to town, so screw 'em. We're working today, proceed as planned. I'm bringing the dozer out and finishing the road. I will not give these tree hugger pieces of shit the satisfaction of shutting us down, even for one damn day. Do what you planned in Grey Canyon but leave early, by 1:00, then we'll go to town or the ranger station in Prospect to report it. Copy that?"

"You sure, Hank? Cops are gonna want to get after these losers. Over."

"Yeah, I want them to know that they can kiss my ass, we are working today. We'll give the cops enough daylight to check this out. Good thing I listened to Becky about increasing the insurance coverage for this bullshit. Copy, gentleman?"

"10-4 Hank, we'll start hiking to the canyon. Over and out."

Sam looked at Jason and shrugged. Jason had been walking around, looking at the ground and studying the damage. "Sam, you want to see something funny?" Sam looked at Jason kneeling and looking down. "Look at these footprints. These radical jack-asses are trying to make it look like skookums did this." Sam walked over, looked down and only then noticed huge and bare, human looking footprints were everywhere. Also a hunter all his life, Sam started following the footprints around.

"Skookums?"

"You know, Bigfoot. That's what we call him around here. I think it's an Indian name."

Walking over looking down, Sam said, "Bigfoot is bullshit. Hmm, these guys even left different sizes. These pieces of shit must think they're pretty smart. I gotta hand it to them, some of these are pretty good. They pulled off giant strides without messing up the prints. Seriously, you sure they're fake, Jason? Ha, got you. Look at this shit though, I mean, this damage is spooky. I'm calling Mulder and Scully."

"Who?"

"Don't you watch the X-Files?"

"No, Discovery Channel and ESPN sometimes. These prints were starting me to wonder Sam, but I stopped wondering when I got to right here. Look, tennis shoes, two pair."

Sam walked over to Jason. "What does that backwards word in the mud say, Vans?"

"Vans, Sam, those are Vans, skate boarder shoes. Those smaller ones might be Converse."

"One of my kids wears canvas Converse," Sam said, then folded his arms and with an awful mock English accent added, "I'd say these two stoner punks were partying with the Bigfoots last night and they all got really loaded and decided to throw rocks at the yarder and crane. Elementary there, Holmes."

"Watson." Jason smiled grimly and said, "They took all the trouble to fake skookum tracks and then left tennis shoe prints. Must be seriously stoned, dumbass tree huggers. These tracks are something; you're right about that Sam, and I like your theory on stoner Bigfoots."

"I know its tree huggers Jason, but this damage does kinda give me the creeps. Like right now, I have this weird feeling of being watched. Do you?"

Both men stepped back and scanned the area.

"I don't know, Sam, I figured it was the damage. To be honest, my hair stood up after we got out of the truck but I'm sure it's just seeing the way they destroyed our stuff. I still can't figure out how they did some of this. Tell you what Sam, I'm for getting out of here. We got our marching orders from Hank, let's head to Grey Canyon. It's only two to three miles, but it ends with a good uphill."

Sam scratched at his beard, shook his head letting out a breath saying, "Sounds great kid, a nice uphill before we rappel how far down, we're not sure, to what, we don't really know and then we might actually start working at trees before we get to climb back up again. God only knows what we'll find when we get there since you say no white folks or maybe any damn humans have ever been to this Grey Canyon, and I'm standing here wondering if friggin' Bigfoots or crazy ass tree huggers are ready to sabotage my ass right now. Shit, what a day already. What the hell, let's hit it, kid. Hank can call the cops when he's good and ready. Just like Hank to make it another day at the office." Sam and Jason retrieved their packs, axes and chainsaws from the truck. "Jason, are you serious no people have ever been down into this Grey Canyon? I should have packed a camera, maybe we'll see a friggin' dinosaur."

"Ever since I was a kid growing up around here, Grey Canyon has been this old legend from pioneer days. I don't know if the Indians have even been there, the story is they've always been spooked by the place. It could be Jurassic Park."

"Funny Jason, let's get this work day done. I was thinking we could get to town early anyway to watch the Beavers pound the Ducks tonight."

"Not a bad idea Sammy, should be a good game. We could clean up at my grandma's place and then head to the Buckhorn, my Aunt Kelly will be there. I'm sure Hank will be ready for beer and football after dealing with this. Hank can call the cops from my grandma's."

"So, Jason, how come you aren't staying at home if you live so close?"

"It's just easier and quicker if I stay with the crew, but it'll be good to see family tonight. I know my Aunt Kelly wants to hear about Grey Canyon."

"Hank mention we saw your picture playing football at the diner when we got into town?" Sam asked. "The waitress said you hold all the rushing records at Walden. Hank said you were good, had a football ride to college. Somehow I wasn't surprised. You're more of a thinker than the average bear."

"Big fish in a little pond when it comes to the football, Sam." Sensing no desire in Jason to speak of glory days, Sam dropped the subject. The two men hoisted their backpacks, climbing gear, axes and chainsaws over their shoulders and headed out, walking through the forest. "This deer trail will get us there in good time, Sam. At least it isn't raining."

# Chapter 7

## DARKNESS

**SLEEPING NEXT TO** the tree, Ian dreamed.

It was pitch black and he reached out, hands only finding dark emptiness. *Where are the walls? I can't see the walls.* Claustrophobic unease crept in as wary fingers searched, reaching for anything. Peering into midnight, more desperate by the moment searching for a point of reference, anything solid and yet only a vague black space surrounded him.

"Daddy?" Ian heard himself say with a trembling child's voice.

Someone or something was with him in the dark. Without seeing, smelling or hearing, Ian knew a presence was there. "Daddy is that-" the boy began to ask again when a feeling blacker than the surroundings came across *and through* Ian. No, it was not his father coming home drunk and mad, the scariest thing he thought he could ever meet in any bad dream. This was worse. Blending into the blackness something else lurked, something ebbing dark, malevolent intent. *What is that?* "Are you a ghost?" the kid voice whispered. It was watching him, waiting, Ian was sure. *Ok I don't like this dream, over now, I don't like this.*

"Ian!?" a frightened little girl called out.

"Nicole!" he shouted into the gloom. "Go away now, don't come here!"

"Ian, where are you?!"

"Run away, Nicole, go now!"

"I'm coming, Ian! I'm scared!"

"No!" The thing in the darkness moved, Ian rushed blindly toward it as he forced himself awake. Something covered him, pushing hands up in panic an evergreen branch flew off. Ian rolled over away from the tree trunk, cold wind hitting as he tumbled into the open. Eyes wide sitting up he only saw blackness, still held in the place of his nightmare. The harsh breeze finished the awakening and Ian's surroundings returned; a gift after the awful, oppressive dream place. Staying on his knees Ian looked into the trees, his terror and breathing gradually subsiding. *Holy shit what a dream, oh Nicole, where are you? We were kids, that thing was there, Nicole can't be there, she can't be there, can't be there, not with that thing.* Ian raised up, cupped his hands to his mouth and yelled for Nicole, listened to the wind in the trees, yelled again and listened, then yelled and listened once more. He felt the sunrise must be very soon, *when the sun is up I will find you.* Crawling back to the tree trunk, Ian picked up the branch thick with soft conifer leaves. *Must have fallen on me, weird I didn't feel it. It was like a blanket.* Resting on his side Ian pulled the branch over, grateful for its cover. After a long, fearful hesitation, he dared to close his eyes again.

# Chapter 8

## GOOD MORNING

**MICHAEL AWOKE CONFUSED.** Why was he in the front seat of the van? Then he smelled stale urine, looked down at his wet sweat pants on the passenger seat and it all came back to him, steps coming up the bluff, those grunts, trembling in his sleeping bag, the smell, the pissing on himself. He had never, even as a kid, even in his worst nightmare been so scared, felt such overwhelming fear. Michael remembered running to the van, fumbling for the keys and getting in, trying to decide whether to drive through the woods in the dark to the highway or not move until daylight, then staring into the trees and scanning back to the bluff for a long time. He remembered really wanting a beer, but not badly enough to get out and go to the ice chest for.

Looking over again into the trees, the early dawn still leaving more shadow than light in the woods, Michael decided to wait for the sun to rise a little higher. Finally, when reasonably sure all shadows amongst the trees were but shadows, Michael opened the van door and ventured out to retrieve his things. Moving at a trot and glancing to the woods he picked up the sleeping bag and then threw it down gagging. The Bigfoot's skunk stench was still on the bag. Then a crazed thought, *the sleeping bag is proof!* He should keep it, put it in the van and did not quite finish the thought when he looked down at a trail of gigantic foot prints, from the bluff to the sleeping bag, then to the trees. He put his own size 12 next to one and said "oh," very quietly, feeling a little weak in the knees.

Walking along the footprints to the edge of the bluff Michael peered down, shaking his head. *I can't believe it walked up this, damn, I met Bigfoot.* Gazing out over the Rogue forest as the November Saturday's first light greeted the Pacific Northwest panorama, an orange sky reaching from the east to meet the western horizon's waiting black and purple storm clouds. The cold bite in the wind leading those clouds hit Michael, *looks like it'll be raining again later,* he thought.

A sudden cracking noise came from the forest, probably just a pine cone dropping, bouncing off branches going to the ground but Michael broke and ran for the van, the ice chest and sleeping bag could wait. Jumping in, he threw the disgusting pissed in sweatpants to the back, started it up and pulled back onto the logging road, driving while leaning forward, eyes avoiding the trees on either side, staring straight ahead until he thankfully reached Highway 62. Michael let his shoulders rest back against the driver's seat and exhaled, mightily. He looked up and down the two lane stretch of highway and did notice how densely and uncomfortably close the walls of forest loomed on both sides of the road. He exhaled again, deliberately now, feeling the tightness in his shoulders and back. He settled a little more into the seat. BAAMMM!! Michael shot straight up, eyes wide. A chunk of tree branch bounced off the van, across the windshield and over the hood. The van tires squealed as he hit the highway turning right. "Ok ok ok, that was a tree branch...just a damn tree branch falling out of a damn tree...ok ok ok, a tree branch...oh Jesus, oh God...ok, a falling branch...a God Blessed falling branch...get a grip now, drive, just drive...breathe and drive...ok, ok..." Michael identified that he was talking out loud and attempted to flush the panic by laughing at himself. Breathing fast, he stared up the road and repeated to himself, *drive Michael, just drive, it's ok... just drive now, just drive, let's just drive.*

# Chapter 9

## ANCESTRY

**"MOMMY?"**

"Yes, my precocious, inquisitive one."

"Big words, mommy."

"Your teacher says you know lots of big words for a first grader, Nicole."

"What are those?"

"Well, precocious means you're adorable and smart and you know it, and inquisitive means you ask questions to learn about things. So what did you want to ask me, sweet pea?"

The Quinn family, six year old Nicole, her mom, May, four year old sister Heather, and dog Bandon camped often at the campgrounds near Mazama Creek, an easy and pretty drive following the Rogue River along Highway 62. They were at their favorite spot at the Natural Bridge Campground, very private spaces with fir tree borders alongside a gentle section of the Rogue. May loved the clean, well-organized yet minimalist, no showers, be grateful for a flushing toilet and tax funded toilet paper, nature of the camping there. "If they put in showers more Californians would be here," she explained once to Nicole. "They can stay at the Crater Lake Lodge or the sleepy bear Travel Lodge in Mazama Creek. We nature girls bathe in the river."

Nicole sat looking across the meandering river this warm September afternoon, the sun's dance of rippling gold and white splashes on sapphire water mesmerizing the little girl.

"Can you hear the singing, mommy?"

May looked up over her mystery novel. "Singing, Nicole? Where?"

"In the trees, mommy, the trees are windy, going, *whoosh,* then they were singing a very pretty song."

"Really? Well, what did the trees sing?"

Nicole turned back looking at her mom with an expression of dramatic disgust. The sunlit river backlighting her brought out the occasionally visible red tint underlying her black hair. "Mom, I mean it."

"I can see your Irish hair, pretty in the sun, a red halo. Ok then, what did the trees sing, my love? Are you sure it's not birdies?"

"Not birds, this," in a little girl's best falsetto voice Nicole sang out, *"Amaterasu, Amaterasuu, Amaterasuuuu,* and then they sing, *Brigeed, Brigeeed, Brigeeeeed...* then they sing some other stuff I don't understand. It's two ladies singing very pretty in the trees." Nicole looked back at her mother again. "What's wrong, mommy?"

"Nicole, did your grandmothers, did Obi-chan and Nana tell you about Amaterasu and Brigid?"

"No, mommy, but maybe Obi-chan and Nana are the ones singing."

"Hmm, that might be, sweet pea."

"Except, they're up in the trees. Why do they sing, Amaterasu and Brigeed?"

Hesitating, May looked at her daughter, seeing both the old

Japanese and old Irish right there in that quite adorable little face. She breathed out saying, "Well, sweetie, Amaterasu is a very important spirit in Obi-chan's temple, her church, and Brigid is the name of a very important spirit in your Nana's old, old family church. The Irish folks say it, Brigeed, her name is Brigid. And there's a Saint Brigid in Nana's and Granda's church, the Catholic church, the one we go to, so we sort of already celebrate Saint Brigid, I just don't remember telling you about her. I know it's confusing."

"They're spirits like angels, mommy, like that saint that helps you find your keys?"

"Yes, like Saint Anthony. When I was a boo like you, your Nana told me ask Saint Anthony, patron saint of lost things, for help to find a lost something. So, that's why I ask him to help me find my keys."

"Does he help you?"

"Well, I always find my keys."

Looking at her daughters, their dog, and out over the river, May thought about her mom, missing her. She then had a moment, soft and warm expanding inside her, a moment of profound gratitude and love. "Thank you, Lord, thank you, Jesus," Nicole heard her mom say, then, "Ok, this might be confusing but we'll try, sweetie. Your Japanese granny, your Obi-chan is my mommy and my da, your Granda live in Ise City, Japan. Obi-chan serves in the Grand Shrine of Ise temple, a Shinto temple for Amaterasu the sun goddess of Japan."

"Amaterasu the sun goddess of Japan," Nicole chimed back.

"Nana is my da's mommy, your great grandmother. She came to see you when you were very little. Kildare, Ireland is where our Irish ancestors celebrated an Irish sun goddess named Brigeed. Nana lives in Kildare and goes to another Brigeed's church. Saint Brigeed was a nun, a church lady who did miracles to help the Irish people a long time ago and she lived in Kildare, Ireland too. Pretty confusing, I know, but interesting, isn't it?"

"Just the part about two Brigeeds. Are you sure they aren't the same lady?"

"That's funny, Nicole, your Gran says Brigeed the sun goddess and Brigeed the nun were the same spirit. Amaterasu and the Brigeeds were all very wise, strong spirited ladies with powerful knowledge about how God has everything work together, the sun and earth and the moon and water to make this such a beautiful world. Amaterasu and the Brigeeds were warriors and teachers and healers and poets, legendary girl heroes to your Japanese and Irish ancestors. So maybe they are angels or your grannies or sun goddesses singing to you. Maybe they're helping Jesus watch out for you."

"Are there stories about Amaterasu and Brigeed and Saint Brigeed?"

"Yes, I suppose you'd like a story."

"About one of the sun angel ladies first."

"The magic word?"

"Please, mommy?"

"Hmm, ok then. Well, Amaterasu, give me a moment to remember, her name means shiny in heaven, and her mommy and daddy were Izanagi and Izawami and they came down from heaven on a big cloud and sailed on their cloud across the seas. They had a giant spear and dipped it into the ocean, and beautiful jewels grew on the spear. The jewels fell off the spear into the ocean and when they splashed they turned into the islands of Japan. And, the islands were so beautiful, Izanagi and Izawami decided to live there instead of going back to heaven, that's how beautiful Japan is. That's what my mommy says. That's why Obi-chan and Granda live so far away in Japan."

"Obi-chan told you this story?"

"She did. Obi-chan told your mommy when I was a little boo that Amaterasu was Izanagi and Izawami's baby girl, the goddess of sun and light in the universe. She was very beautiful. You know the picture of Obi-chan in your room, next to the little shrine she gave you? Amaterasu looked like Obi-chan in that picture but with golden, orange and red rays of sunshine that came flying out from her long, black hair."

Nicole turned back to her mom, "Like my red halo?"

"Just like your red halo. But here's what happened to Amaterasu. Her brother was a real knucklehead and they used to fight, even worse than you and your sister. One day he made her so mad she went to live in a cave. Amaterasu took her light with her into the cave and the whole world went dark. It was night time all the time because she had all the sunshine and she would not come out of that cave. So all the kami, all of the spirits got together and they had a big party out by Amaterasu's cave. It was a very fun party, with cake and presents and music and laughing. Well, Amaterasu heard them laughing and said, "How can they have a fun party without me?" She was mad."

"Amaterasu was a party pooper."

"That's right, Nicole, but then at the party her sister, Sasanoo, she's a goddess of storms and seas, she started to do a dance and it was such a wild dance she started taking off her clothes! The party cheered even louder and Amaterasu had to see what they were cheering for. Just when she peeked out of the cave the kami at the party saw her light and they showed her a mirror. Amaterasu saw how beautiful she was in the mirror and she had to come out to see more of herself. A magic rope was put across the cave door so she could not go hide there again, but Amaterasu decided she and her light were too beautiful to hide and now she shares her light with the whole world every day, the end."

"Good story, mommy, thank you. Do you have a Brigeed story for me?"

"I do, but let's save that for tonight by the fire, is that ok?"

"Ok, mommy. The sunshine on the river is very pretty. I hope I hear the singing again."

"Please tell me if you hear it, ok?"

"Ok, mommy."

May settled back while looking down again to her book, but the words on the pages blurred. Closing her eyes, a vague recollection or her imagination, which was it, she wondered? *Did I hear it too? Did I hear it when I was her age? The forest ladies, I used to call them, I knew their song, I heard it too, I heard them singing when I was a little girl, oh my Lord and then I forgot, mom and I called them the forest ladies ..."* May heard a whispering from a distance, she listened, wondering briefly if it were a memory or imagination or really voices singing in the trees. Or perhaps the birds. She decided not to care and then May knew it was her kin, somehow her grandmothers singing celestially to her and her baby.

"Do you hear them now, Nicole?"

"Yes, mommy."

"I hear them too, sweet pea. I think it is your old Grans, letting us know their spirits are here." Quieting her thoughts to hear the forest lady's voices, she looked at Nicole and Heather playing, Bandon smiling a knowing dog's smile. May closed her eyes again, just listening.

# Chapter 10

## SWEET DREAMS

**TWELVE YEARS LATER,** Nicole lay still on the forest floor, only a few miles from the Natural Bridge Campground. As she slept, an odd dream passed through her. *I'm Snow White,* she thought, smiling at the forest creatures watching over her with a serenity she felt move from them into her. A mother doe and her fawn, squirrels, rabbits and raccoons surrounded her. Birds overhead sung a cheerful sleepy time song, so laying her head back down, Nicole breathed in and thought the deep pine aroma must be the sweetest smell she had ever known.

Now fully aware she was dreaming, Nicole felt weightless, freely drifting upward looking down to see herself, her body anyway, sleeping under the tree and covered by a warm blanket of evergreen branches. Floating comfortably around and through the great old fir, shifting easily with the soft swaying limbs until she hovered about the very top, Nicole considered the misty, moon shadowed forest undulating beneath the night sky. *It's so peaceful here...* From somewhere within the wind she then heard singing voices, "Brigeed, Brigeed, Brigeeeed, Amaterasu, Amaterasu, Amaterasuuu," as she also felt a gentle tugging from behind. Expecting the face of a goddess, Nicole turned to find herself staring up at the shimmering half-moon. *The moon is singing to me, I can feel the moon, I'm smiling at the moon, we're smiling at each other...* Nicole sang joyfully along, "Brigeed, Brigeeed, Amaterasu, Amaterasuu," while dancing in the starry sky above the trees.

Two especially bright stars above her, they seemed to shine brighter in response to her noticing them, began twinkling silver sparkles that broke free, drifting wherever the solar winds may take them. A gentle, lovely warmth flowed through Nicole's loved and formless spirit, a joyful knowing those two stars were Nana and Obi-chan, watching over her. She twirled and pirouetted, singing grateful prayers, *Thank you, Lord, thank you Jesus, thank you for your angels, thank you for my mom and Heather and my grans and thank you for Ian...*

# Chapter 11

## ORCHARD HISTORY

**ERICH LARRSEN PACED** the length of a great wooden table, pivoted on his boot heel and with another pass reviewed the baskets full with pears, apples and blueberries. The orchardist's round, short brimmed Sunday hat provided little shade for his face or neck against the late October, southern Oregon sun. It was not Sunday, but he was dressed in his best knee high, black leather boots. His grey wool trousers tucked into the boots were held up by black suspenders, sharp contrast against a crisp, white button-down shirt. His son, Jeremiah stood at one end of the table, dressed identically. Only his father's trim beard seemed to differentiate. This first son had already reached his father in height of 5' 8", quite average for 1902. They appeared deceptively thin in their church shirts, for each of them were chiseled strong after the five years of clearing the surrounding woods and planting their grove of young fruit trees.

"Kor garmal er du?" the father asked without breaking stride.

"Fjorten, Far, I am fourteen but if I may, English, no Norsk, no Norwegian, as we will be speaking English to Mr. Jack."

"Fjorten, Tecumseh Jack's son would be fjorten. Fourteen."

"Yes, I miss him also. I yet can understand it, Morning Sun thrown from a horse. He was the best rider I know."

"Breaking in a wild horse, Jeremiah, a most strong and spirited beast."

"Yes sir. Would you wish to say Mr. Jack's welcome, again?"

The father cleared his throat, "Waq lis i?"

"Excellent words, Far, only you ask the question after waq lis. Waq lis? Then, i. Waq lis? i. Mr. Jack's language is difficult."

"Klammath-Modoc is more difficult than English, agreed. Thank you for your help son, that rascal surely will have a new greeting in Norsk for me, I must be ready."

"What does Tecumseh mean, Far?"

"It tells his people he is their medicine man. He is also named for Captain Jack, the Modoc warrior chief who won battles fighting the US Calvary." Mr. Larrsen stopped walking at the faint thumping and rattle of horses and wagon. "That will be him. Hjelp meg, Gud," he said quietly.

"God is here to help, I am sure. It is a good harvest."

"Yes son, ros Gud."

"Praise God, my Far."

A lone horse and broadly smiling rider, his long black hair flying behind him and dressed in buckskin came galloping out of the trees and up the trail toward them. "Mr. Jack!" the son yelled as the horse stopped and rider dismounted with a noticeable grimace and grunt. An open, wooden wagon drawn by two horses followed. When it stopped, Jeremiah looked in the back of the wagon, where baskets with several different dried fishes were arranged.

"Hei kompis!" said the Indian in perfectly good Norwegian. Dressed in knee high boots, shirt and pants all buckskin decorated with colored beads, feathers and bear teeth, Tecumseh Jack shook hands with Erich, then turned to shake Jeremiah's hand. Looking into his face smiling, "Hei kompis! to you, Jeremiah."

“Hey friend! to you, Mr. Jack.”

“Waq lis? i,” Mr. Larrsen asked in Klamath-Modoc.

A wry grin appeared on each man’s face.

“Moo dic,” his friend answered.

“I am glad you are well, Tecumseh Jack. Your vision quest, it was good?”

“Yes, Llao’s spirit swam with me in the water of Mount Mazama and stayed with me on the climb out.”

“Would you share your vision?” Jeremiah asked.

“That might be his business,” Erich began to say.

Tecumseh Jack smiled. “Llao’s gift, my vision came not to my eyes, to my ears. I sat on a great, powerful rock after my swim, watching Mazama’s blue water waiting for my vision. After a time I heard my son’s voice singing on the wind, across the water he came to me, singing with the old ones, singing ancient words I did not understand. Singing so beautiful, I know in this heart Morning Sun rests happy with the Great Spirit. My vision was good, my friend.”

“My heart is happy to hear your vision, my family has prayed for you. I’m honored to see you in your Medicine Man clothes,” said Erich with a slight tip of the hat.

“Thank you, Norway Larrsen, I feel strong in spirit still. I will be in white man’s clothes when I return to the reservation. I do not know if I will wear this again.”

“Uufta, you have many more vision quests in you, my friend,” Erich said with a slight smile and direct blue eyes. “I’ll say though, quite a walk in and out of the vulkanen for an old man.”

“Volcano,” Jeremiah translated.

“My backside is sore. This journey was hard. Morning Sun would be of age to vision quest now.”

“I’m sorry, sir, I miss him too.” Jeremiah offered.

"I may be the last Klamath Medicine Man, the end of Tecumseh. The boys only see their quest as a way to get off the reservation. I was angry at them for a time but then I see this is not their fault. The reservation is not our life, it makes us lazy in all ways. But to not seek the Great Spirit, now I cry for them."

Erich answered, "You will stay here tonight, Tecumseh Jack, Matilda will insist. We'll eat, make a fire, have a nip and get you a good sleep."

"Thank you, my friend. A message came to the reservation, did you hear? President Teddy Roosevelt says he can change Mazama's name. He says, Crater Lake is now Mazama's name. Some Klamath angry, some do not care. I tell them, Mazama it has been since Llao, since all things, the mountain knows its name."

"Crater Lake? Hmmph, nobody around here will ever call it that," Erich said, then paused before, "Tecumseh Jack, right off I must tell you I am troubled."

"What is not right for you, Norway Larrsen?"

"Our harvest is less than promised. I have one less basket of pears and two less of apples, less one berry basket."

"The trees look strong."

"They are." Eric Larrsen looked at the ground, then square in the eyes of his friend. "Someone is stealing from us."

"After harvest?"

"No, off the trees, first thought it bears, they climb high in the trees and break off branches, big ones with ripe fruit and take them away or eat them there and leave the branch on the ground. They'll leave cot pits and cherry pits behind, no other mess. A big scat one time."

"A bear you say, Larrsen?"

Shaking his head he answered, "No, it is men. I've found

tracks of two different men, most big fellas, both of them. They wear no boots or moccasins."

"Feet bare? Big men?"

"Yes, even when it's damn cold. I've tracked them deep into the woods and their strides," Erich paused, "they are two most big men, Tecumseh."

"You have never seen these men?"

"No, they only come at night, late. The dogs do not like them. These men are away quick when I come out. And the air is foul after them."

"What is this smell?"

"Awful as a skunk with his hair on fire."

Closing his eyes, breathing out with arms folded the wry grin returned to the medicine man's face. "Yayaya-ash, The Frightener. You lumber-jacked many years, you do not know the hairy man-beast of the trees?"

"Hairy man-beast? You mean skookums? Skookums, you saying skookums are true, Tecumseh?"

"Yes, you will need to learn to live with skookum, our yayaya-ash."

"Skookums, uufta, campfire stories."

The wry grin vanished as Tecumseh looked directly at his friend. "Tonight at our campfire I will tell you of yayaya-ash. I must prepare even to speak of them. Skookum is most real, Larrsen."

"Ros Gud, I heard the Chinook call them skookums when I logged the Puget Sound."

"All tribes have a name for them."

Reading his friend's face and finding no humor there, "Live with them, Tecumseh?" Erich asked.

"Your fruit trees, your home are near den of yayaya-ash. You must respect the many ways yayaya-ash is strong, with many powers. They will take more than fruit," he said, looking at Jeremiah.

"The Chinook are a hardy people and they were scared of them," Erich added grimly.

Sheep and cows scattered as Tecumseh Jack walked across pasture toward the forest that bordered Erich Larrsen's property. Erich and Jeremiah followed until he stopped at a dry creek bed that ran parallel to the tree line. "Next spring after the snow we'll make an all year stream from a well we are digging at Union Creek," Erich explained. "It'll branch the water to all of the trees from here and circle back to the creek."

Gazing out at the open pasture across from the dry creek, Tecumseh Jack said, "Here, Norway Larrsen, this is where you must give to yayaya-ash his own trees. Across from your watering creek here by the forest, your skookum will understand. When the trees here bring fruit I will come and sing to the sky, yayaya-ash will hear me. Perhaps then your skookum will leave your trees and family be."

# Chapter 12

## LARSSEN ORCHARDS

**MICHAEL TURNED OFF** the state highway onto County Road 26 and soon, with blessed relief, saw the LARSSEN ORCHARDS sign and lone mail box. It was barely past 7:00 a.m. and Saturday, but he was sure Eric's parents would be up, so he pulled onto the dirt and gravel road and followed alongside parallel rows of fruit trees, each row interspersed with yellow-orange sunrise bursts. *Pear, cherry, plumbs, apricot and apple,* thought Michael, remembering their sequence, *and the berries are south of the house, pastures southeast...* In the summer of 1982, Michael worked with Eric for Eric's parents cutting and clearing dead fruit tree branches. Working in the trees was hard, dirty work, but Michael would come to think of this as the best job he ever had. Being sore after a day's work reminded him of playing sports and he liked the simplicity of climbing trees and cutting the deadwood. During breaks he and Eric would often stay up high in a tree, sitting in the branches talking, taking the views of the orchard in the forest.

Eric's dad appreciated Michael's good work each day, a no-complaining effort he didn't really expect out of a kid from

California. Bill Larssen also quietly appreciated that having Eric's college friend around seemed to bring a better effort out of his son. Eric's dad even let himself imagine Michael might help his son appreciate the quality of life the orchard and their little forest town offered.

The road curved around the last rows of trees. These were short, stout, and somehow sporting late fall apples amongst brown and yellowing leaves. Michael marveled at those apples surviving and thriving in high altitude Oregon in November. The fact that orchards and pastures had been carved out of this wilderness by Eric's Norwegian ancestors was always amazing to him. Barking dogs greeted the van as he rounded the last row and into view came the Larssen's cabin style home. Dominated by the front steps and porch, the home built from trees cut down to make room for fruit trees stood as it had since 1897, the year his friend's great, great-grandfather Erich Larssen decided he was done with logging and wanted to settle. If one might consider clearing forest and raising fruit trees settling.

Michael made several visits to Mazama Creek with Eric during their time in Eugene but had not been back since 1984. When Eric's mom stepped out the front door as he stopped the van, she at first looked the same as well. It was only when he reached the porch steps that he could see she was still wiry strong looking, her sharp blue eyes smiling to see him, but it still shocked him slightly to see her now in her 70s. "I'm sorry for not calling first Mrs. Larssen, I know it's early. I'm Eric's friend Michael Gardner."

After shooing off the dogs she smiled saying, "Hi Michael, please come in. Eric called yesterday and said you were coming, he should be on his way from Seattle, leaving early to make the Vet's Day game. Bill is really looking forward to seeing you and Eric. I almost didn't tell him in case Eric had some last minute thing. That's happened before."

"Well Mrs. Larssen, Eric better get here, the folks at the Buckhorn are hoping to see him too. My trip was kind of sudden, Eric didn't get much warning. I'm really glad to hear he's on his way." He followed her into the kitchen and sat at the small table there.

"If you don't mind my saying, you look a little rough, Mike. Can I get you a cup of coffee or something to eat? Eric said you were camping at the bluff, is that where you stayed?"

"Yes, Mrs. Larssen, I tried camping at the bluff."

"A little cold, wasn't it?"

"Yes ma'am. Actually, I had kind of a strange night." She set a cup of black coffee in front of him. "Thank you. I was going to go into town to Beckie's, I didn't mean to be so early."

"How about some oatmeal and toast?"

"That would be great, Mrs. Larrsen. I seem to remember you can usually get some pretty good jam around here."

Eric's mom smiled, "So, if you don't mind Mike, you had something happen at the bluff?"

"Yes, Mrs. Larssen." Michael breathed out before speaking. "I think a Bigfoot went through my camp. Most scared I've ever been, ever. It climbed up the bluff, it came over the top of the cliff. The top of that cliff..." She looked back at Michael, her clear, blue eyes widening ever so slightly. "It stunk, it left these huge footprints. They look just like human, but they're way bigger than mine and I'm a size twelve. I could hear it breathing, Mrs. Larssen, like it was thinking about what to do when it stopped by my sleeping bag. I whizzed my sweatpants, it made this wild animal weird scream." He looked up, his cheeks red and she was smiling again.

"Do you mind if I tell Bill?"

"No, Mrs. Larssen."

"I guess we haven't seen you since Eric's wedding, have we?

"Yes ma'am, I think it has been that long."

"Bill and I are leaving pretty quick for the Vet's Day parade." She paused before starting, "Well, Mike, I've lived around here my whole life, never seen a skookum myself. Ask any local and they'll say it's all hooey. Get 'em drinking though and they'll tell you a story about an uncle or a cousin that smelled, heard or saw something that scared the heck out of them. My Uncle Elmer told me he saw one in his headlights out toward the Natural Bridge and swore up and down it was no bear. Even drunk, he'd know a bear. The fact he told the story knowing he'd catch heck just about convinced me." She hesitated again. "But truly, how in the Sam Hill could something like that live in the woods and never get caught or shot or leave scat or a body that proved they were out there? That just doesn't make sense to me."

"I'd say I dreamed it Mrs. Larssen, but those tracks were there this morning. I was too scared to drive through the woods last night. No human could climb that bluff without gear, let alone walk it."

Eric's mom sipped her coffee and looked over her cup at Michael. "Honestly, Mike, I have had a couple times out riding when my horse spooked, usually you figure it's a bobcat or maybe a cougar. This one time though, I was checking fence and my horse stopped, just stopped and all of a sudden the hair on my neck and arms went stiff. I swear I can remember every hair sticking out, it was the weirdest feeling something was watching me. Then, the wind shifted a little and I smelled something rank, like something real moldy. I never had a horse want to make tracks that bad and I didn't argue, we went straight back to the barn. It hit me that it could be a skookum and I got the willies that day." Mrs. Larssen sipped her coffee again. The memory seemed to genuinely disturb her. "When I was a kid we used to hear some Indian stories, some were funny, some scary, said they like to bang branches together to let you know they were there. Indians claimed they travelled all around here through the lava tubes and were scared of them and if they scared the old Rogue and Klamath tribes, well, I always figured those stories were just a good boogie man way to keep Indian kids from wandering off. You know after that time on the horse, I had nightmares about the dang things for a while."

Michael's face got a look that stopped her. "I just remembered something, Mrs. Larssen. About a month ago, I had a dream I hadn't had since I was a kid. It was this recurring nightmare I used to have. We used to visit my grandparents every summer up in Washington, near Okanagon and their house had a basement. I used to have this dream where my kid brother and I were in the basement and Bigfoots were walking around my grandparent's backyard. It always ended with me hearing one walking down the basement stairs coming to us. I used to wake up scared every time, trying to protect my kid brother. I don't think I ever wee'd my jammies though." Eric's mom laughed. "Anyway, I just had that dream again a few weeks ago. It woke me up, Carol said I was yelling in my sleep."

"There's a lot of strange things they say about skookums. Bill and I have known each other from when we were kids. After we were married and I moved out here from town, Bill's granddad told me skookums came down and ate the fruit on the east end of the orchard next to the tree line. He said not to go down there. He had a real Norwegian, real dry sense of humor, so I thought he was kidding."

"That's funny Mrs. Larssen, I remember a section of trees

on the other side of the irrigation ditch Mr. Larssen told us not to clear."

"Those would be them, the wild trees, Bill calls them. Every year, please don't tell Bill I told you this, I don't know if Eric even knows, Bill tells the hands not to pick those trees. He says it's for the birds and critters and keeps them out of the rest of the trees. His dad and grandpa did the same thing. Sounds silly but all I know is we never pick there, whatever kind of year we're having. That section, four trees of everything we grow and some berry brush Bill doesn't cut back either. It's the way Bill's great grandfather laid it out." At that moment the back door opened.

"You ready? Who's car's out front?" Eric's dad walked in and looked at Michael. "California plates, I'll be darned. Been a few years Mike, what brings you? You ready to work? I could use a decent hand in the orchard."

"If you need me, I'm here for you Mr. Larssen. I just needed a time-out, thought coming up here and camping at the bluff would help me sort some things out. I called Eric and left a message. I'm hoping he'll show up. He didn't get much notice though."

"Well, I know his mom would appreciate a visit."

Marcie Larrsen turned to Michael. "Why don't you take a shower and sleep in Eric's room while we're at the parade? When Eric gets here you can go to the game together. And of course, you're welcome to stay here tonight."

"Thank you, Mrs. Larssen. Good talking to you, I appreciate it."

"It's good to see you, Mike."

The shower was a godsend. Michael brushed his teeth and went to Eric's old bedroom. A 1979 Walden High football team picture, a Seattle Seahawks Steve Largent poster, sports trophies and a framed prom picture of Eric and Kelly were still in their places. Michael's eyes held the prom couple for a moment and he thought of Kelly yesterday at the Buckhorn. Her smile was still stunning and he said a quiet prayer hoping she was happy.

It felt so good to get under the covers that he said another quiet prayer of thanks. Michael pulled blankets around him and closed his eyes, deep sleep and dreams without monsters coming quickly.

# Chapter 13

## LOGGER

**THE SUN FINISHED** rising as Jason and Sam marched through the Rogue forest toward Grey Canyon. The woods were quiet and still save for Sam's breathing, which Jason noted was gradually becoming louder. He did not break his pace though, as Jason simply could not slow himself despite Sam or the increasing uphill grade. His day was finally here and he was close now. In fact, the ascending slope he felt beginning to pull at his leg muscles caused Jason to pump his arms and lean his shoulders forward. Striding over the deer trail, pushing branches and brush out of his way with little regard for Sam's proximity behind him, Jason imagined a 200 foot tall, bigger than a house redwood breaking and falling to the canyon floor, parting the mist, the thunderous crash echoing endlessly. This day would put to rest any doubt, his own or anyone else, he was meant to be a logger.

Jason Ibsen knew exactly what he wanted to be when he was seven years old. Before thoughts of football or logging or anything else, Jason believed that any morning he would wake up a real action hero, a Mighty Morphin' Power Ranger. Without fail each day after school, Little Jason got off the bus that stopped at his grandparent's long driveway on Highway 62, ran home and watched the TV teenagers morph into defenders of the world. In the countless crayon drawings Jason drew he was with the Rangers, battling earth shaking monsters and laying waste to swaths of skyscrapers, a necessary price to save the rest of the world from total destruction. Jason would draw himself the Forest Green Power Ranger because he lived next to the forest and his grandpa worked with the trees at his job.

After the Power Rangers show was over he waited for his grandfather to come home from the Mazama Creek Mill, watching out the front window for the pickup truck. Grandpa Jeremiah walking through the door to give Jason and his baby sister Kate a hug and kiss before heading to Grandma Ellen in the kitchen, Jason loved the smell of the mill and his grandpa's sweat but after work. He always showered though, "so that your Grandma doesn't have to smell the mill on me." Then they would sit together for the dinner she made. Jeremiah and Ellen Ibsen, husband and wife for 41 years loved their routine and they loved the two grandbabies they were raising in Mazama Creek.

The Ibsens had endured the greatest of all possible heartaches in 1982. Their son and only child Mathew, a Navy Seal, had been killed in Central America. Details from the military were few, "killed while on maneuvers," the navy chaplain who came to the house and accompanying letter had said. They had become used to waiting weeks or months for a call or letter, Mathew unable to share his destinations.

His military funeral at the Presbyterian Church in Mazama Creek and their daughter-in-law attending with baby Jason brought some solace. They did not know Christine well, as Mathew had met her while stationed in North Carolina. When she confided to her mother-in-law that she did not have much to go back to and she would lose her house on the base in a few weeks, Ellen asked if she would consider raising baby Jason in Oregon. When Christine said Mazama Creek had to be better than back home, Jeremiah and Ellen welcomed her and baby Jason into their house.

Soon however, Christine became bored with life in Mazama Creek and caring for an infant seemed more and more to be a burden to her. Ellen tried not to judge when Christine made out of town friends in Medford and over-night trips became long weekends and long weekends then turned to several days at a time away from the baby. Finally, her concerns had to be expressed, especially in view of Christine's evidently deteriorating health. Their conversation did not go well. After screaming profanities at Ellen, Christine slammed the door and drove away, leaving her wailing baby behind. Two weeks later, Christine was arrested in Medford for shop lifting and possession of meth. When she could not stick with her treatment program and was rearrested a few months later, she was sentenced to a year in the women's correctional facility in Salem. It was there she agreed and signed to the Ibsen's becoming the official guardians of baby Jason. Alone in a small room at the prison on the day they signed the papers, Ellen told Jeremiah that God was easing their grief for Mathew and paraphrased one of her favorite proverbs. "We can't withhold good from those it's due when it's in the power of our hands to give it."

"Ufta," he replied. Ellen laughed while crying. She took her husband's hand and he looked at her smiling and from that moment they raised baby Jason just as they had loved and cared for Mathew. Their niece Kelly stepped up for the Ibsens then too, putting her heart into helping her Aunt and Uncle raise baby Jason.

One fall Sunday three years later, the Ibsens returned home from church to discover a car seat holding a crying baby set on their front porch. Jeremiah read the paper tucked into the baby blanket and handed it to Ellen, then bent down to pick up the wriggling bundle. Barely legible, Christine's note read, "Kate is a good girl. I'm doing crank again. I know you will love her better than me and she can be with Jason her brother. I did good for long time she is ok I tried Im sorry Thank You." Ellen looked at Jeremiah holding baby Kate and then down at her grandson and said, "Lord help us, Jason, this is Kate, your baby sister."

Over the years, the comfortable habits at the Ibsen house rarely changed. Soon after dinner came bedtime for Jason and Kate. Jason liked to listen through his door to his grandparents talking and watching TV. The best part of listening as he drifted toward sleep was that the TV shows or sometimes his Grandma would make his Grandpa laugh. Ellen always did most of the talking, usually about the church or the PTA at Jason's school or she caught Jeremiah up on the doings of their neighbors and other families. Jason noticed one night that his grandpa was talking about the mill. Virtually every day he had heard his Grandma ask about Grandpa's work day and his answer religiously would be, "Fine, nobody got hurt." If she hinted at wanting details, Jeremiah would then say, "I lived it all day. I don't want to live it again at home, please tell me about your day." So the night he heard Grandpa talking a lot about the mill, Little Jason tried hard to hear everything. He did not understand but dared not get out of bed to ask what Grandpa meant when he told Grandma, "If the mill closes, I'll work at Larssen's or we'll have to move." Grandma said something too quiet to hear but Jeremiah answered her clearly, "Screw

Lincoln City and screw Springfield. This is where Matt would want Jason raised and it's best for Kate too."

A few months later, sometime after Christmas and while snow was on the ground, Jeremiah walked into the house, only touched the top of his grandson's head, passed baby Kate's outstretched arms and went straight to the kitchen. Jason could hear him talking to his grandmother through the door. "The bastards finally did it. No BLM cutting for God knows how long. Damn huggers, goddamn owls. We're shutting down, the owners announced it to everyone at the end of day shift." Jason came into the kitchen and saw something he had never seen before, something he would never forget. Tears rolled down his grandfather's face.

"Grampa?" Jeremiah scooped the boy up and held him. His grandmother knelt beside them and put her arms around them both.

"The Lord will provide," she said through her own tears.

"We'll be ok, son, your grandma's right."

"What will everyone else do?" his mother asked. "The town will die."

"I don't know."

The next Sunday as always, they went to church at First Presbyterian of Mazama Creek. After the hymns, Pastor Jones stood before a congregation looking to him as they never had before. He had prayed very hard for guidance. The good pastor had done his best to gauge their ability to take a tough message at a tough time. He looked over a full church, an Easter or Christmas Eve sized gathering. Tears were being dabbed when Pastor Jones instructed to open to Paul's letter to the Philippians, Chapter 4. "Brother Paul, whipped and chained in a Roman prison, does he cry or does he praise God?" The tone of admonishment did not set well with Jeremiah Ibsen.

He folded his arms as Ellen set her handkerchief into her lap. Pastor Jones began, "While in that Roman jail Paul has the strength and faith to write, Rejoice in the Lord always, and again I say, Rejoice..."

After the service, when Grandpa said, "Not today," to Aunt Kelly's invitation to come to the Buckhorn for burgers and pool, Little Jason sensed his grandfather change. They piled quietly into the car, the boy holding his toddler sister's hand.

"I think I'll re-read Philippians today," his grandma said as they pulled out of the church parking lot. And then Grandpa Jeremiah did something again Jason had never seen or heard before. He spoke harshly to his wife.

"Screw Paul. Rejoicing won't put food on any damn table." Grandma Ellen gasped, and then retrieved the hanky from her purse.

The next day all the kids at school were talking about the stupid owls and stupid tree huggers. Riding the bus home that afternoon, Little Jason knew what needed to be done. He now understood what closing the mill could mean.

When he came home, Grandma changed the TV station to the Power Rangers and Jason drew his best ever picture of the Forest Green Power Ranger. A seven year old boy's desperate imagination morphed the Forest Green Power Ranger into a giant robot with chainsaw arms and a forest full of trees flew into gigantic stacks ready for the mill. The skyscraper robot walked towering over the woods when the job was done and everyone in Mazama Creek, most especially his Grandparents and Aunt Kelly, came out to cheer and thank him. The Forest Green Power Ranger stood tall above their town, taller even than the Mazama Lumber Mill smoke stack. Next, Jason wrote a special letter. The boy came into the kitchen, "Gramma, can you help me? I need to mail to the Power Rangers."

"Mail what, kiddo?" He handed her the paper, she opened it and sat down.

Dear Rangers,

I need to be the forest green power ranger. Please. We do not have monsters. We have skookums and coogars but gramma says they are scared of people. I will cut down trees to help my grampa and friends to keep the mill open. To help the Rangers I will go fight monsters with my chainsaw arms with you. I made you a picture of the forest green power ranger. Your friend Jason.

He could not understand why his grandmother was crying again.

"Is it ok, Gramma?" The boy could not possibly know the fullness of reason for his grandmother's tears. Ellen was smart and wise and she grasped well the layered nature of life. The bitter irony that caused a crayon picture to reach so painfully deep inside her was that her husband was once a logger and she had made him leave the work he loved to go to the Mazama Lumber Mill. She had good reason, Jeremiah never denied that. Mathew and his cousin Kelly were sixth graders when Kelly's father, Jason, was killed working in the woods, no more than forty feet from his brother. It took her several years of trying though before Jeremiah would give up logging to become a foreman at the mill.

The brothers Ibsen had followed their father's line to working in the woods. The summer after graduating from Walden High in 1958, Jeremiah started with Gerring Timber. He was hired by Hank Gerring Sr., the owner, and worked side by side with Hank Jr. Two summers later, younger brother Jason would follow the same path.

Their ancestors were immigrants from Norway who settled first in Minnesota because it reminded them of the old country. Many would pioneer to the Great Northwest, where the Norwegian's famously hardy and stoic natures were well suited to the rigors of work in the forest. They would establish themselves in logging camps from British Columbia to the Sierras.

Jason was a 14 year veteran with Gerring Timber when a new faller's rookie mistake caused a tree to fall the wrong way. In one brutal, swift instant, 12 year old Kelly's father was gone. Ellen's begging, pleading, and finally outright threats would eventually break him. Jeremiah left the woods and went to work at the Mazama Creek Mill.

Ellen looked down on her grandson, holding his crayon letter and picture of the forest green power ranger. She knelt to hold Little Jason close, then got up, walked out and returned holding an envelope and stamp.

"Do you know where to send it, Grandma?"

"I sure do, baby." She used the phone book to find the right TV station and wrote Power Rangers and the Medford address on the envelope and they walked out to the mail box together.

The Mazama Creek Mill closed a few months later and Jeremiah was among the fortunate few to land a job at the Larrsen Orchards Packing House. He would also take work in the orchards for Bill Larssen, on those days finding quiet satisfaction climbing up into the fruit trees and using a hand saw and small chainsaw to clear deadwood. Other days depending on where the help was needed, Jeremiah would volunteer to leave the warehouse and join the pickers out in the orchards, challenging himself to keep up with the Larssen's seasonal crew.

A few weeks later, Little Jason received a manila envelope with Japanese writing above the Ibsen's address. He tore into it and found a glossy picture with an autograph from the

Blue Ranger and a card to send with $29.00 to join the official Power Rangers fan club. It did not upset Jason that Grandma told him they could not spend the money, as the Rangers letter did not discuss becoming a real Ranger or using the Forest Green Ranger's chainsaw arms to battle dangerous monsters.

A year later, Grandpa Jeremiah had a stroke while sorting pears at the packing house. Three months after his stroke, he died in a nursing home in Ashland. Like his brother Jason almost 20 years before him, Jeremiah was known, respected and dearly missed by family and community. At his service, Pastor Jones asked if anyone would like to speak about or relate a story concerning Jeremiah. Workers from the mill said that Mr. Ibsen was the best foreman a man could have, and one admitted they joked behind his back about his repetitive safety training sessions but, "we all knew he was the reason no one ever got hurt at the mill."

Another man then rose to speak. In a church full of big, burly woodsmen, he was the biggest man Little Jason had ever seen. A reddish buzz cut and trim beard framed his large round head. Every eye in the church was riveted as he began.

"I'm Hank Gerring Jr. I run Gerring Timber for my dad now, Jeremiah and his brother Jason worked with me and my dad for a lot of years. First off, Jeremiah was a great logger. I haven't seen a better faller before or since unless it was his brother. Both of them were real naturals who worked hard at their craft, cutting big trees. I'm not just saying that because of the circumstance, it's no surprise to hear Jeremiah was a damn good mill foreman, sorry. He was as hard working, dependable and as good a man to be around as anyone I've ever worked with. Jeremiah never wasted words and he didn't tolerate fools as they say either, which I always appreciated about him." Hank cleared his throat to continue. "When he came back to work after we lost his brother, that first day back I offered to put him in the dozer. He just looked at me and said, "can't Hank," that was all he said and he went back out to cutting trees. I'll never forget him walking off with his saw over his shoulder after he said that." The bear of a man paused, then said, "I also know how much he loved Ellen and Mathew. Those years we worked operations all over Oregon and Washington, Jeremiah stayed true to his beliefs and family. He was God fearing and never once gave in to the temptations that come from being away from home. He made the men around him better, myself included. He was a great worker, family man and friend."

Standing outside the church after the service, Hank shook Little Jason's hand, looked down at the boy and said, "Son, if I can ever do anything for you or your Grandma, you just ask. I mean that Ellen."

She only said, "I know, Hank. Thank you for coming and thank you for your words." She took her grandson by the hand, turned and walked away. That night, she took an old scrapbook down from a bedroom closet and showed Little Jason his heritage. He looked in wonder at a black and white photograph of young Jeremiah and Jason, who he was named for, Ellen told him. "He was your Aunt Kelly's dad. He was killed by a tree falling down, Jason. He was a good man like your grandpa." She pointed out the Ibsen brothers posing proudly with other men on a gigantic tree stump. Ellen turned the page and gasped, "oh gosh look at that Jason. That's your daddy, my Mathew, Grandpa and his brother with your Aunt Kelly and Eric. They were such good kids," Ellen said tearing up. They were in hunting gear, rifles over their shoulders except Kelly, who held a bow and arrow. All smiled.

"They were hunting, Grandma. When can I go hunting?"

"I'll talk to your Aunt Kelly about that. She'll be the one to take you now, baby. Tell you what though, tomorrow we go out in the woods behind the pasture and finish building that tree fort you and Jeremiah started. That would make your granddad happy to know we got that done."

"Really, Grandma? You can build a fort?"

"Of course your Grandma Ellen can build a fort."

Fourteen years after Jeremiah's funeral, Jason wondered and hoped his Grandpa's spirit walked with him and Sam to Grey Canyon. Both an explorer's sense of history and dreams of old growth forest dollars pulled at him.

Giant redwoods ancient and virgin had lived in his imagination ever since Aunt Kelly showed him satellite pictures of Mazama Creek and the Upper Rogue on her computer. Initially, they were quiet looking down from the sky at their own shut down mill, the decaying smelter and empty parking lot adjacent to their little town. "God's view," Jason said. Kelly sensed his mood shift and understanding why, toggled north and east to explore their favorite hunting areas. Kelly pointed at the screen. "Those old clear cut sections sure stick out. Been years since they were cut, but still ugly, aren't they?"

"We always replant, Aunt Kelly. It takes a few years to come back but it's not like the old days where they cut and left nothing but stumps. At least Hank doesn't work that way. I know a tree farm isn't the same as old growth but its progress."

"Not so sure about that, Jason. Old growth is old growth. Hey look, there's Grey Canyon," she said, looking at the crooked line of white that looked hand drawn against the surrounding shades of green.

"Now that's cool, can you go closer?" Jason asked. Enthusiasm from her sometimes melancholy nephew was welcome and Kelly happily brought the image down. Jason stared at the screen. "There has to be a river down there, might come underground in a lava tube like the Natural Bridge. I wonder what trees are down there?" He traced the line of mist with his finger near the screen. Only in two places, one north, one south, could the black, rugged ridge line be seen poking through the pale cloud. Otherwise the fog curled over the edge of the length of the canyon. As locals, both Jason and Aunt Kelly knew the legend of Grey Canyon. An opening to penetrate those ridges sought by generations of settlers, hunters and timber men had never been found on either side or end of the mysteriously deep and wide ravine. Eventually it was given up and mostly forgotten. The persistent mist would have the pioneers call it Grey Canyon.

Long before the covered wagons arrival, primordial tales preserved the memory of existence for the Mazama tribe, obliterated about 8,000 years ago when Mount Mazama volcanically blew itself into what is now Crater Lake. The native peoples of the Klamath region told their children the epic battle between Shell, god of the sky and Llao, the god of the underworld, caused Mazama to explode, destroying the Mazama tribe.

The area around and within Mazama, later named Crater Lake, became sacred ground for the Rogue and Klamath peoples. For the native warriors, their vision quest began with the journey up the mountainside, then down the steep caldera to reach the bluest of lake waters. After an icy swim refreshed and heightened the senses, meditative prayer was answered when one fully opened to their vision. The treacherous ascent out of the crater awaited.

Foreboding Grey Canyon, formed during that same volcanic epoch, held the natives in awe as well, though their feeling toward that area were quite different. Children were told the Mazama people's souls were trapped there, the perpetual fog hiding the light that would lead them to the Great Spirit. Legend also said the souls of the Mazama had become trapped and lived in the yayaya-ash, the Frighteners, the hairy wild men of the forest. Another myth said the yayaya-ash were guardians of Grey Canyon, reluctantly holding the Mazama spirits captive for Llao and Shell to fight over. What the Rogue's white settlers did come to know is that no Indian would go there or assist with the search for a passage of entry, no matter the offered price.

"Trees?" Kelly stared at the computer screen.

"Look at the shadow from the south ridge, I'll bet this is taken in the morning." Jason leaned forward pointing at the screen. See how this whole north side is lighter from the sun reflecting. Enough sunlight maybe, it could be like California coast old growth and no one's ever logged it. There might even be giant redwoods down there, Aunt Kelly. A river and dense, really old forest with lots of ferns might explain why the fog never lifts."

"Giant redwoods?"

"Why not?" Kelly sensed her nephew's building interest and was glad for something to spark him. He finished, "Giant redwoods, a rain forest with trees like that one you drive your car through in California." And thus was born the notion that Jason Ibsen would not let go of, that he would someday explore and log Grey Canyon. Whenever possible on time off, Jason hiked in to explore the outer perimeter of Grey Canyon.

When the US Department of the Interior reopened federal land to logging, Jason lobbied Hank to do whatever it took to win the bid and include Grey Canyon in the operation site. Jason had gone to Hank and asked to meet him after shift, away from the crew. Hank was already curious when Jason arrived at a diner near Roseburg with recent satellite pictures tucked into a folder. A timber industry living legend, the big man laughed hard when Jason first dared to show him the satellite pictures and tell the story of Grey Canyon. Seeing Jason patiently waiting out his laughter, Hank listened and looked at the pictures intently. When Hank rubbed his buzz cut back to front, Jason suspected he was more intrigued than he let on.

"Well, that's quite a theory you got there, Jason. Old growth I might buy, giant redwoods though, hmm. Damn nice thought kid, we'd make a fortune. Don't believe they'd be protected if I word the contract right and this bunch of BLM and Interior guys will go for anything." Rubbing his head again, Hank asked, "Redwoods or not, how the hell would we pull anything out of there?"

Jason showed him another satellite image. "This one's taken in August on a real hot day, thinnest I've seen the fog, Hank. See that line there? It's an avalanche chute, I'd bet anything, see how it slopes there. I've been to this spot and we can blast a hole. I think avalanches there have weakened this point, we can cut a tunnel to run a skyline through and get down into Grey Canyon. If you follow to here on the north side you can just make out tree tops poking through the mist. These taller ones are uneven on top but the smaller trees are perfectly symmetrical, characteristic of giant redwoods." The two men stared at the picture.

"That is one ambitious notion, son. I can't believe yet in prehistoric giant redwoods, but you may be right about a helluva lot of untouched old timber." He rubbed his head back to front again and said, "I'll get the bid and I'll talk to my contacts at the Fed about the contract area. This won't be the first time they think I'm crazy." Jason smiled, and they shook hands. "This reminds me of the day you asked me to put you to work. How long?"

"Almost four years." Hank shook his big head.

Three days after graduating from Walden High, Jason called Hank, introduced himself and asked for an interview for a break-in job. Hank was quiet, touched to be reminded of his old departed friends the Ibsen brothers. They arranged to meet at a cafe down the hill in Prospect. After a few minutes of general talk, Hank started asking questions. Jason looked the man in the eye and answered each without hesitation, until Hank got to the last one.

"Does your grandmother know you're here?"

Jason gazed for a moment out the diner window. "No, sir."

"Don't you have a scholarship to play football at Portland State?" Jason looked surprised.

"I read the sports and I kind of kept track of you when I saw your name in the papers," Hank said. "I watched you play last year in Elkton. You can play in college, you know."

"I need to go to work, sir. It's been tough since my granddad died. She wants me to go to school but I really feel like logging is where I need to be and I don't know if I can deal with Portland. The one thing I know is I want to be a logger like Grandpa. Well, and that I don't really like school that much and I want to work outside, Mr. Gerring. I'm not an office or classroom person. I really like being outside, I really want to be a logger, sir." Hank looked at Jason and took a bite of his sandwich, eyeing the lad with sharp eyes that reflected at once humor, compassion, intelligence, and hard-ass. The time it took Hank to munch the sandwich bite before speaking spoke a certain patient wisdom to Jason as well. A grin crept across Hank's face.

"Most likely son, not going to college is something you will regret. I had a full ride to Oregon State and screwed it up. Third week of practice I hit the line coach. He was riding me real good, called me some choice words and I decked him. I told him my old man was the only man who could call me that. That was the end of my playing ball and going to school days. My Pop kicked my ass sixteen different ways when I came home." Hank sighed. "You know, I remember you from your Granddad's funeral, I could see old Jeremiah in you that day. I knew your dad also, Matt was a great kid." Jason saw Hank rub his head back to front for the first time.

"Ok son, here's the deal. You go talk to Ellen. I won't hire you behind her back. I know you're 18 but you need her blessing. She's done a good job of raising you, I can see that. Your grandmother deserves that."

"Yes sir, you're right, Mr. Gerring."

"Jason, there's someone I want to introduce you to. Hey babe," Hank called cheerfully across the diner. A short, smiling round-faced woman came from the counter and put out her hand. "Jason, this is my wife Becky. She's been putting up with my foolishness more years than she deserves."

"Nice to meet you, Mrs. Gerring."

"Please call me Becky. Hank has been looking forward to meeting with you since you called, Jason. He thought the world of your grandfather and his brother. We knew your dad, too. He was a good man, Jason."

"Thank you, Mrs., thank you. I was a kid but I remember Hank coming to grandpa's funeral. I learned Grandpa Jeremiah was a logger that day."

"Alright son, you go have that talk with Ellen," Hank said. "Let me know how it goes. I don't expect it will be easy."

Hank was right of course. His grandmother shed tears when Jason told her what he wanted to do with his life. He did not tell her he could always go back to college and play football, he said he wanted to be a logger. In the end, she could not defeat her grandson's will, and Jason reported to the Gerring Timber Company for work. The hard won respect of the Gerring crew came with sacrifice and time. Four tough years had passed when Jason called his Aunt Kelly with the news Hank had won the bid to log Grey Canyon. "Hank said I'll go in first to check it out." His aunt's first feeling was to share Jason's elation, but then something uneasy worked into her.

"You'll have a crew with you, not just you, right?"

"Oh yeah, we'll plan it out, Hank works safe. I'm gonna head up to scout the area where I think we can get in next weekend. You should come with me and bring your bow."

"I have to work. You're going to find your avalanche chute?"

"That's the spot, Aunt Kelly."

# Chapter 14

## GREY CANYON

**JASON DOWN-SHIFTED HIS** pace slightly to help Sam keep up. They had not spoken for a time but higher ground meant the trees and brush thinned and the hike was actually a little easier despite the increasing grade.

"Sam, if you don't stop looking behind you, we'll never get there."

"Sorry, Jason, I just never lost the being watched feeling. I think seeing the crane and yarder freaked me out some."

"Understandable Sam, those tree hugger dumb shits must have some elaborate stuff to do what they did. I still don't get how they threw some of those big rocks. Might've used a helicopter, but we should of heard it. What a waste. Hank has plenty of insurance but now he's pissed. He sure as hell won't be missing any trees in the bulldozer's path today."

"That's no shit," agreed Sam as they walked past the last line of trees and looked up. Out of the forest floor rose the black volcanic wall, the impenetrable ridge of Grey Canyon. At the very top, they could see the white mist curling upward and then down toward them. Before them, a barren, rocky expanse led to the strange, gigantic rock fortress.

"There it is, Sam, the top of the ridge. We're almost there." Sam stopped to catch his breath and take a pull from the canteen. "We're going up into that? Seriously?" Sam asked between breaths.

"I thought you were in better shape than that," Jason said.

"Working for Hank keeps me in decent shape, I ain't the mountain goat I used to be. More an old goat now, I'll be 40 in a couple of years."

"See that ledge where the fog kind of sits?" Jason pointed up. "The rock I moved to find the opening is about half way up to there. Another 20 minutes."

"This place is crazy Jason. That ridge runs the length of the canyon?"

"It runs all the way around the canyon, first reason nobody gets in. Second is the drop inside. But we know the secret passage."

"My lucky day," Sam added with a tired grin.

Jason worked the steep trail first, stepping around boulders and rock piles, then muscling his way up an eight foot rock face. When Sam pulled himself over the last ledge, he found Jason staring at a rounded boulder tucked into the wall. He was greeted with, "I'll be damned, Sammy."

"What, Jason?" Sam sat gratefully on the hard ground, breathing hard.

"I told you last summer I searched up here for a weak point where we could blast to get to the avalanche chute. I found this boulder that looked kind of funny, it was stuck into the wall but little wisps of mist were coming out around it, so I managed to roll it back and there was this hole here, I couldn't believe it. This is the tunnel to the canyon. I've been trying to get back up here to go down and explore but Hank's schedule, you know."

"Ok, so?"

"Well, somebody came up here and rolled the damn rock back into place."

"No shit. You're sure you didn't put it back?"

"Nope, I thought about it but it took everything I had to move it once."

"Maybe an earthquake, Jason, let's just move it and get this done. I want to get this day over, knock down a few beers and watch football tonight. Any chance of females at this Buckhorn Tavern? I could be open to Mazama Creek mudhoney season."

Jason did not answer, continuing to stare at the boulder. Finally he looked at Sam. "Let's do this Sammy, let's go into Grey Canyon."

When the rock was moved, the two men inspected the oddly rounded opening. They looked into a tunnel twenty feet long and could only see light at the other end veiled in gathering mist. The fog floated towards them until white vapor fingers reached out from the hole. Jason climbed in and crawled his way to the other end. From there he poked his head out and looked down through the clouds to gauge the slope again. It seemed steeper than he remembered from last summer. The broken caldera gravel there was only 60 yards across, bordered by the interior wall, a sheer and rugged drop on both sides. The ridge at the canyon's top created an out cropping that rimmed the entire perimeter of the canyon. From there, the walls curved in as though scooped by giant hands, then fell vertically to a basin floor invisible through the clouds. Grey Canyon, scarred remnant of Mount Mazama's furious lava flows, testified to the unfathomable power and force in the volcanic explosion that would create Crater Lake. Jason had found this the only point, where a massive breaking away of the caldera rock, probably from repeated snow avalanches, caused a sloped drop to the bottom. Or at least he hoped, as it was sloped only for as far as the ever present fog allowed a satellite camera to probe. It was the only place he could see having a chance of rappelling down. It was the only place he could imagine logs being cabled out from, they would blast a bigger hole at the tunnel. A helicopter might liberate the big trees from Grey Canyon. Jason crawled back and began laying out the climbing gear.

"I'll go through first; you'll follow, Sammy. Stay in the hole until I'm out and 20 yards or so down, then you follow me. You won't be able to see the bottom but don't freak. I'm sure from the tree tops in the pictures it can't be more than three hundred feet. Let's check the rappel lines again, you all strapped in?"

If the mystery of the moved rock had created any doubt within Jason, it was gone now. Carrying ropes and wearing the harness with cable attached Jason crawled comfortably through the six foot wide, mist filled tunnel. Without hesitating he dropped out of the opening, rolled onto his side, raising while digging in and pushing up with his legs. Setting his right leg back he pivoted, faced the tunnel opening and set his heels into the black rocky ground.

"I'm going down now, let the line out, Sam."

He worked his way down the broken granite backwards and waited for Sam to come out of the tunnel. It was dark, foggy and cold. The sun would be higher and far enough around to warm this side of the canyon later in the day, in time for a better trip out, Jason hoped. He could still see the opening of the tunnel, and finally the shadow of Sam's head emerged.

"Damn, Jason, this looks like a fun hike. Your tunnel smells strange, kind of like rutting bull elk." After turning around in the tunnel, Sam lowered himself out feet first. Setting his boots in the gravelly surface he gave a hard tug at the rope, yelled, “We’re set as long as nobody moves the rock back or cuts the line. I’d say we are majorly screwed if either of those things happens.”

Pacing himself so Sam would not disappear from sight, Jason looked below hoping to see canyon bottom, but the fog thickened the deeper they dropped. Marching backwards carefully in the swirling mist wore at both men’s bodies, especially the legs, and the mind. “Disorienting if you look around, isn’t it Sam?”

“Taking that ride out on a log with the skyline may be the way to go, my ass has just about had it. Are we there yet, kid?”

Checking back over his shoulder something seemed different about the fog. Stepping back Jason’s boot only found air, grabbing and jerking the line forward he steadied himself, stopped and turned to see a thirty foot vertical drop behind him and barely visible, the canyon floor. Peering out over the ledge he saw a desolate landscape silhouetted in the mist.

“We’re there, Sam. We drop here to the bottom.”

Jason waited for Sam to reach him before dropping himself backwards over the ledge, pushing out with his feet to bounce gingerly down the hard and damp black lava wall. Finally, planting his boots with sweet relief he called up, “C’mon down Sam, now we’re here.” Gauging by the line that was left, it was a little over 300 feet from the tunnel to the canyon bottom.

In a few minutes, Sam joined him. “Looks like the moon,” Sam observed.

“Looks like the Natural Bridge, Sammy. Ever seen that spot on the Rogue where the river disappears underground in a lava tube for a while? It isn’t far from here.”

“Nope.”

Jason took two flares from his pack, tucking one into his

shirt pocket and offering the other to Sam. "Put it in my pack, thanks. Good idea in this fog, but let's not get separated and need them." They unhitched their carabineers, adjusted packs and chainsaws as Sam looked up at their climbing ropes vanishing into the mist along the sheer wall. "Save some strength for the climb out kid, going up this will be another nice workout."

"Agreed, but damn we're here Sam. We might be the first white folks or any human ever to step foot here."

"That's very cool kid, now can we get to work so beer-thirty can get here?"

Walking away from the great black wall the ground remained lava surface before changing to a grainy, grey soil. "Ok, something might be able to grow out of this," Sam noted, "something like a milkweed." The fog allowed 50 yards or so of poor visibility. Sam touched Jason's shoulder and pointed. "There you go, real impressive, dude. Hank called it, ferns."

Scattered ferns and low green brush materialized. The first stand of trees they encountered were thin white aspens. "The big boys are coming, Sam. Listen, I hear water." They walked another 50 yards at a good downward grade when the ferns and undergrowth became denser.

"Oh, here we go Jason, wow, this is more like it." They stopped to behold a mixed grove of evergreens and leafy trees. "Damn, Jason. Those might be the biggest firs I've ever seen. I'm ready to cut. Man, this'll make Hank's day. There's a bunch of different trees."

"Nice variety, old growth style. Not yet on cutting, Sammy, we got a little more exploring to do."

"Damn, that was weird."

"What's that, Sam?"

"When you said, we got a little more exploring to do, I don't know, I just got one of those feelings like I've done this or been here already things."

"Déjà vu?"

"Yeah, that is so weird. Like right now, it just feels like I could tell you what you're gonna say but I can't quite get to it."

"I've had that happen Sam, it's pretty common. I had it happen one time just walking across the field after football practice. Later I figured I might've dreamed it first."

"Maybe, that could be, this place is like a dream. It's like the more we walk, the more familiar it is. The thing is, I'm not sure I like the way the dream ends. One of those dreams you have to wake yourself up from to end it. I gotta stop thinking about this crap."

"Not talking about it would be real helpful too," Jason suggested.

Tromping over and through ever bigger ferns and thicker brush, they passed ever bigger timber stands before the ferns and brush thinned to bare ground, and the trees gave way to a respectful open space. The sound of a running creek came clearer when Sam and Jason stopped in their tracks, mouths open, looking up. Sam spoke first. "That's no fir tree, Jason, that's a friggin giant redwood. My God, that is the biggest tree I ever saw. It's bigger than my house. Holy shit, it's a grove of 'em." The gargantuan redwoods, even with their tops obscured up into the fog, presented immenseness literally breathtaking. Jason set his hand on Sam's shoulder.

"I wish my granddad could see this," he said quietly. After they walked the outer perimeter of the redwood grove, Jason set down his pack, ax and saw. "We'll take down one of these. I want to take a piece to Hank, report the size of these guys. He has to decide how we get a few of these big boys out of here."

"You got it Jason, which one?"

"Biggest one the skyline can handle, Sammy."

"I think these big fellas will be going out in sections. They gotta get through your blown up tunnel too. We'll need an operating base here and we'll need to clear a road to the canyon wall. Damn your right kid, there's a lot of money here."

Jason walked past four of the redwood goliaths before stopping. "I'd say this smaller one, you and I can do it, we can fall it into that opening right there." Striding around to the backside, after a few moments Jason called, "Sam, check this out."

Finding Jason staring down at the ground, Sam followed down to see five rocks of various shapes stacked atop each other. "You did that, that's not funny," Sam said without a smile.

"Sorry, they were like that."

"Those rocks didn't just find each other," Sam said quietly.

"There is a certain randomness, maybe it just happened."

"Right."

"Let's take it as a sign and cut this one."

"You're sure? A sign? You did that."

"Ok, I did it."

"You did it, now no more funny shit."

The men moved to opposite sides of the great tree, about to start their chainsaws when Sam yelled, "Hey, Jason, there's something moving up on this side."

"Squirrels'll jump as soon as they hear the saws."

"I think it's bigger than a squirrel."

"If it's got any sense, it'll jump or fly, right now." Jason yanked the starter rope and the roar of the chainsaw filled the canyon. Sam started his and they attacked the base of the colossal redwood together. Neither of them ever worked longer or harder to fall one tree. When it finally crashed like a mountain falling, the cracking roar and fog parting like Moses' sea was beyond the wildest of Jason's visions.

Sam stepped back and sat down. "I'm done, Jason. Let's

rest and take some of this back to Hank. How did you know redwood like this were here?"

"I thought it was possible, Sam." Jason walked along the fallen giant's length, vanishing from Sam in the still swirling mist, calling back, "In the old days it would take days to hand cut one like this. Be grateful for modern weapons. This is beautiful wood, Sammy. Some millionaire in California is going to have one sweet deck out of this."

"I'll bet a Sierra Club lawyer," Sam added. They both laughed. Jason continued his walk, and then stopped.

"Hey, Sam, come here. You need to see this."

"No, man, I earned this butt time."

"You did, Sam, but I need you to see this."

"Damn, kid."

"Please Sam, come here and look at this." Jason's strange tone caused Sam to push himself up with tired arms. Finding him standing with hands on hips looking into the fallen tree's branches, Jason asked, "What the hell is that? I'm hoping you can pass on some sage hunter wisdom."

"Hmm," Sam grunted, cocking his head. "Don't know, kid. Looks like a big basket or a nest." Amongst the redwood tangle an object about five feet long and three feet across lay entwined. It was fresh fir branches, but somehow crisscrossed and tightly interwoven. Jason reached to touch it and both men jumped back when it moved slightly. He picked up a stick and lifted one edge. "Oh hell," Sam said, "it's a baby bear. I told you something was up there." It was small, black furred, face down and barely breathing. Jason put the stick under one side and lifted it toward him. "Holy shit! Oh God, Jason! Not a bear!" They looked down upon a face. A dark face with open eyes and blood seeping from its nose and mouth.

"It's gotta be bear, the tree smashed it, oh shit, no." Jason saw small, hairy hands.

Sam's eyes were wide. "Not paws Jason, hands, hands! Hands with fingers, Jesus how could it have hands with fingers?"

The creature then shut its eyes, shuddered and stopped breathing.

"Oh my God, Jason, we killed a baby Bigfoot. Shit. Or a monkey, is it a monkey?"

Jason shook his head, staring at the creature in disbelief. "Nobody would believe this. Maybe we should take it... if it's a skookum..." He poked with the stick and turned the nest over to see inside a rounded bark bowl, a partially eaten squirrel, blackberries and two branches full with yellow apples.

"Apples, where in the hell did it get apples around here," Sam wondered?

"Larssen's, only orchards anywhere close. They'd still have some late apples. I'll be damned."

"Jason, somebody was taking care of it." The men looked at each other. "Jason, we gotta get outta here. We gotta tell Hank, he'll know what to do. C'mon man, let's go, right now."

Jason considered their choices. "Ok, you're right, we better go." They backed away from the tree and walked stunned toward their packs.

"Jason, what's that noise?" Somewhere out in the mist, deep in the redwoods something was out there, a low rumbling patter that seemed to grow louder. The men broke into a trot, almost reached their packs when clearly something was thrashing its way through the forest. "It's big, Jason, something's coming!"

"Run, Sam, run to the line!" They took off in a sprint, running as fast as they could through the fog, trees and underbrush. A sound then came from behind them, a shrieking howl that filled their ears. Another screeching wail, long and pained joined it and then two wildly crying screams followed in unison, reverberating in the trees and canyon walls. Running, hurdling over ferns, Jason reached the rappel line first, yelling as he clipped on the carabineers, "C'mon, Sam, run!" Grabbing the line he started to climb, legs digging furiously he bounded against and up the wall. He looked down and back, seeing Sam almost to the line.

"Jason!" He could barely speak for breathing hard. "Don't leave me, I hear 'em coming!"

"Run Sam, climb!" Sam reached the cable, Jason felt him struggling to hook on, looked back and gasped. Huge, dark shapes appeared, snarling and growling, moving fast through the fog. Jason bounded up panicked, then stopped to look below, seeing Sam's head just above the mist. The four shadows grew more gigantic with every stride.

"Jason! Don't leave me! Jason!!"

"Climb, Sam!!" Jason felt Sam secure himself to the line, pull himself up with a grunt, scrambling legs pushing upward, then saw Sam's wild eyed face coming toward him, frantically kicking at the wall with his boots and pulling himself with his arms. "Sam!!" Jason screamed as dark giants, hair and reaching arms broke through the grey clouds. He saw their faces, crazed violent hatred in their monstrous faces. Sam's face vanished.

"Noooaagghhh!!!" They were killing him, wild animal roaring, horrible bone cracking and ripping sounds reaching Jason. He looked down again, red colored mist swirling below and pulling himself up on the line to get away, digging frantically with his boots, a soft thump next to him and something warm splattered on the side of his face. Jason's head turned to see a human hand and arm wearing Sam's plaid shirt ripped out at the shoulder, sticking there before sliding slowly down, a simple gold wedding band on a bloody finger slipping away.

The rappel line shook as Jason held tight and tried to hug the wall. He dropped slightly, the monsters growling and barking now for him. Jason swung back and forth as they pulled and yanked the line, his body banging against the rock. His chest scraped hard and he felt the flare. With his left hand squeezing the line, Jason reached the front shirt pocket and pulled out the flare and bit the cap, tore it off with his teeth and smashed the top end against the rock. It lit flaming bright orange and he dropped it. "Rrrraaarrrgghhh," the beasts roared. They let go of the rappel line and Jason looked down to see them running away from the smoking glow. He pushed hard with his boots bounding the last of the sheer face before rolling over the ledge.

Back on the sloping gravel Jason raised on his knees straining to see through the fog, sure they were coming for him, Sam's voice screaming, "Jason, don't leave me!" echoing in his head. Jason checked himself quickly for injury, found places where he'd be black and blue later, then got to his feet and listened for steps. *They could come from anywhere,* he thought, fighting panic. Jason grabbed the rappel line, still taut and attached to the boulder at the top of the ridge, pulled and strode forward. Step by upward step he put one boot in front of the other, one boot in front of the other over the broken rock, watching and listening, expecting them to materialize out of the fog to kill him too.

And yet through the mist Jason did finally see the taut cable disappear into the tunnel opening. He stepped quietly to the hole in the rock wall, peered in and saw light, the boulder had not been rolled back. Crawling up into the opening laying on his back for a moment, Sam's rutting bull elk smell hit his nostrils. “Skookums,” Jason whispered to himself, then crept forward and stopped, listening before putting his head out. They might be waiting for him, but what choice was there except to move forward, hope and expose his head? Jason did and there was nothing waiting for him but blue sky and the sun. He pulled himself out, stood and looked around while unhitching the clips. In the distance Jason heard Hank’s bulldozer and he sat down, trying to think.

“Ohhh...” Jason said aloud, his voice trailing off. He realized the Sasquatch had destroyed the yarder and log loader last night. Jason worked to clear his mind and it hit him at once. *The skookums destroyed the yarder and crane, then I went to Grey Canyon and killed their baby. I killed a baby skookum and they killed Sam... I left Sam, Jesus, Sam’s dead...*

The echoing crack of the bulldozer taking down a small tree snapped him back. “Hank!” Jason scrambled down the rocks, reached the forest floor and ran toward the trees.

# Chapter 15

## SAINT ANTHONY

**IAN OPENED HIS** eyes, gradually focusing on bright green moss against bark. On his side facing the tree trunk that had protected him well from the elements, he immediately began confronting the events of the night. Suddenly aware that daylight enabled him to see the strands of moss attached to the bark in fine detail, fluorescent fuzzy green interwoven with the grey and brown, rough textured base of the tree, he sat straight. "What time is it?!" Ian yelled at himself. Looking quickly about, heart sinking to see Nicole was still not with him, checking his cell phone reflexively and still no signal. The sun was fairly high and already working across the southern sky as Ian stood, yelling into the woods, "Nicole! Nicole!" The silence was excruciating. *Think! You have to find her or go get help.*

Surprised at how long he had apparently slept, Ian noticed he was thirsty and hungry and took an apple and the water bottle from his pack. Eating the apple standing next to the mountain bikes, Ian looked up at the sky. How could he have put Nicole in this situation? He had been so sure their actions were right. Shifting his gaze down and up the trail, Ian prayed for Nicole to appear. "I'm sorry, baby," he whispered to himself.

Taking both of their backpacks he removed the crowbar, acid jar and other unused instruments of destruction and buried them in a shallow grave under a bush a few yards off the path. He set her pack next to the bikes in case she returned, then took his compass in hand and double checked north. Shouldering his pack, "Nicole!" he shouted once, then yelled, "I'm coming Nicole, EAT ME BIGFOOTS!" before taking a solid bite of apple while stepping forward into the trees. *Head toward the berm, then turn back working your way back and forth, she was right behind you, she can't be that far,* Ian told himself, needing to believe it. In the midst of the forest again, Ian marveled at the difference the daylight made. Seeing the mix of trees and tree starts, ferns, bushes and ivy felt a small miracle after fighting his way through these same woods at night. *I ran this, I ran this twice in the dark. You can find her.*

"Nicole!" Ian called out and while listening for a response, he remembered the eerie howling of the Sasquatch in the night. Another sound did reach him then, a low rumbling hum. Recognizing it from the day before, the Gerring Timber bulldozer was working out in the distance. *Unbelievable!* Ian thought to himself, *Loggers! Sasquatch demolished their shit and they're still out killing trees!*

Ian reached the spot he thought was close to where he last saw Nicole running behind him. *She could have gone either direction from here.* Turning to face south, Ian scanned the vast, dense forest and felt a crushing wave of despair. *I should just get help, she could be anywhere.* Closing his eyes, fighting tears, Ian remembered the promises and prayers he'd made last night. *No, find her now, while you're here, now, Ian! Who did Nicole tell me, ask Saint Anthony, patron saint of lost things, that's who she asks for help to find lost keys and stuff?*

"Saint Anthony!" Ian yelled up at the trees. "I need help, Nicole needs us, for her Saint Anthony, c'mon, help me please!" A great oak stood before him, an imposing cathedral of branches sharp in contrast to the blurred green of the adjacent conifers. The stately tree held his attention, and as Ian stared an odd, old memory came to him. As though standing in his old living room Ian saw himself, strangely watched himself as a kid, maybe eight years old, sitting in front of the TV after school with his mom. She was folding laundry while they watched Oprah visiting with a lady who wrote a book about how to find lost pets, sharing amazing stories of prodigal cats and dogs returning home.

She helped by having their owners focus intently on their lovable doggy or kitty cat's face, and holding that thought before creating a mental image of their pet's favorite place. Perhaps curled up by you on the couch. Last, you repeat to yourself, "Come home, come home to me Sparky, home now, Kitty." She spoke of communicating with animals, simply by understanding how they visualize things, not thinking in words but understanding mentally conveyed images, could one send a message to a dear lost pet. "Be still and very quiet in your mind, just see Sparky's or your kitty's furry little face," she taught the audience and Oprah. "When you see Sparky's face so clear you can smell his doggy breath, then call to him with your mind, come home Sparky, come home Sparky, and feel free to think of home, create an image of Sparky's or kitty's favorite place and then come back to visualizing their happy face, see them happy, smiling his Sparky smile or contented kitty cat purring look."

"She's probably nuts, but other nuts will buy her book," Ian's mom suggested. The author then related more miraculous stories of pets returning home, sometimes over amazing distances to their joyful owners, using her method. *Nicole's face, Nicole's face, shut up Ian and just see her face. You have to find her, you have to! See her face, Ian, see her face, just see her face, Ian, shut the fu- sorry Saint Anthony, but shut-up Ian, just see her...* and finally an adorable vision, Nicole wearing her beanie, smiling and clapping her mittens at the silver pine last night flashed bright and in front of all other thoughts. Ian concentrated to hold her image walking off the narrow deer trail, pushing brush away. Zigzagging methodically south and east, looking about crouching low checking under brush and branches Ian stopped every few steps to renew Nicole's face in his mind. Seeing an old cut tree trunk Ian went to it, stepped up and surveyed the area.

"Nicole! Nicole!" He listened, waited, called again. An odd heap of fir branches on the forest floor caught his eye. Jumping off the trunk, Ian ran toward it and stopped at seeing a light beneath the oblong green pile, then sprinted. It looked like a grave, pine boughs with someone buried there. Ian dropped to one knee and pulled away a branch, revealing Nicole's face. The stillness of her lips and closed eyes scared him. "Nicole! Nicole, wake up!" He brushed her lips with his to put air into her mouth. She stirred, slowly opening her eyes.

"Ian? Ian, that's you? Where are we? What happened?"

"You're ok! You're ok! I got you baby, I found you!" Ian interrupted her with shouts, looking at her face to believe it. Nicole sat up, groaning.

"My head," she said while reaching behind her ear. Bringing her hand back she held her palm open and they looked down at a small, flat river rock wrapped in green moss. "That was stuck on my head. There's a lump and it's sore there. What happened?"

"We got scared and ran, Nicole. We ran and got separated.

You don't remember? I'll tell you about it. Can you get up and walk?" Reaching over to shut off her lamplight, "We need to go home," Ian said.

"I want to go home, Ian. My head hurts. I think I remember running..." She felt the tender spot. "Ian, feel this knot. I must have tripped and hit myself on that root there."

"On the back of your head? Do you remember the yarder and crane, do you remember the Bigfoots?"

She thought for a moment. "Oh my God, that wasn't a dream? I sort of remember. We were at the logging stuff, weren't we? They were there. Oh God, the logging stuff was destroyed." Sitting up, Nicole blurted out, "The eyes in the trees Ian, the eyes in the trees! It came out of the trees right at us. That face, that face, Ian!" She turned to him. "We ran... I got lost. I was lost without you!" She slugged him hard across the upper arm.

"Oh God, baby I looked for you, I looked for you in the dark, I couldn't find you. You were right behind me, I looked and you were right there. A Bigfoot followed me, I went back to the trail and the Bigfoot growled and threw a pinecone at me, he wouldn't let me go back to find you." Ian glanced away from Nicole's eyes and a curious look came over his face.

Turning to see a strange stack of good sized river rocks, Nicole put a still gloved hand to her mouth. At the base of a rock sculpture sat an apple sized, rounded rock supporting a larger, football shaped long rock and it topped by one softball sized and shaped grey river rock sporting a thin white stripe around it. "Ian, somebody did that, just like somebody put that rock on my head where I hit it."

They looked at each other and had the same thought. "Bigfoots?" they said together.

"If you didn't do it, I didn't do it. Bigfoots, crazy Nicole."

"Ian, look at these branches on me. It's a branch blanket. All the branch ends are out away from me and the nice soft evergreen part is covering me. It's really nice and warm."

"Crazier, Nicole. I'd like to get under the tree blanket with you but we need to get home. Can you walk?"

Nicole smiled, "I think so, let's go home, baby."

"Wait, I just remembered I had a pine branch that was on me during the night. I noticed it when I woke up from this crazy scary dream. You were in it. I'll tell you about it later, let's go home." Leaning against him, Nicole pushed herself up. "Ok, baby?" he asked.

"Yeah, I'm ok. I have to keep this rock they put on my head."

"Must be some magic Bigfoot powers in that rock," Ian said cheerfully.

"Thank you, Bigfoots," Nicole called out, and they began walking hand in hand through the forest, back toward the trail.

# Chapter 16

## HUNTERS

**HARPER SMITH POURED** Crown Royal into his coffee. "Let's get some Bailey's tonight, it might actually help this shit. The Crown can't hurt. I forgot how bad instant coffee sucks."

"You're welcome, Harp," Brian answered. "Sorry it's not your Starbutts triple latte foo foo shit."

"Relax, Brian. Forget last night. We'll go back to that hole of a bar and find that nimrod that gave us those bullshit directions. After we kick his ass it'll be done and we'll both feel better. Let's eat a tasty survivor man breakfast and go kill Bambi, then that little hairy turd."

Brian shook his head. "I figured it couldn't hurt to ask directions from a local. I'm gonna kill that hairy little dumb ass."

"Maybe next time we'll just go with the internet directions," Harper said dryly.

"You really want to start again?" Brian worked at bacon and scrambled eggs in a frying pan sitting on the campground fire pit grill. "What's the name of this campground?" he asked.

"Hell, I can't remember," answered Harper, putting on his USC baseball cap. "I know it isn't Deer Creek campground. Does that help? Might be the, no showers, shit in a hole in the ground and wipe your ass with bush leaves campground, from what I see."

"Why don't you get the ATVs ready? That would be useful. Oh, I tried to call Trish, cell phones get no action up here."

"Why would you want to talk to your wife? Getting the hell away from the ball busters, isn't that why we go someplace every year?"

"Yes, blessed escape. I'm here to escape, just wanted to let her know we got here ok."

"That's sweet. You know, I checked the map. We could divert to 395, hit Reno on the way back and do Mustang Ranch or some cat house. If somehow I don't score with that local barmaid tonight, hitting some strange on the way home might be helpful."

"We'll see, Reno's pretty far out of the way, even for a guaranteed piece of ass. Hey, I got one for you," Brian said grinning. "Ya know what one saggy tit said to the other? If we don't perk up, people will think we're nuts."

Harper laughed, then added, "that barmaid at that tavern had some seriously perky tits. Giving her the big Harper wang dang doodle tonight would make getting lost almost worth it."

"Ok, but before you apply your Jedi magic pick up tricks on her, we find that stupid furry little shit and shave his ass."

"A fine plan, Brian my man. And from this day forward we go with the printed directions."

"Oh shut up about that. I should let the hillbillies shave your ass. They might enjoy that before they do the Deliverance dance up your bunghole."

Harper smiled. "Easy there tiger, save the hate for Bambi or little hairy man."

"They're both dead today," Brian said, walking to the ice chest. He pulled out and opened a beer.

“That’s better, el tigre,” encouraged Harper.

“If we go back to that bar, the Buckhorn, that pretty little waitress might kick your ass,” Brian advised. “You’re a real smart ass after pounding bourbon from LA to Oregon.”

“Oh, that’s too bad,” Harper said. “She was pretty. I said something about her rack, didn’t I?”

“You compared it to an elk’s.”

“That could hurt my chances. Dammit, not a good start,” Harper mused while slurping the whiskey laced Instant Folgers. They ate the breakfast and finished the awful coffee before reorganizing their packs to ready for the day. Harper opened a rifle case and removed an old 30.06. “Check this out, Brian. This was my grandfather’s deer rifle. I borrowed it from my dad. I took it to a range last week to practice. I think it can tell we’re in the forest. My granddad actually killed deer and a bear with this baby. I remember eating deer jerky he made when I was kid.”

“You got something gourmet planned for your kill?” Brian asked.

“No, just a deer head to hang in the man cave, that’s the goal today.”

“My rifle only knows it isn’t at the Big 5 anymore,” Brian answered. “I’m sure it’s very excited.” They both laughed. Finally packed and ready, they mounted their all-terrain vehicles and fired them up, their roaring engines blasting the empty campground and surrounding woods.

“Let’s just head out this trail until we find a good spot to hide and watch for Bambi’s daddy,” Harper shouted, pointing north. “We’ll see where this takes us.”

# Chapter 17

## OLD FRIENDS

**MICHAEL WOKE WHEN** the door opened. Eric was smiling at him.

"Who's sleeping in my bed? Hey man, great to see you."

"Good job getting here. What time is it?" Michael said yawning.

"One, the Walden game just started. I hear you had a coyote come into your camp last night."

"Coyote, that was it, tell your mom thanks for leaving it to you to mock my close encounter. At least she humored me."

"She says you actually had something happen out there. You game for going back later to check it out?"

"Yeah, sure. I need to go get my ice chest anyway. Carol would be pissed if I didn't bring it home. And it still has beer."

"Good deal. Get yourself up. We'll catch up with my folks at the Vets Day game, then go to the bluffs and then we get to kick some Beaver ass tonight. Could you ask for a better Saturday?"

"Nope, you can't. I'll be right out. Oh, I committed to CP yesterday we'd be at the Buckhorn to bring some Duckness to the Beaver crowd."

"That's cool, it'll be good to see those knuckleheads. I'm

glad you're here. I've been needing to get down for a visit."

"So I've heard. Your folks and the Buckhorn people are looking forward to seeing you."

Michael and Eric caught up while driving to the game in the van.

"How's work, enough bad guys out there to keep you busy?" Michael asked.

"Stupid people needing to go to prison are still plentiful, staying busy is not a problem. Staying busy is easy, way too easy. I bring work home most nights to be ready for trial. I turned down another offer to go private a few weeks ago. It was a lot of money. Veronica would kill me if she knew."

"How are she and the girls?"

"Good, the girls are good. Smart and pretty, like their mom. I see them all the time, do what I have to do to make cheerleading and jazz band competitions. You wouldn't believe what a racket cheerleading is, that's Brianna's deal, gymnastics and dance lessons, travelling to games and these all-day cheerleading competitions."

Eric pulled a picture of his daughters from his wallet. "Kylie is really getting good at piano. She made the junior high jazz band; they do competitions all over the state. It never ends but Veronica would say I'm an even bigger loser if I don't get there to see them perform."

"And you would be. So, how is Veronica? Your lovely ex being civil?"

"Still hates my guts, as far as I can tell. At least she doesn't poison the girls, all I can really ask for."

"You have a girlfriend?"

"No, no time."

"I saw Kelly at the Buckhorn yesterday."

"She's been married to a forest ranger for a few years now.

I don't get to talk to her much." They passed a mailbox next to a gravel road. "That mailbox we just passed is Kelly's aunt's place. That's where Kelly's nephew Jason grew up. She helped raise him. He had a football ride to Portland State and became a logger instead. Great kid, though. How was Kelly yesterday?"

"I remember he was a baby when we were in Eugene. He came up yesterday at the Buckhorn because he's logging in some place called Grey Canyon."

"Seriously? Wow, that's amazing. Grey Canyon, no shit, Jason is?" Michael was taken aback by his friend's reaction.

"Yes, he's on a logging crew that knows how to get in there."

"I'll be damned," Eric said shaking his head.

"Anyway, I could tell Kelly will be glad to see you. Man, she's still really pretty."

"The Buckhorn is coming up here on the left. It'll be closed for the Walden game, packed though for the Ducks-Beavers tonight."

They entered town, passing the Larssen's packing house before pulling into the Walden Stadium parking lot. "It was good to see your folks this morning. They seemed to be in good spirits. They're amazing, I don't know how long they'd been up and working when I got there about 7:00."

"They don't change much that way." Eric said quietly.

Walking across the school parking lot, Eric pointed to a window on the second floor. "That first window was Mrs. Kirkpatrick's English class. That's where I saw Atticus Finch."

"You remember when we got loaded and watched *To Kill A Mockingbird* at the midnight movies on 11th Street? I remember you telling me that's why you were going to be a lawyer."

Eric laughed. "I also remember that Woody Allen movie you took me to where they kept saying all the lawyers were gay." *To Kill A Mockingbird* may have won author Harper

Lee the Pulitzer Prize, but in the spring of 1980 Eric Larssen found it a classic bore, another act of reading agony running Mrs. Kirkpatricks's American Literature gauntlet. The Great Gatsby, The Sun Also Rises, the brutally long and meandering, The Hamlet, were among the over-rated snoozers he had endured. The Gilded Age had been an exception, Eric appreciating Twain's layered, dark humor and its exposing the worst in us. To Kill A Mockingbird had its moments, but it was no Maltese Falcon. Now that was Eric's idea of a great American novel.

Eric was happy to walk in one day and see the projector aimed and ready at the screen. Movie days were always better than in-class readings and Mrs. Kirkpatrick's sad daily attempt at inspiring thoughtful literary discourse. She hit the classroom lights and started the projector while warning her students yet again that a Hollywood movie could never convey the rich depth of a good book. And yet Eric absorbed *To Kill A Mockingbird,* and it would be Gregory Peck playing protagonist attorney Atticus Finch who changed his life that day.

When Eric announced he was applying to the University of Oregon to study pre-law, not agricultural science at Oregon State, his parents understood the recently improved homework effort and corresponding better grades. They were also not too surprised he had found motivation by charting a path away from the family orchards. Eric's choice would also be a town topic in Mazama Creek. They wished Eric well but people wondered who would someday run the orchards and the packing house, as his older sister was married and lived in Spokane. Twenty-five years later, it was still an unanswered question.

Eric kept working to get the grades and entered the U of O in September, 1981. His first few weeks in Eugene were overwhelming though. Homesick and missing Kelly, Eric wondered if he wasn't wasting his time, that he was simply fated to live and die in Mazama Creek. Larssen Orchards were surely meant to be and surely also meant to be his, and who was he to mess with Norwegian generational history? One day though, he met Michael Gardner in the dorms, a freshman from the California bay area. Indian summer in Oregon that year, as they usually are was sensational, and the Saturday afternoon they saw the Ducks 7-7 tie a great USC football team (Marcus Allen and Ronnie Lott!) at Autzen Stadium, Oregon Duck football became a sacred thing. A week later, Michael drove Eric and their dorm buddies in his 1970 Torino the five hours to Seattle to see a Rolling Stones concert (Mick and Keith!), their first of many road trips. The next weekend Eric brought Michael to Mazama Creek, and in those three weeks they cemented a life-long friendship. Eric's new friend helped him settle in to the dorms and college life, and he and Kelly planned for her to move to Eugene the next year.

But on her first visit, she soon found she did not care for Eugene or some of Eric's new, smart-assed college friends. She liked his new friend Michael and could see he was helping Eric deal with Eugene, but most of the college students seemed spoiled and trying too hard to show off their brains and parent's money for her to want to be around them. And she did not appreciate that in the winter it rained even more in Eugene than Mazama Creek. When her cousin Mathew died and Little Jason became Uncle Jeremiah and Aunt Ellen's responsibility, Kelly knew her place was in Mazama Creek helping them.

Bright and industrious enough to manage the U of O party lifestyle and get the school work done, they rented a duplex apartment near the university together the next year. Their place became a popular destination, famous for a keg of Henry Weinhard's perpetually tapped in a refrigerator on the tiny back patio. When they graduated, Eric in Psychology, Michael's degree in History, Eric headed to a Seattle law school and Michael went to look for work in California before going back to get a teaching credential. He never got back, eventually settling in at a huge grocery warehouse in Tracy, east of the California bay area. Busy lives and distance meant few visits over the years, only seeing each other at their weddings or an occasional Duck football game. Eric had now been an Assistant District Attorney for King County for 16 years. Before this weekend, they had not seen each other since Michael flew to Seattle to see the Ducks play Washington shortly after Eric's divorce was final two years ago.

It was likely the entire towns of Mazama Creek and Prospect were in the covered stands at Roosevelt Field. Following Eric up the stadium steps, Michael enjoyed watching him greet virtually everyone, including CP and Dewey with alto sax and trumpet respectively, in the Walden Alumni Band. Michael smiled to see Kelly sitting with the Larssens and Ibsens and after Eric hugged all around, was re-introduced to her Aunt Ellen and niece Kate.

"Gosh, you were a baby the last time I saw you," Michael said to Kate, shaking her hand. A small boy, Michael assumed Kate's, played with Star Wars action figures next to her. He seemed to be the only one not thoroughly absorbed in the football game.

"Jacob, say hi to Eric and his friend Mike," Kate instructed. The lad remained fixated on Chewy and Hans Solo. Jacob held out Chewy to Eric.

"Thanks. I see you have Hans and Chewbaca, who else do you have?" Eric asked. "Princess Leia?"

"No," Jacob answered emphatically. "Darth Vader. He's in the car."

Kate laughed, "He refused to let me get him a Princess Leia. I'm getting my own Princess Leia to play with."

"How was camping, Mike?" Kelly asked.

"It turned out to be a wild night. I'll have to tell you about it."

It took Michael one play to identify what was odd about the game. "Eight man football," he said to Eric, who responded, "Football the way God meant it to be played, we say here. You'll like it." It was a fun game to watch, the more open field contributing to some nice runs and good action. After the Mazama Creek running back broke tackles to score a touchdown, Eric noted, "He almost looked like Jason on that play. Where is Jason, Michael said something about logging Grey Canyon? I was sure CP was messing with him or something."

Kelly answered, "It's true, he's working on the crew that's logging the BLM. Hank Gerring got that bid. I can't believe where Jason is today. He's going into Grey Canyon, down into it, really. He's probably there right now."

Kelly's aunt and the Larssens stopped watching the game to look at Kelly. "What do you mean Jason is going into Grey Canyon?" asked Aunt Ellen. Kelly explained the satellite pictures and Jason's old growth forest theory.

"I'm surprised old Gerring went along with something like that," said Bill Larssen.

"Gerring's not really from around here," added Aunt Ellen.

"He really found a way in, some place with a little tunnel and an avalanche chute you can climb down," Kelly said. "He promised he'd come by the Buckhorn tonight and tell me about it."

"Kelly, please call me when you hear from Jason or when he gets to the Buckhorn tonight," Aunt Ellen requested. Michael found the concern in her voice interesting. He would have to ask Eric about Grey Canyon. They all turned back to the football game.

# Chapter 18

## HANK

**THIRSTY, JASON'S MOUTH** and throat were very dry and legs sore but he knew Hank would have water and used that to keep running. Never in his life had he felt fear in the woods, until now. At the edge of his vision, bare tree's branches or a deadfall's upturned roots were extended arms with claws. Every sound was them coming for him, each shadow hid something terrible. Jogging the same deer trail he and Sam had taken, the rumble of the distant bulldozer's motor was Jason's beacon.

Nearing the dozer Jason stopped, feeling something was not right. The dozer was running but no gears shifted and the cracking sound of clearing small trees and brush was absent. If he were on break, Hank would shut the tractor down to save fuel. Jason crept forward, moving quietly, reached a brush pile and hid, looking at the stationary running tractor. Hank was not in sight. Stepping out of the brush, Jason sprinted to the dozer and climbed up into the cab. Hank's water bottle sat in its rack and Jason grabbed it and took a long drink. Choosing not to call out, perched on the seat of the cab eight feet high, he scanned.

"No!" he gasped, stomach turning. Hank's ball cap sat upside down on the ground a few yards in front of the dozer. Jason followed that sight line and sunlight reflected bright on a big fir tree caught his eye. Jason strained to see what it was and felt his stomach turn tighter, something red was shining on the bark. He climbed down from the tractor and walked forward, each step more dreadful. When he was within a few yards, he could see it was blood. Under the tree he dared to look up, seeing only pine branches. Jason scaled the trunk to reach the lowest branch, hoisted himself up to sit there, looked up and jerked away from blood droplets. Raising himself standing on the branch, Jason parted boughs until he saw an arm and a leg hanging down. "Oh, God, no," Jason whispered. It appeared they had thrown the giant of a man 20 feet up into the tree. Jason was sure Hank was dead, a lower leg grotesquely at a right angle from the knee joint, the pant leg blood soaked, the arm dangling from between two branches, dripping blood. Then he heard Hank moan. "Hank, I'm coming!" Jason pulled up gripping the next limb and climbed the tree to reach him. Hank lay sprawled across branches, his head facing down. Jason got his feet set and pushed branches away from Hank's face, then closed his eyes. His head was completely purple and black with bruising, eyes swollen shut, blood everywhere. "Hank, I'm here, it's Jason. I'll get help Hank, I'll get you down, we'll get you-"

"No." Hank could barely speak, pausing between each word to draw breath. "Done, back broke. Bigfoot, stomp me. Fought 'em, got one good."

"Hank, let me try-"

"No. Can't feel. Heard back break. Done. Love Becky. Go home. Go home. Where Sam?"

Jason cried. "I'm sorry, Hank, Sam's gone, it's my fault, all my fault, Hank."

"Oh. No, me, me. Say love, Becky."

Hank breathed out and did not breathe back in.

"I'll tell her, Hank, I'll take care of Becky." Jason cried quietly next to Hank until the dozer's motor shut off, apparently out of gas. In the silence, Jason thought of Hank's words, "go home." Jason moved above Hank in the tree to get a better view out. Checking his watch, it was 2:20 p.m. With three hours of daylight and about six miles using deer trails and off highway vehicle roads to get to the highway, depending on where he came out, his Grandma Ellen's house, the Larssen's place or the Buckhorn Tavern would be closest places to get help. He would also have to cross the Rogue somewhere.

About to climb down he heard movement in the brush, Jason froze, crouching next to Hank, peering through a small opening in the branches. Suddenly he felt the hair on his neck stand on end, the brush parted and a Bigfoot walked into the clearing, striding nonchalantly to the dozer. It stood nearly even with the tractor cab, Jason seeing it was about 8 feet tall. Hanging reddish brown hair covered it, yet he could see massive, defined muscle outlined underneath. *Skookum,* Jason thought, scared yet transfixed, studying carefully, *human gorilla, a human gorilla.* The creature's shaggy head, vaguely simian with a slightly rounded crest, sat almost neckless on massive muscular shoulders that extended into long, powerful arms with big, hairy, five fingered hands. Only around the eyes, nose and cheeks was it hairless, the skin there a weathered brown. When it turned, the sun hit its face fully showing Jason watchful, oval eyes, dark and set deep in high cheekbones and thick, furrowed forehead. Its nose, rounded at the end but otherwise flat and it took Jason a moment to realize the nostrils faced downward, completely human looking above a full lipped mouth. There was also no doubting the humanity Jason saw in the Bigfoot's face. Deep wrinkle lines and sunlight exposing grey hairs woven with the red-brown, *He looks like an old red Viking,* Jason thought. Its mouth was closed as the Sasquatch raised its head and smelled the air, Jason instantly grateful the western breeze put him downwind. Closing his eyes he saw the dead infant skookum laying in the fallen tree in Grey Canyon. *That little face, oh Jesus I'm sorry, I killed their baby.*

Hearing steps, Jason looked to see an even bigger creature, its hair black, shorter and thicker than the other Sasquatch. He stood taller, bodybuilder physique even more obvious underneath the bushy fur. Jason saw intense anger in the dark face and knew he'd seen this one running first out of the fog to kill Sam. A dominating broad, flat nose, narrowed eyes and grim lips reminded Jason of old, black and white pictures of American Indians. *An Indian war chief and an old red Viking,* Jason thought. *Chief and Old Red.* He also saw blood and a swollen, bruised lump over the black haired Bigfoot's left eye. *You did get him Hank, you whomped Chief a good one.*

Leaning toward Hank's body, curling into a fetal position setting his legs on a branch, upper body against the dead man's back, Jason closed his eyes, listening. The skookums began sniffing the air, snorting and making low growling sounds. One of them began to beat its chest and the other joined in, the repetitive thumping and growls growing more menacing. The grunts, snarling and chest slapping escalated in intensity and pitch and just as he wondered if the Bigfoot were about to fight each other, they stopped.

Jason heard them breathing fast walking toward the tree, then standing below him growling low. A fetid odor reached him. Closing his mouth to stop gagging, claws scraping tree bark pushed Jason to panic before a sudden, determined grunt and the branches shook violently. One of them was climbing the tree. *Jump!! Run!!* Jason's mind screamed, *please God, please God, please God...* CRACK!! A limb snapped, the tree shook again and Jason heard a loud thud and "uunngh!" As the skookum dropped from the tree lay there, the other Sasquatch made weird hoots and "aahk aahk," sounds. The beast was laughing at the fallen one. *They're smart, my God, it's laughing.*

From out in the brush came a series of strange coyote yips. The laughing Bigfoot stopped and called back in the same manner. Jason listened to the two walk quietly back to the bulldozer. He waited, then looked carefully out and could see two more skookums, one of them a smaller male, the other a female standing with Chief and Old Red. The smaller creature was man-sized, a six footer but with less black hair covering his face and Jason thought, *he looks like a junior high kid, a really big, strong kid.* This younger one had several wavy, tan and brown wisps mingled in his shaggy black hair. Jason saw his brown eyes moving back and forth from the female to the black haired male.

The other Bigfoot was brown haired, clearly female as he could see plump breasts showing through the hair on her chest. Her face also less hairy, her eyes had an almond shape and were a deep brown, though Jason saw they were red and puffy, he was sure she had been crying. Her lips were full, set in a strong, slightly protruding lower jaw. The young one stayed close to her and his black hair and watchful eyes resembled Chief. Jason was sure he was observing a family when they began conversing, only the smaller one not speaking, the others barking and discussing something very important.

"Rrekk!"

"Aahkk"

"Kahr!"

"Barbb-ak!"

*Their thoughts are ahead of their words,* Jason thought.

The female raised her arm and pointed north. "Kahrr!" she roared. *She's pointing to Grey Canyon, please go back there,* Jason pleaded to himself. The two males gestured to the west with growls and then roared at her together, turned abruptly and walked into the brush, heading southwest. Standing with the young male, her eyes not following the two but instead looking north, toward Grey Canyon, Jason saw tears and the depth of pain in her eyes and knew she mourned her dead baby. With a grunt the young one followed the males into the brush leaving her alone. Only then did her gaze homeward break. She turned slowly as Jason watched her broad shoulders sag before walking after the others.

Waiting long minutes before whispering, "I'm sorry, God bless," to Hank and climbing down from the tree, Jason ran past the dozer praying they weren't hiding, watching for him, then started jogging south through the forest, desperate to reach Highway 62 before dark.

# Chapter 19

## SKOOKUMS

**THE MOTHER BIGFOOT** stayed a distance behind her son and the two males, needing to walk by herself. She did not repress her grief, surrendering to tears and the aching pain inside her. A living spirit can never die, she understood that, but now to whom would she teach the art of living in the forest, to whom could she pass the wisdom sacred and feminine? Her baby girl was such a precious gift.

Her ancestors likely migrated with humans across the Bering Strait to North America around 14,000 years ago. Or it may be they were already here. As the first peoples settled into tribes and tribes became tribal nations, the mythology of the giant, hairy man-beast of the wilderness travelled with them. Many centuries later, native legends and their own frightening, legendary tales worked their way into white explorer and pioneer letters and journals.

Many of the eastern and plains tribes believed Bigfoot to be a spiritual entity not of this world, capable of moving through various dimensions, transverse plains of existence appearing here or in dreams, to whomever they wished and always for a reason. Tribal elders often took a sighting as a sign their people needed to return to an older, more natural way of being.

The great Iriquois nation shared what would become the northeast United States and Canadian wilds with Ot-ne-ye-hed, or *Stone Giant.* Wendigo, the terrifying, shape shifting and human devouring monster of their Algonquin speaking neighbors may well have its roots in ancient Bigfoot encounters. Further west across the Great Plains, the Sioux named them Chiye-Tanka, Chiye meaning*, great or big,* and Tanka, *older brother.* In the Pine Mountains of Kentucky are the legends of Yeahoh, a hairy man-beast who made home in deep, underground caves and is known for a willingness to share food with hungry hunters. In Oklahoma, the Choctaw fear Shampe, creature of the deepest parts of the woods. When pursued by a Shampe, Choctaw hunters say drop small game to distract and throw them off your trail.

The Great Northwest and western tribes knew them to first be earthly creatures, physical beings the natives simply coexisted with. Throughout the mountains and wild lands of the west, Bigfoot has many names. The Wenatchee tribe of central Washington called them Choanito, or, *night people,* and further east they are Scweneyti, or, *tall, hairy, smells like burnt hair,* to the Spokane nation. The Chinook tribe of the Puget Sound called them Skoocoom, *evil god of the woods,* a nickname that migrated to other parts of the Cascade region. Steneyahx, the *stick people,* taunted and scared the Yakima people at night by poking long sticks through the flaps of their tee pees. The Yokut tribe of central California left a rock pictograph of a Mayak datat, or *hairy man* family estimated over a thousand years old.

Bigfoot creatures however, do not assign themselves names. From the earliest of times they were nocturnal and usually avoided overt contact with humans, especially after the arrival of firearms. Incredible physiques and thick hair enabled survival and their desired solitude in the harshest climates and most brutal terrains, but only in concert with ancient wisdom of their habitats could this be possible. It was the female Sasquatch who carried strongest this primordial, metaphysically molecular understanding, for she sensed the living power that exists in all things. A mother Bigfoot's greatest joy through the ages then, has been teaching a beloved daughter what her mother taught her. She learned from but did not dwell in the past, living each moment utterly aware in her wilderness surroundings. Rarely in a lifetime would she fret over the past or future, for without the burden of abstract thought and complex language the female Sasquatch thoroughly engaged each moment in her forest home, opening herself to the source of everything, and the Source came naturally through her.

For epochal generations hers was the sacred ability of discerning the powers of plants and minerals. By feeling and seeing what a plant or rock radiated, knowing the traits of the thing she touched or smelled the moment she reached out to it, she provided to her kind the land's nourishing and healing gifts and thus, survival in the wild. The moon's dance with the waters unveiled the pattern of the tides to her, and so also the best time for harvesting rivers, lakes and ocean. In the woods, buried bulbs and roots, ripened berries or a deadfall laden with tasty bugs presented themselves first to her. Before the weather turned, she had her clan building shelter or on the move to a warmer or cooler place, depending on their need. In these ways the female Bigfoot guided her species over the tens of thousands of years, holding the bigger, stronger males in reverential awe. The terrible thing that happened in Grey Canyon shifted a delicate balance. She did join the violence against the human after finding her dead baby girl, wildly tearing at the screaming, writhing tree man and wanting desperately to kill the other tree man swinging on the rope above them. Now though, she felt weary after watching the males including her son, kill the big human driving the machine. She only needed to go home and take her baby girl to the place of peaceful spirits, to her resting place.

But her mate, the one Jason called Chief and Old Red, a wanderer Bigfoot, were far too excited by the killing of humans. The fear and screaming pain in Sam's face thrilled and empowered them, but Hank fighting hard for his life before they beat and stomped him, then threw him up into a tree stirred something even deeper within. They would track and kill the other tree man, he was somewhere in their woods and they would find him and rip him to pieces.

Despite already realizing the sudden power found in killing humans had taken the males over, the female Sasquatch was shocked when her mate and the old male defied her to hunt the tree man. They had never refused a decision of hers before, but the look in their eyes told her she had lost them. She also knew her son would go with them and they now might kill any human they came across. A fear of even greater catastrophe came over her, burying her baby girl would have to wait. First she needed to save her son.

# Chapter 20

## PROMISES

**IAN AND NICOLE** held hands walking past a blackberry bramble. "You said they were owls or raccoons, Ian." Nicole was getting her energy and memory of the prior night back. "Can you believe we saw Bigfoots? Can you believe what they did to the logging stuff?"

Ian answered, "I'll tell you something else that's crazy. I heard the logger's bulldozer when I was looking for you. They were out working somewhere past the berm this morning. I guess nothing stops those guys."

"Not even Sasquatch, wow, Ian."

"I wonder if they know who smashed their shit."

"Ian, please don't cuss."

Ian stopped. "Oh! Oh! I can't believe it!"

Nicole laughed. "Believe what?"

"Aahh! I can't cuss. I can't smoke pot either. Aw, crap! I made some promises last night and this morning. I found you, now I have to keep my promises. St. Anthony and I cut a deal this morning."

Nicole looked at him laughing, "You and St. Anthony?" Ian squeezed her hand and started walking again.

"We should be close to the trail, you veered left pretty far."

"I like it better out here in the daytime," Nicole said.

"I was thinking that looking for you this morning. I could see so much better, I was totally good with the difference after last night. Everything seemed really sharp. I mean I was scared and my adrenaline was pumped but I knew I would find you." Ian stopped, Nicole turned and watched one tear roll down his cheek, he caught himself, breathed out and Nicole threw herself against him, holding him tight with both arms. Ian let himself cry. "Sorry," he said, letting her go after a time.

"Don't be," Nicole answered softly. They walked on before stepping between two massive fir trees and saw the friendliest dirt path ever, their OHV trail. "Thank you, Lord!" Nicole said cheerily. "Home," she added, "I just want to go home."

"Me too, even going to my house sounds good right now. The bikes are under some bushes up there. How's your head?"

"It's a little sore where I bumped it, but I'm ready to ride." She reached into her sweatshirt pouch and held out the flat stone she had found stuck to the back of her head.

"Amazing, Nicole, its tree moss and mud wrapped around the river rock, I'll bet it worked like an icepack."

"Bigfoot Ian, I'm glad I saved this rock. This is too wild baby, the evergreen blanket they made me and that rock formation was just the wildest thing ever. Oh Ian, we didn't get a picture, please draw the stacked up rocks the way they had them when we get home, ok, please? They really took care of me. It had to be the Bigfoots."

"Yep, or the forest spirits really were with you," Ian said.

"Forest spirits, what do you mean?"

"Remember after we got off our bikes, just before we hiked in last night you said the forest spirits were with us, you said you could feel it in the trees."

"I kind of remember. I guess I was feeling my grannies with me. My mom says both my Irish Great Nanny and my Japanese Oba-chan have strong spirits watching out for me. They're both alive and strong and mom says they are very attuned to her and Heather and I even though they live in Ireland and Japan. My mom's side has bloodlines going way back in the Shinto religion in Japan and my Irish Gran says her family women were powerful leaders and priestesses many centuries ago, like before the Druids."

"I can see the Braveheart and Ninja warrior combo resemblance," Ian said with a smile. "Plaid kilt and red stockings with black ninja hood, deadly with a sword, flying from tree to tree, it's you, baby, I can see that."

"Braveheart and Ninja, you're mixing Scotland and Ireland, fool, but I'm good with that, my ancestors were kick-ass girl warriors too, so watch out, foolish one." Pausing, Nicole looked up at the tree tops reaching for blue sky and white clouds. "But not just warriors, more like beautiful and entrancing goddesses of the forest. Dancing in the trees with the moon... oh that's weird, Ian, really weird. I just flashed on something, like, why do I think I remember dancing with the moon last night looking at the forest from way up high?"

"Maybe you and the Bigfoots danced, why not?"

"That is so weird, Ian. I totally have this picture of me dancing with the moon, the moon was right there, singing. I was singing with my grannies or forest moon goddesses or my grannies were forest moon goddesses, or they were stars. I can't figure it out Ian, but I think I did some trippy dreaming last night."

"Ok, now you're a little freaky on me Nicole, but it's all very cool. You and the forest spirits and the Sasquatch and your grandmas all partying with the moon, I think I got the picture. Maybe you fell down and your face landed in magic mushrooms."

"Funny. I know both my grans were there, singing and dancing and I was flying or floating at night way up in this big fir tree. It was a really nice dream I can kind of remember."

"My dreaming wasn't fun, I think. Do you remember at the logger stuff, when the Bigfoot stepped out, his eyes were red from the headlamps but I could see his face, plain as day."

"All surrounded by hair, his face was like a mask or something with fur all around."

"You could only see it for a second but that Bigfoot face has been bugging me. I think it reminded me of someone."

Nicole laughed. "No way, I remember there was something really weird about it. It was so human, but it wasn't. I thought he was coming straight for me. That big hairy hand reached and pulled him back, oh my God." Ian put his arm around her and they walked silently.

"What was your crazy dream, Ian? I was in it and you said it was scary."

"I kind of remember. It woke me up, so weird, we were kids, you and I were both kids. It was really dark, we couldn't find each other and some monster or something was with us. I thought the monster was my dad at first."

"Your dad?"

"Sometimes I have nightmares from when he used to drink. I thought it was one of those."

"I know you don't like talking about that."

"It's ok, since he quit drinking doesn't come home mad all the time. Not after he started going to his meetings. I get sick of the self-righteous bullsh- sorry baby, I'm trying. Anyway, I don't need to hear him preaching but at least we can live with him. He quit because he loves us, that's what matters, I guess."

“It is what matters, baby. Mom kicked our dad out because he wouldn’t stop snorting crank. He loved that more than us, I guess, but mom loved Heather and I enough to give him the boot.”

“That shi- stuff is so nasty, I don’t get crank at all. Is your old man still out by Cottage Grove?”

“Yeah, in his Uncle’s trailer working in their orchards still as far as I know. He sent a card, or more likely Uncle Rick sent a card for my graduation. It had ten bucks in it, so I bought a picture frame and put a picture of me, Heather and mom and sent it to him. My uncle called and left a message saying thanks. My mom wasn’t too happy. I think it made her sad. He wasn’t always a loser if mom loved him.”

“You tried, that’s good. Right around this bush Nicole, here’s where I tied the signal hanky.” Their bikes were waiting with Nicole’s backpack undisturbed. “We probably should keep our head phones off so we can hear if the cops show up. It’s sketchy we haven’t heard them yet to check out the logger’s stuff, I guess they started working someplace else and haven’t seen what your Bigfoot homies did. If we see cops, you and I are just out biking after camping in your car last night. Or we go off trail.”

“Right Ian, where are the tools and the acid?”

“Buried over there under a bush, we’ll need to come back in a few weeks to get everything. If we see troopers, off trail, baby. If the cops or loggers chase us we’ll take the bikes off trail into the trees. Ditch the cops on bike in the woods, how killer would that be?”

“Right, Ian, and why are we ditching the cops if we are just out biking?”

“Better if they don’t know us, they’ll investigate the logger damage, big time. I’ll say I thought I had a joint on me if they did get us. They could never catch us on bike in the forest."

"Maybe true, but you are still a crazy fool, Ian. You are right on one thing. They could blame us for what the Bigfoots did. Who would believe us if we said it was Bigfoots?"

Ian nodded. "The FBI might have a tough time explaining how we threw boulders at the yarder and crane." He gave her a long hug as she closed her eyes resting against his chest. "Let's go home, baby."

With the sun warming them, they pedaled west at an easy pace up the tree lined trail. "I remember riding through the fog around here, that was awesome, I think this is where we came out, everything was so clear, like we blazed but we didn't," Nicole said, pulling up alongside Ian. She smiled and asked him, "So, who were you making promises to last night?"

Ian grinned. "I don't know, Nicole. The stars, the trees, God and Jesus and the Bigfoots, anyone who would listen and bring you back to me. St. Anthony came through big time this morning. I'm good with God today. I am cool today with God. The stars say today's a great adventure day, its great adventure day. You're here, Nicole, that's what I know. That's what I know and that's what matters. Cussing and smoking weed don't mean anything, I was so scared I lost you." Ian's voice cracked, Nicole looked over to see a tear he quickly wiped away. "Cried enough, I need to get you home," he said.

The wind picked up and they pushed their bikes against it, looking over the trees to looming grey and purple rain clouds, though a fat sliver of blue sky and sun remained over them. Ian circled back toward Nicole. "The clouds are awesome today. I can't wait to get home. Nicole, I am so sorry we did this, so sorry I got you lost."

"No more life changing decisions made when we're loaded. This was really stupid and it was both of us. We still have to fight for our trees, Ian, we'll find a better way."

"The Bigfoot are fighting for their trees," Ian said, feeling his determination returning. "Find a way to help Bigfoot fight for the Rogue. Environmental lawyer might be the way to go."

"Sounds way better to me, Ian, you do the law and I'll do the science. We should be helping the Bigfoots."

"Do the science of Sasquatch, Nicole. Wild and beastly yet smart enough to live in the woods, makers of home-made ice packs and evergreen blankets, rock formation artists, pinecone throwers and boulder flinging destroyers of logging equipment, the amazing Bigfoot! Seriously, Nicole, the new spotted owl strategy will be about Sasquatch habitat."

"I wonder what else Bigfoot can do," Nicole considered. "Just think about living totally in forest, just out here completely wild and smart enough to make a natural ice pack."

"Those eyes were way up in the trees, they must be eight footers. They could play some serious hoops. Portland Trailblazers could use a Bigfoot. Maybe they could beat Shaq and Kobe for once," Ian said hopefully.

"Bigfoot versus Shaq, the Blazers might have a chance, maybe," Nicole said laughing.

"Kobe would still find a way to rip the Trailblazers hearts out. God I hate the Lakers. Isn't your sister hooping this weekend?"

"Yes, she and mom are up in Salem for a tournament. If they won last night they'll have the late game tonight. They're good this year and Heather made varsity as a sophomore. I wish I kept playing basketball sometimes."

"Snowboard season is almost here. I was thinking about doing the racing team, you should do it with me. There's a couple of races at Bachelor and one at Mount Hood."

"Seriously, you'd join the racing team? You said those guys

were all lame posers," Nicole asked with surprise.

"They are completely lame posers, but it would be fun to whip their poser asses. Just thinking about it, snowboarding is a club sport at Berkeley. They go to Tahoe."

"Hmm, do the cheerleaders go to the races? Maybe I'll do that, I already have a cheer for you. Snowboard, snowboard Ian rules, fly right past those other fools! Gooo Ian!"

"I'm inspired, baby."

"I'll work on that. Hey, aren't we almost to the car?" she asked.

"Almost, another 10 or 15 minutes, let's beat the rain. Keppler! Nicole, its Keppler, nemesis dude sits behind us in Cardwell's class! That's who the Bigfoot face looks like."

Ian did not understand Nicole's expression, for a moment thought she was being funny, her widening eyes and gaping mouth puzzling him. He turned as the monster stepped out of the trees onto the trail. The Sasquatch roared swiping with claws tearing at his chest, knocking Ian flying backwards off the bike. Nicole screamed as she braked hard and stopped with Ian lying in front of her. She looked down at four red, jagged rips across his sweatshirt and yelled "Ian! Ian, get up!" Groaning he opened his eyes, reached for Nicole's handlebars and pulled himself up to her. They turned and faced the goliath. The black haired Bigfoot stood watching, dark eyes riveted, a deep growl coming through an awful smile. Its knees slightly bent, impossibly long arms away from its body ended with clawed fingers spread open. Ian saw the gash and lump just above one eye that Hank Gerring's fist had made. "Ride, Nicole!" Ian yelled at her, "Go!! I'll hold him off!"

She took a panicked glance at Ian. "No, we go!" she screamed. But another Bigfoot stepped out onto the trail and stood next to the other, blocking their way. Somehow Ian stepped forward, watching the beasts watch him as he knelt to pick up his bike.

Ian begged her as blood flowed from the chest wounds, "Please go Nicole, please ride, go off trail, you can do it!" He turned to look into her eyes, "I love you, go!" Ian grabbed the handlebars to push Nicole away but a crashing in the brush made them turn, Nicole screamed when a third Bigfoot jumped out to the trail. It met her eyes and she knew it was the monster from the night, the one who had stepped toward her from the trees at the berm. Now though, Nicole saw something inhuman and beyond animal in those eyes, an evil, violent intent. It reached to her and Ian swung his bike with the handlebars as hard as he could, the frame and back wheel smacked against the thick shoulder and head, knocking it off balance. It glared and growled at Ian. Nicole saw the other two Sasquatch looking on, perversely amused. Another Sasquatch was coming through the brush and the three creatures looked in that direction.

"Go Nicole!!" The Bigfoot closest turned back to them, eyed Nicole and reached again. Ian swung his bike screaming, "Go!" and she pulled around right taking off into the forest pedaling fast, riding and bouncing hard not caring if she hit roots or rocks. She rode until she heard Ian scream. A single note of pure fear and pain that stopped suddenly, then echoed in the trees before vanishing with the wind, as if his spirit itself carried away from her. Nicole stopped and looked back.

"Nooo," she wailed starting to cry but through tears, in the shadows she saw a huge dark shape stepping from the trail. Before she could shift the bike it moved toward her, a ray of sunlight striking the creature between the trees showing Nicole the Sasquatch was female, having breasts. It moved again and Nicole saw her face, the eyes of this one were different. They were soft, maternal, *looking* at her and sad, very sad.

"You took care of me, why, why?" Nicole said to her sobbing. She saw another giant shadow coming up behind the female Bigfoot, turned the bike, pushed and rode into the trees. Pumping her legs without thinking, taking the bike over and around ivy and ferns, through tree groves riding as fast as she could Nicole caught air hitting a root, came down hard and checked with a quick glance, grateful her tires held. Looking for a trail, she suddenly careened down a steep grade, working the handlebars until it finally bottomed out. She pushed until a long deadfall stopped her. Easier to carry the bike over rather than find a way around, she hoisted it to a shoulder and hop stepped up and across the log. Resisting the urge to sit down and rest she jumped back on with a grunt moving the bike forward, gathering momentum for crossing the forest floor.

# Chapter 21

## KELLY AND ERIC

**IT WAS HALF-TIME,** Walden and Prospect were tied at 12 points each. Eric's dad asked Michael if he had played football. "Yes, sir, I played high school. I had a couple of small schools looking at me and I thought about walking on at Oregon. But I hurt my shoulder making a tackle in our last game, which also took care of my baseball. I liked baseball better and wasn't bad. I watch my kids play now. To be honest, I never really encouraged my son to play football."

"Why's that?"

"He's a funny kid, kind of laid back, intense if it matters to him. It would have been good for him in some ways. Football is the best game I know for teaching anger management at an early age. Most people don't realize the mind set it takes to play. If you're not as teed off as that guy across the line from you, you'll get killed. We played some pretty rough east bay schools in Oakland, Antioch and Pittsburg. It wasn't just the trash talk. It got nasty in the piles some nights. Guys trying to plant their cleats in your nuts, fun stuff like that."

Michael had the attention of the Ibsens and the Larssens. "I tried explaining to Zach that when you line up against some guy bigger and meaner than you are, football will put you in a fight or flight situation like few things in this world can. He tried out his freshman year and didn't get through two-a-days and it didn't really bother me. Right now though, he needs to find something. He's a very skilled skateboarder, which doesn't mean squat to me but maybe it counts for something. I don't know, I just want him to find something worthwhile he'd be passionate about and dedicate himself to it. He messes around with this guitar we got him and is getting pretty good, but he doesn't try that hard. My greatest fear is he'll end up in a b.s. job working for somebody else and kick himself later for not trying harder at something." Looking out across the football field, Michael smiled, "You should see my daughter, Megan, play soccer though. She works hard, practices every day. I can't believe some of the stuff she can do with her feet and a soccer ball."

"Good for her," said Kelly. "Send her up here and I'll take her bow hunting."

"I don't know if she's a deer killer, but I wouldn't put it past her. I've seen her take some pretty good hits on the soccer field and bounce right up. Sometime later in the game, she usually knocks somebody on their ass for make up." Michael smiled again and added, "I think she gets that from her mom."

"Girls kick ass," Kelly said.

"I'll tell her about your invite to go hunting. Megan would like you, Kelly. She's an action girl and a smart, funny kid. She'll probably want to go deer slayer with you. I've needed to get both the kids out in nature more. That would be one way."

"Have her start practicing archery if she wants to come up, Zach too. I could teach rifle, but bow hunting is natural, quiet, we'll be Indians."

"Kelly was archery state champion," Mrs. Larssen said to

Michael. "She knows her stuff."

"She can track a deer with the best of them, too," Eric added. "We haven't been hunting for a long time. I think I'm overdue for a nature trip myself."

"We could go tomorrow if it's not raining too hard," Kelly said. "I haven't been out since Jason and I went last year."

The second half did not go well for Walden High. Smaller in size and number of players, Prospect wore them down and won 32-18. As they filed out of the stadium Kelly asked, "You boys are coming to the Buckhorn for the Ducks-Beavers, aren't you?"

"Next best place to Autzen Stadium. If we can't be in Eugene, we'll hit the Buckhorn," Eric said. "Besides, Michael made a promise to CP he has to keep."

"I think you mean the promise to Dewey, Duck losers buy rounds after the game," Kelly replied. "Don't forget to bring money." Eric walked over and leaned toward Kelly and whispered. She smiled saying, "Sure," quietly.

In the stadium parking lot, Eric's dad took him aside and spoke to him briefly. When he walked away, Eric told Michael, "That was interesting. Mom must have told him about your camping buddy last night. He told me to swing by the house and pick up a rifle to take to the bluff." Eric grinned and looked at Michael. "He said, don't take a .22."

"Now I feel better," Michael said, grinning back at his friend.

"I need to ask you a favor first," Eric said. "I need to talk to Kelly about something. Do you mind hanging for a while at Edna's? It won't be long, then we'll head to the bluff."

"No sweat. Take your time."

Dewey and CP strolled into the parking lot carrying their trumpet and sax cases. "Hey, guys," Dewey said. "Sad game for old Walden, good thing I'll have the Beavers to cheer me up tonight."

"Setting yourself up for the pain, I see," Eric replied.

"What are you boys up to," CP asked? "I would say we head to the bluff, but my volunteer shift at the museum starts in a few, time for my civic duty."

"I've gotta run a couple of errands," Eric said. "You should take Michael. Old history major, you want to check out the museum?"

"Glad to," Michael answered. "I like museums."

"Why don't you take CP," Dewey asked Michael. "I have to go tend the garden. I'll pick you up later, CP. We can go to the Buckhorn from the museum to see the Ducks suck, and suck hard tonight."

"That works," said Eric. "I'll have Kelly drop me by the museum. Michael and I can go to the bluff from there." Eric walked over to Kelly's jeep and climbed in, Michael half expecting something leering or smart-ass from Dewey or CP, but they watched and said nothing.

Kelly drove west on Main with Eric. "Sorry I don't have more time. I promised I'd go to Medford for Jake to get a big screen for the game tonight. I have to leave pretty soon."

"Oh, no problem Kell, I just wanted see how you're doing."

Kelly smiled. "Thanks, I'm ok, same old. Buckhorn's still there. Mark will be back for Thanksgiving. Then he'll be stationed at the Prospect ranger station in January."

"That's good, Kell, glad to hear it. Mark is a good dude."

They were quiet as Kelly turned the jeep off of Main and drove down side streets of old and either quaint or dilapidated houses. She stopped the jeep in front of the modest but clean and trim little house she had grown up in. "I need to grab a couple of things and feed Max. You want to come in?" Eric reached for the door handle, but then saw Kelly's elderly neighbor watching from the yard across the street. Eric waved and the old woman waved back.

"I'll wait here," Eric said.

He watched Kelly walk to the front door, noting her rump still perfectly round in snug blue jeans and sighed. As she went through the front door he sat back, pondering the choices he had made. Eric loved prosecuting for King County; that was one thing he could be sure of. He also loved his daughters and he desperately missed his ex-wife, Veronica and clearly he would always, always love Kelly. Those were the things he knew to be true. How those things were to somehow work out or make any sense he had no answer for and so it was easy to run the, *what ifs* over again. What if Kelly had tried moving to Eugene 25 years ago? What if Mathew had not been killed and she had not taken on helping her Aunt Ellen and Uncle Jeremiah raise baby Jason, surely they would be married. What if he had accepted life as an orchardist? Eric looked at the old lady pulling weeds in her flower garden and thought it a good thing she had been there. *This is Kelly and Ranger Mark's house, you jack ass. You're the last pain in the ass Kelly needs.*

Kelly stood in her living room and out the front window watched Eric sitting in her jeep, staring past the windshield. She knew he was thinking about her and it made her heart hurt. She might have let herself cry but there wasn't time, so she called out, "Max! Maxine Kitty, where are you? Here, kitty, kitty." A grey and black striped cat sauntered in and jumped onto the couch, then looked up expectantly. Her cat sat on a new couch but in the same spot where Kelly used to sit on Eric's lap watching TV, jogging a memory.

One day after school, freshman year, she leaned back without warning and pulled off her shirt. Kelly giggled aloud at remembering Eric's goofy happy boy grin. *He was so cute,* she thought looking out at him in the jeep, his face about as far from happy goofy as it could be. Kelly picked up her feline and held her, stroked Max and said, "Oh Max, oh Eric. Dammit, Max, dammit, Eric. Mark will be home soon. He loves me, Max. We'll do fun things when Ranger Mark gets home. Eric has babies to take care of in Seattle. That has to be that, Max."

Eric, Kelly and her cousin Mathew were inseparable growing up. Born only a few months apart, they grew up playing cowboys and Indians or sports as equals. The boys had little choice as Kelly was simply as good or better at anything they ever tried. In the fall of 1970, Kelly, Eric and Mathew were nine years and old enough at last to deer hunt with their fathers, or, at least the boys were. Kelly begged her dad, Jason Ibsen, to go with them on the first hunt of the season, the boy's first hunt. It was all Eric and Mathew could talk about. Jason Ibsen reminded his daughter that she had been knocked on her fanny by the kick back from a 30.06 at the rifle safety class she and the boys had taken. "You can use a .22 squirrel hunting. I'll take you on Uncle Jeremiah's property. We can thin out the squirrels for him. Its good practice until you get stronger."

"Squirrels Dad!" Kelly stomped into her bedroom and slammed the door, refusing to come out, even for dinner. When she emerged the next day after the hunting party went without her, Kelly walked past her mother without speaking and went outside to the back shed. There, she rummaged until she found her father's old hunting gear, rummaged further until she found his old bow and arrows. In their younger days Jeremiah and Jason learned bow hunting first but now always used deer rifles. Mathew and Eric would be learning to hunt with rifles first.

Kelly made a target, hung it on a tree and shot arrow after

arrow in the backyard. When her fingers rubbed raw, she taped and bandaged them to keep practicing. Two weeks later her father came home from his logging job with his brother Jeremiah. Jason fully expected another battle with his daughter about her going on the deer hunting trip the next day and was not surprised to see her waiting for him in the front yard. When Uncle Jeremiah pulled his truck into their driveway Kelly greeted her father with, "Daddy, I need to show you something." Clearly his strong-willed little girl meant business.

"Can Uncle Jeremiah see it too?"

She looked at her Uncle and said, "Sure daddy, I think that's a good idea." They followed Kelly around the house to the back, and there was the target hanging on the tree, the bow and arrows propped underneath. Without speaking she retrieved the bow and arrows, turned and marched back across their open yard. She set herself, the bow looking ridiculously big to her father, but he simply folded his arms and watched. She fingered an arrow and placed it on the bowstring, pulled back and let fly. The arrow struck four inches left of the bull's eye. "Dang it," she said under her breath. She set a second arrow, aimed and released, this time hitting dead center. Kelly said nothing. The third arrow struck the bull's eye also, just right of dead center. Holding the bow comfortably, rather naturally her father noted, she looked at them saying, "I want to go deer hunting tomorrow. Please."

"Let me talk to your Uncle Jeremiah about it. Go inside, I'll be right there. Good job, Kell." They watched her walk in before the Ibsen brothers looked at each other and laughed.

"One heckuva kid you got there," Jeremiah said.

Jason grinned, "It'll be more dangerous if I don't take her. I'll call Bill Larssen, I'm sure he'll be fine with it."

After that hunting trip until he was killed working in the

woods with Jeremiah four years later, Jason Isben never hunted again without his daughter, teaching Kelly everything he knew about the upper Rogue forest. Uncle Jeremiah and Eric's father always took Kelly with Mathew and Eric, continuing the lessons after her father's death. Eventually, Kelly would be the one to pass this sacred knowledge on to little Jason.

"You ok there?" Eric had not seen Kelly coming to the jeep. She looked at him as she climbed in.

"Yeah Kelly, sorry, I was just thinking about hunting. I miss our group. I need to get my dad out to the woods. Watching the football game today had me thinking about your nephew, I hope we get to see little Jason tonight. I really need for dad to go hunting next season with you guys. I really need it." Starting the jeep she managed a smile for her old boyfriend.

"Mathew would be really proud of Jason. So would my dad and Uncle Jeremiah," she said softly. "I miss hunting with our group too, so get your ass down here next deer season, I'll get Jason to schedule it and you get your dad out. It'll be good for all of us."

"I will, I'll make sure of it." Eric leaned over and gave her a hug and she held him tight. He felt her tears on his neck. When Eric let go, Kelly smiled and only said, "Sorry for crying."

"I really miss you, Kelly."

"Why don't you call me sometime so we can just talk like friends? That would help."

"That's a good idea, Kell." Eric sighed, "Sounds' easy enough."

They drove to the museum and Eric told her what his daughters had been up to. "Brianna is a cheerleader? A cheerleader? How the hell did that happen?"

"I don't know. Cheerleading is different now. She does gymnastics, takes dance classes. They go to these competitions."

"If you say so," she said pulling the jeep up to the museum. "Thank you for checking on me, Eric. Sorry we don't have more time."

"I'll see you at the Buckhorn tonight. Don't let Jake go cheap on the big screen. What are you getting?"

"I don't know, he said buy American. There's a sale at Fred Meyer."

"How much did Jake give you?"

"About five hundred bucks."

"For a big screen?" Eric laughed, taking out his wallet.

"Eric, you don't need to-"

"It's ok Kell, just do me a favor and don't tell Jake, he'll think he owes me. Besides, I want a good one for the game." She reached across and hugged him again and Eric squeezed, not wanting to lose the familiar feel and smell of her hair against his face.

Finally, Kelly let go. "Damn tempting to jump your bones, old man."

"Good to know you're tempted, your bones feel pretty good too."

"Gotta go buy a TV, you and Mike have fun at the bluff, wish I could be there. I gotta hurry or the TV will be late for kick-off."

# Chapter 22

## HUNTING

**THEY WERE GIDDY** as school girls getting off the ATVs after romping along the forest OHV trail, but after hiding and waiting next to brush on a meadow's overlook for an hour, Harper and Brian were restless. "Ok, even if the ATVs scared off the deer, they should be back by now," Harper offered while taking off the Crown Royal cap and gulping another shot down. He handed the bottle to Brian, who did the same.

"We could move around some," Brian suggested. "I'm ready to get off my ass."

"Can't hurt, what the hell, let's be scouts," Harper said grinning.

They stood, surveyed their surroundings again and headed further into the woods. Sunlight stripes slanted through the trees as evaporating mist rose slowly off the damp green, lichen covered branches. "I'm glad we're here," Brian said. "It's peaceful, quiet, really pretty in here. I could use this once in a while. LA is such a cluster."

Harper stopped, looked around and answered, "Jeremiah Johnson."

"Jeremiah Johnson?"

"My old man took me to see Jeremiah Johnson when I was a kid. I wanted to be Jeremiah Johnson after that."

"Robert Redford, right?"

"Yeah, great damn movie. Sad in places, I remember being really pissed at this preacher in the movie that gets him in trouble with the Indians. His squaw and kid get killed, then Jeremiah takes it out on the Indians."

"They go through a sacred burial ground or something."

"That's right, the damn preacher screws up everything. Jeremiah was trapping, hunting, doing just fine living like an Indian. I wanted to live in the forest after that. Shit, I haven't thought about that for a long time. That was one of my old man's, one of our better days." Harper breathed out. "This is a good timeout, dude, I'll give you that, even if we don't shoot anything."

"Let's rent Jeremiah Johnson after we get back," Brian suggested while adjusting his Lakers cap.

"Good idea." They walked on through the trees.

"Here's a nice view," Harper said. They stopped on a rise with another small meadow before them. "We can hide by these trees. Look at that grass and those berries over there, what deer wouldn't find that tasty? This has to be a prime spot."

"I'm down," Brian said. "Ready for lunch?"

"Sure, I might even take a nap after. Smells better than LA out here, doesn't it?"

"Sure as hell does. We haven't seen sky that blue forever."

"I can see why hairy little shit and his redneck friends like it up here."

"We still have to kick his hairy ass tonight."

"And we will. Then little miss perky tits might get the boning of her life too," Harper said wistfully stroking his goatee. "Damn she was cute, real spunky as I vaguely remember."

Brian pulled a pack of salami, cheese and rolls out of his back pack and began assembling as Harper opened two beers. "Thanks, dude," Harper said reaching for a hearty sandwich. "Jeremiah Johnson, damn," he added before tearing into a bite. Suddenly a deer, an adult female sprint bounded across the meadow. "Shit!" they yelled together, grabbing for their rifles. When they raised their guns, the deer had just entered the trees. Harper shouldered and fired quickly as the deer vanished, bark from a struck tree flying as the shot reverberated around them. Brian fired a second later, that bullet's destination a forever mystery. One could safely assume it missed the deer.

"Balls!" Harper yelled.

"Man, that deer was making tracks," Brian exclaimed, "like it was getting away from something."

"No shit, did you see its eyes? Wide, like it was really freaked out. Shit, oh well, let's be ready for the next one."

"Well I guess we're in the right place, anyway. Let's hang here for a while." Harper and Brian grinned and tapped their beer cans in agreement.

# Chapter 23

## MUSEUM

**SERIOUSLY CONSIDERING THE** offer from CP on the brief drive to the museum, Michael studied the deeply green pot bud CP dropped from a film container into his hand. "No thanks CP, I'll wait to burn with Eric, maybe for the Ducks game. I haven't been loaded for a long time and this looks and smells like real ass kicker. Nice work."

"Thanks, Dewey and I teamwork it. I'd say a run to the bluff while you and Eric are here tomorrow definitely needs to happen."

"That'll be great. I don't have to be home until Monday so we can let it rip."

The Mazama Creek Natural History museum had a covered wagon in the lobby, an excellent tribute to those who pioneered the Oregon Territory. Michael looked at the wooden seats and wagon wheels bare of anything resembling absorbent rubber and marveled at the determination and toughness of generations past. He remembered whining in his parent's station wagon during family vacations and shook his head.

"Check it out, it's actually a pretty cool museum," CP told Michael as he settled in at the front desk. "My section, the part they let me put together is in the far back. Do you have any interest in skookums, Bigfoot?"

Michael laughed. "When I lived in Eugene, I thought it was interesting how once or twice a year I'd read in the paper about a Sasquatch sighting. Always the same, somebody saying they knew it wasn't a bear." He chose not to mention his encounter of the previous night.

CP said, "When the mill closed I tried to get the town to use skookums as a tourist attraction, but they wouldn't go for it. Eric's old man was really down on the idea, said last thing we need are fools in our woods hunting for something that isn't there. No arguing the fools part."

"I could see Eric's dad being that way. Keeping the idiots away is never a bad idea."

"I guess. They do bring money. Anyway, I have a section of old newspaper articles and other stuff. Let me know what you think. Personally, I haven't seen one but I've heard some wild stories from old-timers around here. You read those articles; the consistency has to mean something. How many times do you have to read similar descriptions, the same noises, the smell, make imprints of tracks before there's a clear enough pattern? The locals always say, 'well, if they were that big somebody would have found a body or shot one.' The thing to me is, they're nocturnal, and they use the lava tubes. The lava tubes are the key. We have hundreds of miles of underground caves that go from Crater Lake to all over around here, especially around The Rogue. Just like Shasta, St. Helens, Mt. Hood, Three Sisters over by Bend. They all do; all throughout the Cascades. That's where they are. They travel the lava tubes, no doubt in my mind."

"Makes sense, CP," Michael offered.

"See Mike, the Indian stories go way back. We call 'em

skookums, but that actually comes from a tribe in Washington. Skookum means mountain devil. The Indians were scared of them, said they ate humans, carried off young ones and women, real scary stuff. The name skookums just worked its way down with the Norwegians that settled here. Did you notice the sign for Skookum Ridge just west of here? That name stuck since wagon days. That should tell you something."

"Hey, what was Dewey giving you a hard time about yesterday, Grey Canyon? I noticed Jason's grandmother seemed upset at the game when she found out he was going there today."

"Oh well, ok, Mike. Grey Canyon is this totally inaccessible place a few miles north they say no white man has ever stepped foot in and the Klamath tribe would not go into for anything even if they could. Kelly's nephew, Jason is on this crew that got the logging rights to work Grey Canyon. He thinks he knows the way in and where they can pull the timber out." CP adjusted his glasses. Michael could see he was happy to have an audience. "Jason going in there is really a historical situation and nobody knows. Pioneers tried and tried to find a way into there. The Indians here said no one should ever want to go in. The fog never lifts there; really weird. Evil spirits, skookums, really bad energy, the natives say. Did you know we get a high incidence of UFO sightings around Crater Lake also?"

"Nope."

"Anything is possible, Mike. UFO base at the bottom of Crater Lake, skookums and aliens connected some way and the US government knows all about it. Nimrods here can call me Conspiracy Paul all they want. The truth is there for those with eyes to see, there will always be deniers. You think anyone around here will pay up on my bets on weapons of mass destruction in frickin' Iraq?"

"Nope, I suppose not. Where's your Sasquatch section, CP?"

"Past the natives, dead stuffed animals, Crater Lake, the Vet's section and in the back is Bigfoot." Michael left CP to wander the museum. He paused at a replica teepee and model Klamath tribe members gathered round. Indian artifacts such as bow and arrows, baskets and grinding stones were positioned in the foreground. The next section featured stuffed animals, including a huge elk standing tall to a mountain lion in attack pose and another where a black bear fended off a bobcat.

Beyond the wildlife exhibit, a large topographical model of the area surrounding Crater Lake showed the descent of the Rogue River and described the formation of the lava tubes that honeycombed for miles. Reading the description of massive volcanic eruptions over thousands of years finally collapsing Mount Mazama's top, creating the crater that over geologic time filled with snow and rain water, Michael decided he'd try to work in a run up to Crater Lake before going home. Taking his time reading how lava tubes are formed he made a note to also stop by the Natural Bridge. Leaving the Crater Lake section, he passed through pictures and biographies of military veterans from the area, Civil War to Iraq. Normally a place where Michael would linger to absorb stories of history and individual lives intertwined he paused only at Kelly's cousin Mathew's picture, young and handsome in a Navy uniform. A need to reach the Bigfoot exhibit suddenly taking hold, he moved on.

Rounding a corner Michael stopped cold and a bizarre, never felt before wave of nausea and fear invaded him, first in the stomach, then down to wobble his legs. He stood before an 8 foot high poster picture of a Bigfoot, the famous outtake from the Patterson film shot in California in 1967, the beast or beast costume with its head turned back toward the camera walking way. A deep breath helped Michal clear his head, bring strength back into the legs. Remembrance of his reaction to last night's encounter, peeing in his sleeping bag, the paranoia afterward in the van returned and Michael was now disgusted by the unmanly way he'd responded in a shocking situation. *Now that was a real fight or flight and all you did was flight your piss right into your sweatpants. Way to handle the test, Gardner,* he told himself bitterly.

He studied the Sasquatch's huge back and shoulders, the long arms and human-seeming gait and settled himself gradually, wondering how someone in 1967 could have faked those calf and hamstring muscles. And seriously, are those really breasts, Michael pondered, *who the hell would put knockers on a fake Bigfoot?*

CP had arranged a montage of newspaper clippings from various Northwest papers, some from the 1800's, some very recent, surrounding the picture. Michael read them, especially the older stories of explorers, trappers and pioneers. He smiled as they described the smells, sights, sounds and fear along with the frequently said, "It wasn't a bear," all recurring with remarkable and interesting continuity. This seemed to calm him, the shared experience as it were being helpful. He studied a plaster cast of a giant's footprint, eerily similar to the prints near his sleeping bag. Looking up to the Patterson film outtake, locking eyes with the strolling lady Bigfoot he breathed in, exhaled smiling and thought, *actually hope I get to see you again sometime, I'll try not to freak out.* Telling Carol and the kids about his Sasquatch adventure would be great fun he suddenly looked forward to. Michael would ask them to keep it quiet though, sharing with Eric and his parents should be the end of any further reporting outside of family. *Maybe I'll leave out the whizzing my pants part when I tell Carol and the kids.*

*Nah, I'll have to tell everything.*

"Hey, is that your buddy?" Michael turned and laughed at the grin on Eric's face.

"Yeah, I was just thinking I'm glad she or he wasn't horny. I was vulnerable."

Eric walked up close to the picture and shook his head. "I read somewhere that mountain gorillas were considered an African myth until about 1950, who knows? You ready to go get your ice chest and confront your sleep disturber?"

"I'm ready to knock down the beers in my ice chest, then we'll see about a confrontation. He or she might come back frisky, you know. Sure, let's go. I've gotta tell CP he's done a nice job back here."

# Chapter 24

## HER IRISH SIDE

**NICOLE'S LEGS WERE** done and her head hurt, she really wanted to quit the tough biking through the forest. Navigating the terrain kept moving her toward home though, and the intense focus required along with the tired pain her body felt enabled not thinking of Ian, hearing his scream again and again. Sure she had put some distance between herself and the Bigfoot, expecting to hit a real trail any time and still very sharp in her survival mode thinking, Nicole intently biked the rough open spaces between the brush and trees. But as thoughts of Ian would escape and run through her head, Nicole resisted by remembering other things, like childhood things, fleeting but clear moments from school, playing with friends or camping with her mom and sister... *yes, camping with mom and sis, that's a good one,* Nicole thought, *when mom told Heather about the Brigeeds, that was a fun one....*

It was after a fish dinner mom cooked over an open fire, the three Quinn ladies, May, Nicole, Heather, and dog Bandon, watched the sun go down behind the hills, the pinks and oranges of sunset mirrored in the Rogue River gliding by their camping spot. Nicole sat glumly in her camping chair, a

Gameboy held limply in one hand, watching her mom stack wood for the night's camp fire. "I'm bored, mom. I don't see why I couldn't bring my friends."

"That sunset's beautiful, Nicole."

"Can you tell us a story, mom?" Heather asked as Nicole rolled her eyes.

"Sure sweetie. How about a story, Nicole?"

"Whatever."

"Do you remember the Amaterasu story?"

"The sunshine hair lady," Heather chimed in. "I like that one."

"How about something else, mom?" Nicole asked.

"Like a swift kick, miss attitude?" Mom answered.

"I can't help being bored, mom."

"Oh nuts Nicole, please, you know better. Look at that sunset and how pretty it is around us. Why don't you draw that? Did you finish the Harry Potter book?"

"Hours ago, it was ok, not as good as the first one. Ok, tell Heather about the Brigeeds, mom, the Irish goddess saint ladies."

"Ok good one, Nicole. Well, your great Nana told me about the Brigeeds, girls. The first legendary Brigeed was a lot like Amaterasu, her parents were warrior gods who came from the heavens to fight with swords and shields and magic to drive mean kings out of Ireland."

"I like that the girls were warriors," Nicole shared with big sister wisdom to Heather.

"Oh yes, in the olden days there were many great lady warriors. When the great warrior king of Ireland, Dagda had a baby girl they named Brigid, her spirit was so bright and strong she shot like a flaming arrow up into the sky. A special cow from the heavens came to give her milk when she was baby. The Irish say her name, Brigeed. To say it properly you roll the g and make Brigid, Brigeed. She grew up to be a strong girl, a warrior poet princess who made her own swords with metal and fire. She also learned the secrets of the forest, like which plants were good to eat or could help you feel better or fix a wound from battle. When she grew to be a big girl she became a teacher and maidens from all across the land came to her school. She put her school by a special oak tree that had magical powers. No stranger could take their weapon past that tree, it helped protect Brigeed's school. They also had a special campfire, just like ours but it never, ever went out. Many years after Brigeed was gone, 19 maidens took turns keeping the sacred fire burning, one each day to celebrate Brigeed. But on the 20th day, no maiden would go near the fire."

"Were the maidens afraid the fire will go out?" Heather asked.

"They were not afraid because on the 20th day, Brigeed's spirit takes care of the fire with old wood from the sacred oak tree. When the maiden came to take care of the fire the next day it was always burning bright and warm."

"Is the fire still burning?"

"There are those who say Brigeed's fire still burns at the church your Nana in Kildare, Ireland goes to. We know the nuns at Saint Brigid's church at Kildare took care of the fire for many centuries."

"Mommy, is there a Saint Brigeed story?"

"Well, Nana told me there are many legends about Saint Brigeed. Some say her father was a druid king and warlock, a magic wizard who was captured by pirates. While a pirate captive he fell in love with another prisoner, a lady Pict warrior. The Picts were a tribe that lived in the woods, very knowing about nature and their girls were action girls, fierce warriors with arrows and bows and spears. They wore wild scary make-up and fought with everybody. So, the magic king and the warrior girl fell in love and had a baby girl, also named Brigid, who grew up a prisoner of the pirates."

"Maybe they named her after the first Brigeed?" Nicole asked.

"That always seemed possible to me too, Nicole," her mom said. "Your Nana says the Quinn's are descended from both Brigeeds, she says they're the same angel. Nana's a funny old girl. Your Oba-Chan says our Japanese side is descended from Amaterasu. It's fun to think about. It might be why we hear the forest sing."

"I haven't heard singing in the trees since I was little but we are definitely princess warriors, mom," Nicole said so matter of fact, May laughed.

Heather added, "Except Bandon is a handsome prince warrior."

Laughing harder, May began again, "So, the wizard father cast a magic spell over the pirates and the warrior mom and daughter Brigeed fought the pirates with swords. They killed those nasty pirates and escaped to Ireland. Because her Da was such a gifted wizard they lived with the King of Leinster." May got up to add a new log to the camp fire and she finished the story as the girls and Bandon watched her tend the flames. "Nana says as a young lady Brigeed was the priestess spiritual leader of her people and after a time in Ireland she came to find a very strong faith in Jesus. Her faith and wise spirit gave her a special connection to God for doing miracles to help the Irish people. Her miracles of feeding the hungry were told all over Ireland and Europe. She also started a school and a church at Kildare where goddess Brigeed's school was. Right in the same place, so the great oak tree protected them too. The

Catholic nuns were brave and kept the first Brigeed's campfire always burning for many centuries. That is the church your great Nana goes to and I need to take you there someday. The end, who wants smores?"

Nicole saw something she didn't like up ahead, jolting her from the friendly memory's distraction, though not sure what it was. Something dark appeared on the ground and as it came closer, the darkness spread. She braked hard and stopped, peering down at the edge of a ravine. Too wide to jump easily and unable to see the bottom of the crevice, she dismounted and set her bike against a tree. Nicole walked up and down in both directions, taking sips of water, looking for a way across. Doubling back toward the Bigfoot, even with her car on that path did not feel like an option.

Standing with hands on her hips, looking over a spot that might have room on both sides for a take-off and reachable landing, she heard something strange. A far-away rumbling, thumping sound, over and over, growing louder, coming closer, rumbling steps and clearer, running steps, some kind of stampede was moving swiftly toward her. Nicole gasped, thinking, *they're running after me!* Suddenly she heard them close, heard them breathing and dove behind a tree rolling and stopped, facing down into the ravine. They were not slowing down. Nicole told herself, *"Stay here, they'll fall into the hole!"*

The first Bigfoot reached her and Nicole curled up tight and closed her eyes but opened them when she heard it rush past to see a hairy giant incredibly in mid-air, flying like a track long jumper across the ravine. The beast landed with yards to spare on the other side. Nicole watched another monster leap across and then two more, side by side. They bounded and ran immediately into the woods, except one of the last two. Snorting, turning its head Nicole froze, knowing he had smelled or sensed her. The young Bigfoot's eyes grew wide and spreading his arms smacked his chest twice, all the while staring at her. It grinned and hideously, there was movement in the tuft of hair that covered his crotch. Smacking his chest once more, he turned running into the forest after the others. Nicole knew the young Sasquatch would come back for her, for she knew in the most sickening possible way how he wanted her. *Get to the car before he comes back, get to the car!* Scrambling to her bike, she grabbed the handlebars, pushed herself forward and started pedaling back across the forest floor, toward her car.

# Chapter 25

## NOT A .22

**MICHAEL AND ERIC** stopped at Roy's Shell to fill up, get ice and beer and after Eric chatted with Roy, who came out to pump the gas and clean the windshield and rear window as per Oregon custom and law, then headed to Eric's folk's place to pick up a deer rifle.

As they pulled back out of town Michael asked, "How was the visit with Kelly?"

Eric took a moment, answered, "She seems ok. Honestly Michael, I've been confused as hell about my feelings lately, my feelings for her, how to feel about Veronica. So, today sitting in Kelly's jeep outside her house I decided my feelings in particular don't mean dog shit. Kelly's married, no changing that. Veronica thinks I'm a piece of shit, no changing that either. Being a good dad for Brianna and Kylie is the only thing I can control, so that's what I need to work at. The rest is just my own bull that's nobody else's problem. This approach to feelings I think will be liberating. Far simpler anyway."

"I can appreciate you having feelings for Kelly and I can see Veronica being tough once she turned on you." They drove along the tree lined highway in silence, then Michael offered,

"For what it's worth, my brother, I'm still married because Carol and I figured out love is a choice. You think it's some eternal rush that goes on and on and has something to do with personal destiny or something. Horseshit, we make our choices and live with them, or not. Carol and I would have said, "screw you" and split years ago if it weren't for Zach and Megan, and the crazy thing is by hanging in there we've, what, forged, forged is a good word, forged enough actual love for each other it carries us past all the crap that pisses us off about each other. Barely, a few times too. There's no magic, dude, it's a choice, pure and simple, let love in or don't. But the heck of it is, by making that choice, we've created real love. We're still a royal pain in the ass to each other, but she's my best friend. You know, Kelly is amazing but I still don't see her living near Seattle. Do you mind if I ask, why don't you take a run at getting back with Veronica?"

They reached the Larssen Orchards sign and mailbox and Eric sighed. "My mom and dad have been married for 49 years," he said as they turned onto the gravel road. "I just took for granted that getting married meant end of game, you do what you have to and it just works. I suppose I could ask her to forgive me, but man, I screwed up so royally."

Michael answered in the matter of fact way and tone that Eric had always appreciated about his friend. "Could it really hurt to try? Would her telling you to take a hike hurt any worse than the way you feel now? A one-time piece of ass while in the grips of good tequila might eventually be forgiven, maybe."

"I don't see forgiveness in those eyes when I see her."

"Might start by saying sorry again and asking for it, you never know."

"That'll be asking for it alright," Eric answered as they pulled up to the house.

Eric walked out a few minutes later holding the rifle as Michael waited in the van. Bill Larssen stepped out onto the porch behind his son. "Eric, you understand there's a reason I told you to take the deer rifle?"

"You always have a good reason for everything, Pop."

"Dammit Eric, I'm serious. What Mike had happen last night, from the sound of it, you need to respect. Just take my word. One of these days we'll talk some more."

"Ok, Pop, I'd like to hear about it from you. I'm not leaving until Monday, how about tomorrow?"

"Tomorrow, fine, tomorrow. I'll sit you and Mike down and we'll have a little talk about skookums."

"Great, Pop. We're gonna watch the Ducks-Beavers game at the Buckhorn later. You and mom should come out."

"I'm pretty tired, long day with the parade and all."

"You got it, Pop." He gave his dad a quick, awkward hug and said, "I love you."

"Love you too, son, we'll talk tomorrow. And take off from the bluff before it gets dark."

# Chapter 26

## THE HUNT

**OUT OF WHISKEY** and down to sharing their last beer, Harper and Brian trudged the darkening woods, reasonably sure they would soon return to the ATV trail and their off-roaders. The rain and chill wind found them beneath the trees.

"Rain *and* freezing-ass cold, nice combo, Brian. I could be hunting two-legged deer in Vegas, but you gotta watch some survival bullshit on the Discovery Channel and take us to Freezin' Ass, Oregon."

"Freezin' Ass, Oregon, that's a good name for this place and like you weren't all ready to play great white hunter, Harper. Jeremiah Johnson, my ass. Where is that damn trail? I'm so ready to hit that bar, shave and skin the hairy little shit that got us lost, eat their food and blow. I can see why village idiots like that hairy little shit like it up here. This place is for Hobbits."

"I guess he's all we're gonna kill today. We haven't seen squat since that one deer."

"I know it's weird, one freaked deer and no squirrels, no rabbits, nothing. There's supposed to be all kinds of critters running around up here. Hey look, there's the trail."

"Sweet, about time, ATVs should be this way. It's getting

dark, let's just go get a room in town or we could head to that town, Medford, at I-5. Maybe they got a girlie bar."

"Hobbit babes with hairy armpits, that'll be a lap dance to remember."

"Beats this bullshit, I don't care if we head back in the morning. We could hit a Reno cathouse. A diversion true, but legal guaranteed ass."

"If it stops raining, we could try for Bambi again tomorrow. We'll need booze though," Brian suggested. They stepped past a big hemlock tree and stopped. "What the hell?" Brian said angrily, staring at his upside down ATV. It rested on its seat and handlebars, the four fat tires sticking up in the air.

"Hairy little shit!" they yelled together.

"He followed us out here! We gotta kill him. Where are you, you little asshole!" Harper hollered at the trees. A thick chunk of tree branch flew out of the brush, sailing just over their heads. They ducked reflexively, but Harper stood and shouldered his rifle.

"I'm gonna shoot your hairy ass!" he yelled again, and fired a shot up into the sky, the boom echoing around them. Peering through the rifle scope into a mixed tree grove, Harper growled, "I think I see the little bastard, something's moving over there. Eat hot lead, you little assho... mmm, that might not be him, I think it's big, I think it's a bear. Brian, can you see this? Freakin' bear is in those trees. Is it bear season? What the hell, bear skin rug baby, bonin' on a bear skin rug. Mm Brian, are you looking at this, is that a bear? What the hell, it's walking, walking around... holy shit Brian, what is that? Brian, what the hell that big is walking around over there? It has a face let's get outta here man, this is freaking me out!"

Harper pulled back from the scope and turned to see huge hairy hands, one digging claws into Brian's neck and shoulder, blood trickling down while the other hand held the top of his head. Long, red furred fingers covered Brian's face, Harper saw his friend's eyes bulging between them. The hand on the shoulder shot out yanking the rifle from Harper's hands, tossed it aside and gripped Brian's shoulder again, squeezing down hard. Brian winced, mouth opened and a whining moan escaped. Looking desperately at Harper, his head twisted suddenly, neck breaking with a sickening crack. Brian dropped to the ground and Harper only saw reddish brown hair. He stared up into the face of Old Red, teeth barred into a fiendish grin. The Bigfoot reached with both hands sinking claws into Harper's shoulders, looking into the terrified face. Seeing this human also would not fight, knowing he only had to decide how, Old Red's horrid smile widened. They would play first with this one.

# Chapter 27

## THE BLUFF

**THE RAIN FELL** softly as Michael's van stopped at the bluff, the deer rifle lying in the back. His ice chest and sleeping bag were still there, apparently undisturbed. Eric walked immediately to the set of tracks starting at the cliff's edge, veered toward the sleeping bag and followed them to the trees. "Kick me in the ass," he said in genuine disbelief. Eric put his foot next to one print and shook his head. "I've lived and hunted around here all these years and did not believe. One night and they come right to you."

"Maybe someday I'll appreciate that. Did your mom mention, I peed my sweat pants when it screamed after stopping by my sleeping bag?" Michael carried the rifle from the van and handed it to Eric.

Laughing, Eric said, "No, she left that part out. She said it gave you a good start."

"Your mom's a saint."

Eric nodded. "That's a fact, if she can forgive some of the dumb ass things I've done."

"God bless forgiving mommies," Michael rejoined. He pulled two beers from the ice chest. "Still nice and cold, some ice still in here, pretty brisk today." He opened them and the two friends clinked bottles and took their spots sitting at the edge of the bluff.

"So, what does bring you up here to camp in November?" Eric asked.

"It was going to be camping with my kid. I really wanted to get Zach up here. I hoped a little back-to-nature time might light some kind of fire for him, inspire something, anything. Play his guitar, want to be a biologist or a forest ranger, I don't know, just be happy doing something more meaningful than video games and skateboard. Sit and think and wonder about God the way I used to out here, believing in God through nature. But he blew me off to hang with his buddies, some new video game is out this weekend." Michael exhaled looking across the rugged, tree covered hills. "So while I was driving up here feeling sorry for me, I rounded the bend on I-5 where Mount Shasta's right there in front of you. It has snow already, it really looked cool, majestic. I'm driving and looking at Shasta, pretty soon I thought, damn, I'm the one that needs the back-to-nature time. Yesterday, I realized my mistaken belief while driving and meditating on Mount Shasta. I really believed I'd done my job and repressed all my latent and current disappointments sufficiently to avoid mid-life crises, but no, Carol has been good enough to let me know what a grouchy pain in the ass I've been lately. As I was driving up some things hit me and then I spent the afternoon and evening here, trying pathetically to recapture an old buzz, the one you and I had that first weekend you brought me here back in '81."

"Oh, Kelly's margaritas with Dewey and CP's green bud, that was a great buzz. A tough buzz to recreate with just beer," Eric said with a grin. "Damn, that was a long time ago."

"It felt like a long time ago yesterday."

"Sounds like trying too hard, or you just need to cheat with weed and tequila like the rest of the seeking world."

Michael laughed, "Completely trying too hard, I could not shut up the voice in my head. I come all the way up here, sitting in God's country and I just wanted a moment like I used to have when I was so completely, magically sure the natural world I was looking at was created with some great purpose. Is that too much to ask for?"

Eric considered, then answered, "I guess you can ask for that, but you have to let it happen. When I was a kid, I thought if I could just shut up the voice in my head I could hear what God was thinking or saying to me."

Michael answered, "I remember you told me that when we were sitting in a tree in the orchards. That was a great summer, that summer I worked for your folks. The just listening trick, you called it. But you did that when you were a kid, right?"

"Yeah, ten or eleven, maybe, I remember it because I used to try to use that when I worked in the orchard. If I could just listen to all the sounds around me, the other pickers speaking Spanish, the wind, the trees make noises too, just listening without thinking about what I was listening to, the time went by so much faster and I always did good work. I could keep up with the pickers and not realize it until the basket was full. It was a way to make the time go, but sometimes it was actually fun. I think I forgot how to do that when I hated working in the orchards later on."

"Maybe that would help at my job. It's madness daily, just constant shit. I bounce from one thing to the next continually, a worker problem or some corporate deadline bullshit crises. I really need to find a quiet space somehow to keep my mind right."

"I know, I haven't thought about the just listening trick for a long time. I could seriously use it myself."

"When we were here that first time, that October, that's what I wanted to feel like." Michael said wistfully.

"Freshman year, after the Stones concert in Seattle and the USC game where Vince Goldsmith stuffed Marcus Allen on 4th down. I remember."

"We both just read The Peaceful Warrior. I was trying to breathe properly, quiet my mind, stuff like that."

"Really tasting food, appreciating every bite," Eric said chuckling.

"That was about creating some quiet space, as I remember."

"That's funny, we were working on that here," Eric said. "You gave me The Peaceful Warrior to read, I haven't thought about that book for a long time either." They both took healthy pulls on their beers and were quiet for a time. Eric spoke first. "So, while you couldn't stop thinking yesterday, did you hit any great conclusions? Ya gotta come out of this trip better for something."

Smiling, Michael answered, "Oh, I already have; no worries. Just seeing you and your folks, trust me, just the being here is making me better by osmosis. I can feel it, hell, I felt it walking into the Buckhorn yesterday."

"Good."

"And I gotta believe my crazy ass Bigfoot moment has to be some sort of sign of something." They both laughed, tapped bottles and finished their beers.

Looking down, Eric said, "I can't believe that skookum walked up this thing, it barely slopes from the bottom."

"It was a steady clip too. One strong mofo," Michael added, pushing himself back on his butt to swing around and get up from the bluff's edge. Taking Eric's empty he recollected, "And stank, just like they say about 'em but worse up close. Sorta moldy skunk smell, putrid."

"Skookums are real, man that's wild." Taking the fresh beer Eric asked, "So you care to explain how seeing the majesty of Mt. Shasta leads you to conclude it's finally mid-life crises time? Maybe you're just naturally grouchy."

"Oh, I really learned it on Oprah, but wasn't ready to face up, I guess." Eric grinned and Michael said, "I actually learned how lamely typical my worries are. One night Carol's watching Oprah in bed, I'm reading next to her, and this very attractive woman psychologist, blouse unbuttoned just right to initially get my attention, she explained it all so nicely, so formula, it depressed me just hearing how garden variety my personal crap is. I learned though, I've fully hit two, but only two out of three mid-life crises warning signs." Eric grinned, nodded and let Michael go on. "Let's see, first, my kids hit teenage, so they don't need me like they used to and to boot, they can at times be complete ingrates, especially my son who reminds me of me, which makes it worse." A wind gust caused Michael to stop to grab his ball cap, the rain fell harder.

Eric advised, "Good storm coming and we should hit it pretty quick, but please go on. It's reassuring to know I'm not the only mess I know."

"Glad to help," Michael responded. "Where was I, ah yes, item number two. The job loses meaning. The same old crap is just older and crappier. It's a joke how busy I am at work. They wouldn't let me replace a supervisor that quit and now I pull 11 and 12 hour days routinely. Work has never been a source of great personal enjoyment other than bringing home a paycheck and providing our fabulous California lifestyle and now it's really wearing me down. It was an ok place to work before we got bought out. All they care about is the quarterly reports and the stockholders. Carol says go somewhere else, but everyone I talk to says it's the same everywhere. I just need to ride it out a few more years."

"Hmm, so what was the third Oprah item, which mid-life red flag have you managed to avoid?"

"Oh, hormones. The lady psych said hormonal shifts in women in their 40s render them unhorny. It goes back and forth creating male confusion and depression when she suddenly changes from nympho horn-dog to Home and Garden Channel granite counter tops are way more interesting than your big wang. Some men take that personally."

"We're such insensitive jerks that way."

"Just ask Oprah."

"But you, my studly friend have somehow defeated the laws of hormonal nature?"

"Well, so far. All I can say is Carol and I are a testimony to good friskiness helping overcome other relational differences. We aren't setting records like we used to, mm, maybe a couple of age-group records. It's all good at least on the frisky front."

Laughing, they hit bottles once more. "So Michael, do you still need a miracle as we used to say, or was your day at the bluff helpful?"

"Strangely in some ways, it was helpful. During the sundown, I really wished Carol had been here to see it."

"That's a good sign."

"I'm taking it that way."

"Michael, you mind if I say something?"

"No, I'm counting on your sagely wisdom."

"Michael, take it from a guy who screwed up his marriage. Veronica and I had plenty of crap to work through, but I choked. If I didn't like my job and have my daughters to keep it together for, I don't know what I'd do. If your work sucks that bad, you either change the work or how you deal with it because you're bringing that work sucks attitude home. And you know your kids *see* that. Either you conjure up a way to deal with work or I'm with Carol, start your ass looking for something else." Michael breathed out and took a good swig. Eric finished his beer, went to the ice chest and opened two more. "I always thought I was doing Veronica a favor not telling her about the disgusting things I see prosecuting criminals," he started. "But now I think it would have been helpful if I talked more. She might understand better why it matters to me, why I bring work home, why more money wasn't worth leaving the DAs office. I expect Carol's not too used to you coming home and talking about your day."

"No, I hate talking about work. It sounds boring to me when I talk about my job."

They were quiet before Eric said, "Michael, I know you're good at what you do and you do have a nice house in one of the most expensive places to live in the world, but take this in the right spirit, you're bitching because you got complacent a long time ago. You're talking to someone who knows what you're capable of. Can't you still be a teacher?"

"I'd love to, but they make under forty thousand to start. I don't see that math working out for us."

"You doing anything with your photography?"

"Nope, I always planned to take it up again after the kids are gone."

"What about starting a business? You're good at distribution stuff. There must be something you can move from one place to another better, faster, cheaper. It's still America, dude."

"I've thought about it. I actually have a couple of ideas. Damn."

"I don't mean to make it worse."

"No, no, thank you, Eric. I need to hear it. More than any of my other stuff Eric, I really fear for my kids, especially Zach. I think that's been weighing on me. I work my ass off to support them, but usually I'm gone before they get up in the morning and lately I miss way too many dinners, too many soccer games. I actually think Meg will be ok. I needed to just sit here again and meditate on what I can do better for them, Zach especially. I see myself in my son and it's sad I don't like what I see sometimes. He's a good kid, but he could do so much and I pray, I mean really pray, he finds something he loves and works hard at it and grows up getting to do that thing. If that happened for Zach and Meg, anything I've done to put them in that position would be worth it."

Eric was quiet again, then looked at Michael and said, "Don't you think you'd improve their chances for having that prayer answered if you were doing something you liked, you know, setting that example yourself?"

Michael looked across the Cascade's rolling hills, mountains and trees. Dark, full storm clouds ruled the sky. "I figured it was too late for me a long time ago. I know I can do them better by going out the door and coming home happy. I guess I haven't done a great job lately of hiding that work sucks feeling."

"You can't hide that from your kids and Carol pushing your ass to change isn't about granite counter tops, it's about a happy you. C'mon dude, start doing something about it. Really explore starting a business or get with Carol and figure out how to make teaching or taking pictures happen. Or do whatever it takes to get your attitude right at the warehouse. No faking it either, you made smart kids with good bullshit detectors."

Michael laughed. "No, Zach and Meg would smell out me faking it real fast. My spirit must be true."

"So, you gonna tell them about your skookum encounter?"

"Of course, I'll tell the family. My mom will really get a kick out of this. After that I don't know, I may keep it quiet. There are some friends I could tell, but not everybody."

"Who wouldn't you tell?"

"Oh, we have some friends from church, our small group. We love 'em, they're sharp, great people, but several of them take Genesis literally, six days to make the world, the universe, everything we're looking at, all of it 6,000 years old. We've already agreed to disagree about it, but it gets uncomfortable sometimes. I don't know if they're ready for this, assuming Bigfoot is really proof of an evolutionary process. My Genesis friends tell me humans and dinosaurs coexisted and humans helped hunt them to extinction. I tried once to suggest if Jesus speaks in parables why not accept Genesis as allegorical? It's actually in an old Hebrew poem form I think expresses our separation from God by attachment to the world really, really well. Anyway, they really didn't want to hear it so I just stay quiet now on that one."

Eric laughed. "Humans taking out dinosaurs before hunting rifles, I appreciate your conflict."

"I think I'll keep the skookum story in the families; mine and yours."

"Who knows, still, the fossil record," Eric mused.

An echoing rifle shot from somewhere in the woods caused both to flinch. "Somebody's T-Rex got out of its pen," Michael said.

"That wasn't too far," Eric said looking back. "A mile or two, a little late in the day for deer hunting, it's going to be dark soon. Hmm, you ready to head back? We didn't bring a camera for your skookum tracks. We'll come back with Kelly, Dewey and CP tomorrow."

"CP will want plaster casts. Ok, Ducks, baby," Michael said

grinning. "To the Buckhorn for Oregon Duck football, yeah I'm ready. Partying out here tomorrow sounds fun. Maybe we'll see colors. We'll try the listening trick."

They rose and walked silently alongside the Sasquatch tracks toward the van and Eric asked, "Can't you tell your church friends about meeting a skookum? I mean, it's a great story. Is finding out God's world is more complex than it is simple, would it really mess with their beliefs that much?"

"I need to pray on that. Who the heck am I to cause someone to question their faith?"

"I guess that's my point. What if they find out Bigfoot is real or that spaceship they sent to Mars discovers life used to exist there? I don't see how something like that invalidates what Jesus did, what the Gospels say. God working through evolution, I'm ok with that. Jesus a step in the process. A big step." Eric set the rifle down across the back and chuckling said, "Taking down a T-Rex before modern firearms sounds like a real stretch, Michael. Man, I don't know about that one."

# Chapter 28

## JASON'S RIDE

**THE SHARP CRACK** of a rifle shot stopped Jason in his tracks. The shot was close, near his planned path to the highway, a trail he was sure was close, and he still had at least three miles to go. It was late in the day for hunters to still be out and Jason considered skookums might be the cause of the shooting. Parched, sore and exhausted, he could divert southeast to avoid the area, adding miles and time that would ensure darkness falling before reaching the highway. But deer hunters might be able to help him, and having a rifle near if Chief and Old Red found him was a good sounding proposition. Jason desperately wanted to be out of the forest before dark, but the thought of holding a rifle pulled hard. He headed in the direction of the rifle shot.

Jason drew near to where he thought the shot had come from, moving from tree to tree. Raining harder, the wind kicked up and in the roaring whoosh of the storm in the trees, something metallic caught his ear. Creeping forward, Jason's heart leaped when he saw it was rain drops hitting an All-Terrain Vehicle. About to spring to the ATV he stopped at hearing a faint voice, a whispered groan, "no... no... no..." over and over coming from behind a berry bramble across the trail. Crouched behind a fallen log he saw two ATVs, one turned upside down, the other sitting with keys in the ignition. He circled the log staying low, crept around a tree, stepped on something wrong and looked down into the dead, wide open eyes of a man with his head ripped backwards. Jason's boot was on the man's back. Next to the man lay a rifle, the barrel twisted crazily.

Another noise from behind the bramble, steps, the skookums were coming back. A quick glance to his left, without another thought Jason dashed, jumped on the upright ATV and turned the key, it started with a roar. Pulling the wheels hard around he opened up the throttle and hit the trail, mud flying. He reached 40 mph on a straight stretch before the trail curled away and then rounded back. When it circled Jason searched the woods and saw them, four gigantic shadows moving through the fading, misty light, passing in and out of sight in the trees.

Checking a mirror he saw one come onto the trail, a Bigfoot running at a steady gallop behind him. It was Chief, fast for his size, leaning the upper body stiffly forward yet moving athletically, the long, hair covered forearms pumping low with the hands and fingers relaxed, pumping along with its massive legs. Jason looked forward while his mind raced, trying to confirm which trail he was on. *It should bend a few times and pick up Union Creek.* A rock came flying past his head, Jason ducked and a broken tree branch just missed him. They did not seem to be tiring. In the mirror Chief was not gaining, but maintained his distance of 40 yards or so. Jason made a sharp right turn staying with the trail and swerved as swiping claws burst through the brush, just missing his head. He straightened the bouncing ATV and gave it gas. Another bend to the right brought the trail alongside river rapids. *Flat Creek! Outrun them and figure out how to cross*, he told himself.

Then he remembered the ramp. He and Kelly were annoyed by motorcycle noise when they hunted here last year and they'd come across kids jumping the creek off a ramp they'd built. Jason had agreed with Kelly it was crazy, for they had chosen the widest and deepest run of rapids on this section of Flat Creek to catch air over. "Maybe that's why they put it here, too safe anywhere else," Kelly said, and they'd laughed at the reckless abandon of kids these days.

Jason briefly calculated his chances. He'd get to 40, maybe 45 miles per hour before taking the ramp, but the ATV weighed considerably more than any dirt bike. Two of the monsters were chasing him on the trail now, Jason had flying thoughts, *Old Red and Chief, you bastards don't quit,* as the two big males kept their pace, *just go away,* Jason begged, then remembered, *I killed their baby.* The brush cleared and Jason saw the opening to the strip of beach. He turned sharply at the Y in the trail, pulled the throttle back as hard as he could and went straight at the ramp. He hit it hard and was airborne, flying over the rushing creek, the cold wind and rain pushing against him. Jason glanced down and realized the water would be freezing. The ATV splashed in, the front left wheel bounced hard on a rock and he tumbled over the handle bars. The snow melt water jolted him, Jason screamed, "aaahhrrrgh," as he surfaced. He floated down stream, gasping to breathe and smashed into another rock. The impact turned him perpendicular to the bank and he kicked his legs and threw his arms forward furiously, knowing the intense cold would soon kill him. He felt one hand hit a rock and then his boots hit bottom and with one last push Jason could crawl dragging himself over the rocks and sand. Turning painfully onto his side Jason saw Old Red and Chief standing together at the ramp, watching. The Bigfoot howled a banshee scream at him, pounding their chests with their hands. But they did not step into the rapids. Another pair of Sasquatch, the mother and son, joined them. Chief and Old Red stopped screaming and the four creatures simply stared.

"I'm sorry," Jason said to them, but the skookums maintained their glare until Chief first, then Old Red and the young one flared their nostrils, showed their teeth and growled in snarling reply. The female Bigfoot stood by mutely. Jason forced himself to his knees, met her eyes and said, "I'm so sorry," again to her.

Knowing he had to move, Jason pushed a deep breath and a searing pain emerged through the numbing cold where he'd hit against the river rock. Touching his ribs on his left side, *really bruised, might be cracked,* he thought. Jason looked back and the skookums were gone. Rising to his feet, every breath daggers in and out he fought to control his shivering to slow his breaths. The wind and rain were in his face as he stepped forward, walking painfully where motorbikes had worn a turnaround and a narrow path heading south. Leaning into the bluster, working to warm his body by jogging when open space allowed, Jason moved through the darkening woods again.

After a distance the riding trail ended and Jason struggled to find a deer trail in the thick creek side undergrowth. Following Flat Creek would take him to the Rogue and he could cross the Rogue at the Natural Bridge footbridge, maybe find someone to help him. From there the highway and flagging a car were nice things to think about. Grandma Ellen's house and the Buckhorn would be close also, imagined glimpses of home or Aunt Kelly at the Buckhorn helped him move forward. The pain in his ribs subsided from sharp to merely throbbing as Jason picked up his pace thinking, *Home, please just want to go home, home God let me see home...*

# Chapter 29

## SINGING

**WALKING MIGHT BE** easier than riding across the soggy pine needle floor, Nicole considered when her back tire popped, settling the matter. She pulled her bike under a huge conifer and sat comfortably between two roots, her back resting against the trunk. Setting the backpack in front of her, the thick branches were a canopy, the headlamp shining the rain drops falling all around her. Nicole shut off the headlamp and was startled at how instantly the forest became pitch black. Soon though she took comfort in the solitude of the darkness, the fear her lamp a beacon to the Bigfoot now gone. Nicole drank the last of her water and munched a breakfast bar. Closing her eyes she tried gauging the time and decided it might be eight p.m. Her mom would not be home from her sister's basketball tournament until late and Ian's parents would simply assume he was camping another night or had gone to her house. Nicole was sure she would not be missed for several hours.

While feeling in the pack for more food, Nicole found her compass. Squeezing it hard in her hand Nicole thought, *Ian's last gift to me,* while starting to cry softly. She raised her eyes to the tree's glistening lower branches. *Silver pine,* Nicole thought while breathing in the surrounding evergreen aroma. Finally she let her tears go and immediately caught and told herself to be quiet. Crying silent tears without sobs until her throat hurt, sharp pains radiating down to her chest, she cried for Ian, cried for being scared and alone in the dark with real monsters somewhere near. Nicole cried for wanting her mom.

Somewhere in the crescendo of the storm's howling she discerned another sound. Turning her head to find it, a murmuring whisper quiet and distant seemed to ride the wind swirling about her. Was it a song? She stopped crying to listen. *Quiet!* Nicole shushed at herself. *Quiet!* She scolded herself again, closed her eyes and took a deep breath. When she exhaled, Nicole heard two voices singing to her. "Oba-chan? Nanny?" she asked out loud. *Both of my grandmothers singing to me?!* One soprano, deeply Irish, flowing majestically and intertwined with another voice female, celestially beautiful and Japanese, their ethereal trill enveloped her and in that moment Nicole remembered her dream. *I was Snow White, but then I was floating like a spirit above the trees and laughing with the moon ...* Nicole took another deep breath as the singing grew louder and this time when she exhaled, recalled her night's dream vividly, and with it, the simple and beautiful realization that she had nothing in this world to fear. *I wasn't floating like a spirit, I was my spirit floating, I met my spirit! My spirit is loved!*

Opening her eyes, Nicole was pleasantly astonished to see wisps of white fog drifting toward her under the branches. Tiny, silvery sparkles danced in the gathering mist, floating with the siren's song, entrancing her. As the fog enveloped, Nicole felt her grandmother and great grandmother with her in strong spirit, utterly sure it was their voices somehow together, somehow singing to her, somehow bringing comfort in the dark Oregon woods. Sparkling, singing mist surrounded her beneath the tree, *everything will be ok,* she knew in her heart.

After a time, sad when the fog and heavenly duet vanished slowly, dissipating together, Nicole whispered, “Bye, Nanny, bye Oba-Chan, I love you.” As the last of the mist faded she looked up and realized the rain was now falling freely into her face, she was not protected by the tree. She turned, the tree was gone. Standing up and switching on her headlamp Nicole screamed, “Oh! Oh, thank you! Thank you, grandmothers, thank you Lord!” She stood in the middle of a two lane dirt trail, magically transported, it seemed. “They moved me, this is the trail, I’m here, I’m here! My car is that way!” Nicole took off running.

# Chapter 30

## THE BUCKHORN

**AMONG THE THINGS** that Michael and Eric appreciated from the beginning of their friendship, especially when taking road trips together, was their ability to drive for miles without the need for talking. They likely realized this reminded them of their own fathers. Eric almost took up conversation as Michael drove the minivan on the logging road from the bluff, as he sensed Michael's discomfort with the closing darkness, but he leaned back quietly instead.

"Kind of odd, somebody shooting this late, wasn't it?" Michael eventually asked.

"Yeah," Eric answered, "most anyone from around here would have enough sense to be home or back at camp that close to night. Might have been out of towners with late season permits, they aren't too sharp sometimes."

"Oh hell, there were two guys like that at the Buckhorn yesterday. SoCal boys, Dewey gave them bullshit directions to a campground. They were idiots, it was funny at the time."

"Always, until somebody gets hurt," Eric said, chuckling and shaking his head.

The rain fell harder when they reached Highway 62. "Yeah,

baby," Michael said with unashamed relief at being off the narrow logging road. "This morning, when I was right here leaving, this big branch or something crashed on top of the van, gave me a damn heart attack."

Eric laughed. "Must've been your skookum saying, get your ass back to California. I say on to the Buckhorn and a serious Beaver ass whoopin!" They drove west, passing the mail box at Kelly's aunt's place. The trees soon parted and the Buckhorn Tavern & Grill, sporting a very full parking lot appeared.

Michael and Eric walked into the Buckhorn and twenty eight people booed. Eric struck muscle poses and pointed to the University of Oregon 'O' on his sweat shirt. Michael removed his green 'O' baseball cap and doffed it to the crowd. CP alone stood and applauded. After laughter and friendlier greetings to Eric and Michael, all eyes shifted from the door to the bar, or more precisely up the ladder behind the bar where Kelly was working with wires and cables to hook up a new big screen television, set a few feet down from the great elk head. Dewey sat next to CP, anxiously checking Kelly's progress and offered, "No pressure or anything Kelly, but kick-off happens in like, 37 seconds."

"Hey, Dewey, if my hands weren't occupied," Kelly returned, "at least one would be single digit saluting your fat ass." At that moment the big screen snapped into a moving picture and the crowd cheered heartily. Kelly leaned back with a remote control in hand, worked with it and Autzen Stadium, the football home of the Oregon Ducks burst into view. The crowds at both Autzen and the Buckhorn were going wild.

"Thanks, Kelly, you saved me again," said Jake, steadying the ladder.

Dewey yelled, "The amazing Kelly! Hottest, smartest, greatest all-around bar wench in all of Oregon!" The Buckhorn patrons whooped in agreement. Kelly smiled and provided parade queen waves as she descended the ladder.

Michael and Eric sat down with CP and Dewey. "Well said, Dewey," Eric added, then looked to Michael and said, "Kelly ranks number one bar mistress of all-time, her greatness surpassing even Brittany the Psych major at Taylors in Eugene and Jennifer at Flanagan's in Medford."

"Ah, Jennifer," recalled Michael fondly, "an oasis of intelligence and beauty in a butt-nugget of a Medford bar. And yes my brother, couldn't we both use some of Brittany's in depth analysis right about now? There was Tillamook Terri, and the hippie girl at The Place that took care of us on Robert Cray nights. Yet, Kelly does surpass them all." All gents at the table drank deeply together. Another cheer rose at the big screen sight of the Ducks kicking off to the Beavers. Kelly came to their table and Eric stood to give her a hug. Michael recalled the prom picture in Eric's old bedroom and wondered about their time together this afternoon.

CP had a question for her. "Has Jake been skimming your tips to buy a new TV? I can't believe he sprung for it."

"Nice, isn't it? I went to Medford after the Walden game to get it. It was painful for him but check it out, great picture." Michael noticed the quick smile she passed to Eric.

"Pitcher of Mirror Pond, boys? How was the bluff?"

"Raining but great," Eric answered. "You were right Kell, we all need to go out there tomorrow."

"10-4 that," CP agreed. "We'll party like olden days."

"Hey, CP, when we get to the bluff tomorrow there's gonna be a surprise for you," Eric said with a smile looking at Michael.

# Chapter 31

## A PLAN

**THE WOODS WERE** black, rain clouds hiding moonlight that might help Jason find a trail. He used the creek, kept in hearing distance to his left as his guide, pushing his way through a willow cluster. The thicket was a gauntlet. His side throbbed still, thin branches rubbing as he passed bore excruciating pain and then one snapped back hitting hard, dropping him to a knee. Jason stayed down, waiting for the pulsating agony to subside enough that he could breathe. Despite the pain, for a moment it felt safer to be crouched down low, but closed eyes brought back the horrors of the day, Sam screaming, "Jason, don't leave me!" reverberated.

Jason raised himself up. The wind in the trees and the rushing creek melded into a continuous, flowing roar. Aware he would never hear the skookums coming when they attacked and hating the claustrophobic fear he stepped forward, hands before his face. Only by putting one boot in front of the other and working through the plan did he manage his mind. Forward movement was keeping him alive; the November night, soaked clothing and skookums be damned. Jason repeated it once more, *Get to the Natural Bridge and cross over the footbridge. Go up 62 if you don't see tourists, hike the back way to Grandma Ellen's house. Get Grandma, Kate and Cody, grab a rifle, jump in the car and go. Stop and get Aunt Kelly at the Buckhorn, call the state police, call the Larssen's* ... These words were Jason's mantra, the vision held fighting his way through the rain and underbrush.

Gauging he was far enough south, he worked away from the creek toward the Natural Bridge. The ivy, ferns and bushy terrain thinned and he started making better time. The trees became bigger with more space between them, he could stride without his face getting scratched, a change he was grateful for. Scanning the dark perimeter for a tell-tale space between brush indicating a deer trail or better yet a hiking path, he moved at a good pace now. The creek's noise subsided as he veered west. A momentary respite from the wind quieted the trees. Jason heard himself breathing and the oddly reassuring sound of his boots scrunching on the damp pine needles. Listening to his inhale, exhale while watching steam come rhythmically out of his body was settling and he stopped a moment to peer into the darkness ahead. *Good night vision tonight,* he thought as two Shasta red firs, pillars side by side attracted him, and between them a continuous open space in the trees and brush presented itself. Jason laughed walking through them before laughing harder when in four steps found himself standing on a bark hiking trail. Just before taking off he stopped, crouching, checking all around for movement, lifting his head and smelling for them. *They aren't here. I'll bet this goes to the Natural Bridge, they could be waiting there ... gotta go across there, then go to Gramma Ellen's, Buckhorn to get Aunt Kelly, call the Larssen's, the cops, watch for Chief and Old Red ...*

Jogging the trail, the plan quieted and Jason alertly

smelled the air with each breath in. Stopping to pick up a good sized rock, kneeling down remembering, *you whomped Chief a good one, Hank.* Jason rose, pushed himself forward and liked running with the hard, cold weapon filling his hand. He imagined his old baseball throwing motion, heard his high school coach, *feet set, turn the shoulders toward the target, see the target, step into the throw, follow through.* Seeing himself nailing Old Red right between the eyes, *I could do that, I'd get one chance,* and he watched for another ball sized rock for the other hand. Jason knew well the sound of a river, the resonant hum of rushing water over great rocks, yet in his state disbelief held sway until with more steps clearly, undeniably not a trick of the wind, the Rogue River finally called out to him. Moving forward cautiously at the edge of the trail next to the brush and trees until his boots hit something hard and flat, Jason looked down at wet, shiny black ground. Putting numb hands against man-made pavement, pressing until there was pain Jason lingered for a moment, down on one knee. *I really want to go home, Lord.* Standing, then stepping forward until he found the wire and wood protective fence, Jason went down to one knee again, grabbed and held on needing to believe the fence was real, that he'd reached the Natural Bridge tourist platform.

Downstream the sound and motion of the river's wild flow could be made out in the darkness. Dead ahead though, the river was strangely still and quiet. *Dry summer, it's gone down the hole,* he thought, meaning this was one of those years low river flow caused the riverbed itself to be exposed between the lava tubes in and out openings, creating the natural bridge. A light on a post at the other side of the walking bridge spotlighted swirling, illuminated rain in its circle, framing the footbridge.

Quietly Jason backed from the overlook, crouched behind a big conifer watching for movement at either end of the bridge. Moving low, forward to the next tree, Jason ducked down reflexively at the smell of something rank on the wind blowing toward him. Hiding behind the tree, waiting, peering into misty woods the shadow of something big moved near the bridge entrance on Jason's side. It stopped and Jason knew it was one of them, standing guard. The shadow vanished backing into the trees.

Looking down at the Rogue, he charted a path behind a row of big rocks where rapids would usually be, the boulders exposed, deciding he might make it across the riverbed. Calculating the western wind would protect his smell and the river and wind cover his noise, *Stay low, out of their sight, I bet they see real good in the dark,* Jason coached himself.

Backtracking tree to tree, around the overlook fence he surveyed another path between boulders, down a steep embankment to the riverbed. Reluctantly setting down the rock in his throwing hand Jason began the climb down. Able to stay behind huge rocks Jason reached the bottom, laid down flat and immediately started soldier crawling. The recent rains did provide a sheen of freezing water over the smooth, hard lava and river rock bottom, which hurt like hell to crawl across. Still, he was able to move steadily behind the river boulders keeping the bridge out of sight. Spurts of river water, miniature geysers escaped from small holes around him as Jason worked through a small rivulet, turning his head letting the icy water into his mouth. Again, he forced away memory of Grey Canyon, walking in with Sam the morning of this hellish day. "It looks like the Natural Bridge," he remembered saying. Stopping at the edge of a big rock cluster, he knew he'd be exposed for a few yards before reaching a man sized, watermelon shaped boulder. Hugging the ground pushing one painful forearm and knee at a time he reached the giant rock and lay prone, breathing hard.

Jason tried to stand but a wave of breath stealing cold went through him, he gasped twice without drawing breath. The hurt in his ribs reached into his aching lungs. On both knees, his head dropped, then lifted and air rushed in as though emerging from deep water. Shivers hit next though and Jason tried forcing the freezing shakes away. *Get up, move!* He closed his eyes, drew and pushed a breath, opened, a row of boulders revealed themselves behind the big watermelon. Jason saw where he needed to go next, forced himself to his feet and scurried up the river bank. Cresting the top without hesitating despite knowing they might be waiting for him, Jason rolled over the edge, came up on his knees, looked around and then rose. Staying low for several yards before running between trees, suddenly into the open, Jason stood in the empty Natural Bridge parking lot. Crouching low again, feet apart and hands raised defensively, pivoting slowly to scan the full circle around him, hearing and seeing nothing more than the trees, Jason started sprinting toward the highway until his aching legs and screaming ribs forced him to slow to a brisk jog. Nearing the highway, he heard a car coming. Jason ran harder but was too late, the SUV passed without seeing him. He looked left and right, seeing only the shrinking red tail lights.

Now Jason had another decision. Another car would eventually come, he could follow the highway west to the long driveway at his grandparent's house, but would he be drawing Chief and Old Red to his home, putting Grandma, Kate and Cody at risk? Another two miles past the driveway was the Buckhorn, back the other direction south and east was the Larssen's place. Or Jason could cross the highway and work his way through the familiar section of woods that backed up to his grandma's property, a considerable shortcut. The rain was bitterly cold, driven by the harsh wind and while the road seemed safer and another car might come along, in the dark and alone Jason knew the skookums would not care where he stood, they would come out and kill him. He jogged across to the south side of Highway 62 and walked back into the trees. Even in the dark, he would know the trails there once closer to home, so he chose the shorter path, through the woods. *Stay with the plan, Natural Bridge crossed, get to Grandma's now!*

# Chapter 32

## KAHRR

**STRETCHING HIS HAND** over her pregnant belly, he felt the pulsing warmth in his finger tips and smiled. He knew she carried a daughter because she had told him. As he pulled his hand away she reached and grasped the forearm, met his eyes and conveyed the time was near. He assured her they would return before sunrise, only going to the trees bearing sweet food. Their boy paced impatiently a few yards away.

A wind gust moved the surrounding fog and looking up the mother enjoyed glittering stars in the black night sky above the trees. The father turned, grunted at the adolescent son and they began walking away, gradually enshrouded by the returning mist. Not wanting to let go of them, the mother narrowed her eyes and their shadows became opaque, vibrating colors, purples and blues at the edges, orange and red inside. She watched until they dissipated, then settled back upon her pine bough and bark mattress. Gazing up at the stars until they also disappeared, she rocked gently side to side, knowing her baby liked this. Rarely did she consider the future, but now in her quiet serenity and inspired by the stars, allowed a vision of guiding her daughter in the ways of the forest, as her mother had taught her.

Opening her eyes awake, the mother Bigfoot emerged from her dreaming and immediately the exquisite joy from letting herself believe her baby girl was still inside her vanished, replaced by the cruelest pain. She closed her eyes for wanting to go back, but the sound of wind, trees and river shouted their harsh reality, confirming her return to the world her daughter had come into and then been taken so ruthlessly from. Sitting up, rubbing her eyes to see her son sleeping beside her, all the corrupting violence of the day struck her, and she looked into his still face with a sense of loss as deep as for her taken daughter.

The father Bigfoot turned away from the bridge to see their son asleep on the ground, mother sitting by him, her hand gently stroking the head. Her gaze remained distant as he told her they would wait for the old one to return from his search. The tree man would surely be going to the car road to find other humans and here, the human's bridge would be his likeliest path across the river.

She stared out into the night, and he realized hers was a look he had never seen upon her face before. His anger subsided, creating a void immediately filled with shared grief and pain. Kneeling by them putting his hand over hers, he told her they would go back home after the old one returned. Standing up to resume his watch the mother grasped his hand, breaking her stare to meet his eyes saying, thank you. She suggested they walk to the sweet food trees and eat before the trek back to home. He glanced away and she knew again the desire to kill remained, and how desperately her mate still wanted to find the tree man.

When the old one returned without seeing or smelling Jason, the father pointed north toward Grey Canyon, grunted

"Kahrr," then motioned for the mother to wake up the boy. "Kahrr," replied the old nomad Bigfoot, looking down at the mother and waking son. She stood to face him, her eyes and clenched jaw saying clearly, time now for you to move on, old one, time for you to leave my clan. Her mate walked over to stand by her, but as the young one rose the wind shifted suddenly swirling, and Jason's smell reached them all at once. The two adult males looked at each other, eyes widening, mouths apart, grinning. They began to beat their chests and the son joined in, grunts and growls building ferocity, for tree man was somewhere near, the direction unknown but near. The males ignored the mother sitting back down crying, her hands over her face.

The Bigfoot clan of Grey Canyon and the wandering old one perfectly understood the tree men invaded their home to kill their baby girl by cutting down the tree she nested in. They understood it happened because they attacked the human's tree machines, and their actions had cost them dearly. The baby's death weighed painfully hard on each of them. Still, the humans killing their living baby for throwing rocks at machines offended an innate sense of decency and respect for life in the Bigfoot, stirring anger and hatred never felt in any of them before.

The males shared desire for violent revenge resurrected after smelling the tree man again. They would move out first to see if the tree man were approaching to cross the river, sure they'd find his trail and track him down. If necessary the sweet food trees would be a good next stop to both search and eat before invading the nearby human's houses, killing as they went. They would then go to the building many humans gathered to eat and drink, perhaps finding the tree man and killing every human there. Whether the son or mother followed them was not the father and old one's concern. The two males would hunt together until their prey was caught and killed.

The mother cried, exhausted and sure the hollow ache of mourning would be a forever, endless pain. Desperately she needed to go and take her baby girl to the special place by the waters, laying her to rest where loving spirits would guide her back to the Source. But watching her son walking away with the males, she stood again and followed, hoping to hold him back as best she could.

Only she had discerned the tree man crawling over the river bottom, catching a glimpse of his life colors between the rocks, seeing also see the colors ebbed, a thin light blue surrounding pale orange and yellow. He would likely die soon anyway from cold.

Destroying the tree men's great machines the night before had been the most exhilarating thing any of the Bigfoot had ever done, until the killing of humans. Both fascinated and awe-struck by what we share, and by our differences, Sasquatch secretly observe the homes, cars, hunting rifles, the miraculous human things while keeping their safe and solitary distance. But ripping Sam to pieces and seeing his fear no different from a trapped, doomed deer's inflamed a blood lust they had never tasted when killing for food. Fighting with Hank aroused them further. Old Red and Chief found each of their kills interesting and different. Now, after smelling him again, they would not be satiated until they found the tree man and slowly tore him apart.

Meeting her eyes briefly, Chief turned his back and strode away, but then stopped. He turned and locked eyes with their son, who followed. With a glare and snarl he directed the young one to remain back with his mother. Not wanting his father's anger to turn on him, the young one nodded he understood.

# Chapter 33

## CIVIL WAR

**IN THE PACIFIC** Northwest they call it the Civil War, an apt colloquialism even for those understanding quite well it represents a mere football game. Still, in the hearts and minds of many Oregonians, the Union and Confederate analogy resonates. Only 40 miles separate the two campuses, yet perceptually they reside in different universes. Oregon State University, located in Mayberryesque Corvallis and viewed as a relatively wholesome aggie and science school, remained the favorite in the smaller towns around the state.

The University of Oregon in Eugene, home to pot smoking tree hugger hippie elitists was not the place to send your children if you did not want their college experience to be corrupting. In the recesses of many old-timers, the U of O could never be forgiven for students and agitators burning down the ROTC building during the Vietnam protests. 'Berkeley North' is a nick-name not generally considered complimentary outside of Eugene and Portland. Mazama Creek was typical, where only the oddly disenfranchised such as CP associated themselves with the Oregon Ducks. The two rival's proximity and contrasting cultural styles make for a football rivalry that generally causes allegiance to one or another, at least in Oregon, and as big football games do require nicknames, Civil War became a nice historical way to express their Ducks and Beavers feelings for each other.

At the start of the game, the boisterous Beaver fans at the Buckhorn reveled in reminding Eric, Michael and CP the outcome of last season's game, an Oregon State pounding of the Ducks. Dewey had gleefully rubbed it in, "Was that 50-21 last year, or was it 150-21? Must've felt 150 to nothin' to you poor Duckies, Nike money couldn't cover your asses," he taunted. But this year's game would be different, Dewey and his Beaver friends in orange and black feeling subdued, drinking quietly by half-time with the Ducks ahead 28-7.

"At least it isn't zero-zero," offered CP. Eric and Michael looked at each other. They were students in 1983 and could thus reliably claim they had actually witnessed the infamous 'Toilet Bowl' of that year, when the Ducks and Beavers bumbled and fumbled their way in torrential, sideways rain to a 0-0 tie. The futility of both teams that day has taken legendary status, especially among old-time fans of two college football programs who then knew well the pain of persistent losing.

Eric leaned back and smiled. "Dewey, CP, let me tell you a little story about the Toilet Bowl," he said. "It's half-time and Michael and I are sitting there in Autzen and the rain won't stop for anything, only the Quervo or Jack in the boda bag keeping us alive. We know it was one or the other as the tradition was to switch his favorite, Quervo, to mine, JD, and back each home game. Anyway, Michael here, from out of nowhere, with no apparent prompting, suddenly announces and loudly, for him, to anyone with ears to hear, "the game will finish zero to zero."

Eric paused, ensuring all were attentive, Michael enjoying

that years of arguing cases to juries had honed his friend's natural gift for storytelling. Eric continued. "People turn to look at Michael like he's crazy, and a little pissed because they can't believe they're going to suffer these miserable conditions for zero to zero. And to suggest we wouldn't beat the Beavos, well come on, sacrilegious." The table laughed, Eric looked at Michael with a grin, finished his beer, poured another from the pitcher. "So, as the second half progressively gets worse, still raining, passes dropped, missed field goals, a Duck running back had the ball just fly out of his hands to the Beavers and twice, twice, the Ducks actually scored touchdowns and gave 'em back on penalties. But, instead of getting pissed and booing like most everyone else, we just laugh harder as it went on. Michael's prediction was an omen calling on something predetermined, ordained by the football gods and he and I are the only two people laughing about it, the only two in the whole stadium getting the joke. People nearby are getting irritated, shooting us dirty looks but we don't care. Both teams sucked that year and the further it went, the more you could see it coming. Finally, as the clock ran out the Ducks missed another field goal, Michael and I both stood and raised our arms, which was pretty blasphemous. This was the Ducks-Beavers after all! Boys, I'm here to tell you, this man made one of the great football calls of all-time that sorry day." Michael doffed his cap to the fellas at the table as the second half of the 2005 Civil War kicked off.

"Hey look, it's foggy at the game," Dewey said as they all looked up at the big screen. Fog indeed had rolled into Autzen Stadium, somewhat obscuring the field and players from the TV cameras. "Maybe the fog will slow your asses down," Dewey added hopefully.

# Chapter 34

## SWEET FOOD TREES

**BILL LARSSEN STOPPED** watching the football game to listen, not liking the way his dogs were barking. "Is that Eric?" Marcie Larssen called to her husband.

"Sounds more like something they don't like, maybe its Mike's car," he answered. "I'll go see." Bill Larssen got up, put on a jacket and baseball cap, took a flashlight in one hand, a rifle in the other and stepped onto the porch. The dogs were at the edge of the apple orchard, running back and forth. Bill saw their back hair standing and their barking did trouble him. They barked, growled and whined simultaneously, moving as a group along the road but not passing the first row of fruit trees into the orchard. Eric's father went out to them, the rain hitting his face. "What's going on Bear?" he asked the leader, a mostly black Australian shepherd mix. Shining the flashlight out his heart jumped, a reddish brown Bigfoot stood under a tree pulling down an apple.

He had seen this one a few times over the years, Bill believing they might be about the same age. Turning the flashlight on himself he raised the arm holding the rifle, put the light back to the orchard and could see three more skookums gathering around the old red male. They were familiar, a family he thought must live close by, though he had never seen any of them this near to the house before. Bill noted the young male stood at least a foot taller than the last time he'd seen him a few months ago with the father, the huge black haired male now strolling next to the red-brown creature. He also saw the mother and realized immediately she was no longer pregnant. The males glared at Bill, then through gritted teeth growled back at the dogs. Two of the dogs broke and ran to the barn. Bill watched the big male skookums make brief eye contact with the female before they shifted back, eyes following up his arm to the rifle. The old red Bigfoot reached for another apple, took one and put it whole into its mouth turning away walking into the trees, the family following.

The Larssen's remaining dogs flanked Bill, the fur on their backs bristling, teeth showing, holding their ground when suddenly their ears pointed up and they stood rigid at the sound of the Bigfoot running, not walking. Shouldering the rifle until in a few crashing steps it became apparent they were running west away from the orchard, Bill waited rifle ready until the skookums could no longer be heard tromping out. Wondering why they weren't eating the late apples in their trees, Bill also felt most disturbed by the look in the eyes of the males, a malevolence he had never experienced in a lifetime of sharing his orchard with them.

After locking the dogs in the barn with the exception of Bear, Bill went back inside, bringing Bear with him. "Not sure what they're barking at, probably just raccoons, maybe a deer," he told his wife, then stopped. "Oh hell, I'm talking to Eric and Mike tomorrow. Sweetie, damn, I have to apologize for something."

Looking up over reading glasses with bemused expectancy she said, "Yes, dear?"

"Marcie, can I tell you the truth about skookums?"

# Chapter 35

## HOME

**WHEN JASON WAS** eight years old, soon after his Grandpa Jeremiah's passing, Grandma Ellen began allowing him to play on his own in the forest behind their property. He explored and wandered, walking or riding his bike throughout the area. Usually alone he built forts, climbed trees and practiced Aunt Kelly's lessons on tracking, like staying upwind to observe animals without detection. Aunt Kelly also taught him the basics of archery and he would play Indian for hours. The boy would come to think of these woods as his own.

The rain stopped, shuffling his boots through pockets of floating mist Jason found a familiar deer trail he had helped to wear down. He reviewed the plan yet again. *Get Grandma, Kate and Cody, get a rifle and go. Warn Aunt Kelly at the Buckhorn, get to town, call the State Troopers, call the Larrsens.* He forced the repetitious meditation that kept unbearable cold, pain and painful thoughts away. At first passing the familiar places brought comfort, trees he'd climbed or built a fort in, then the fallen log he'd hidden behind to watch a bobcat, but those thoughts led to more memories and eventually one would trigger back this horrible day, to Hank and Sam. He moved quietly through his old familiar woods, repeating the plan.

The rain started again as Jason reached the tree line next to the fence and the four acres of open pasture he would cross to get to his Grandparents house. He tried to hear, but the windy trees still masked anything that might be coming for him. Stepping into the open, Jason went to the gate he had passed through a thousand times and opened it, then latched it behind him as grandma had told him as a boy, never forget to do. He looked to the house across the open field, dark but for the flickering light of the TV in the living room. *Someone's awake, probably Kate, oh thank you, God!* Home, Jason could see home and yet he stood not moving, and not understanding why. Raising his right forearm to his eyes to see what he denied, his arm hairs stiff and straight, he reached back touching every hair on his neck standing on end. *No, God, please no, not here!* He ran against the stinging rain over the wet grass to reach the house, staggered up the porch, turned the handle and opened the front door, falling in.

Kate jumped in her chair. "Jason! Jason, what's wrong? Jason, what happened to you?!"

"Kate, get Cody, get Grandma!" Jason said pushing himself to his feet. "We gotta go now, right now! Don't ask, just get them! I'm getting a rifle, get Cody now Kate, get Grandma! Now! The car keys, Kate, c'mon just do it!"

"Jason what-"

"Now Kate, we have to go now!" Kate got out of the chair and went to Grandma's room, Jason went to Grandpa Jeremiah's antique gun case. "Where's the key?! Where's the key to the gun case?!" His grandmother was coming down the hall, putting on her robe.

"Jason, what on earth is going on?"

"No time, Grandma, where's the key to the gun case?!"

"Oh, I just moved them because of Cody. Where did I put them Kate? Maybe over the fridge, Jason, what happened to you?"

Kate joined them in the living room, then followed Jason into the kitchen. "Jason, you're scaring me."

"Skookums, dammit! Where's the key to the gun case?! Where's Cody?!"

Five year old Cody appeared behind his mother, his eyes wide. "Mommy, I see Chewy outside." Kate frowned, then gasped at the sound of the front door being jostled roughly. She stared at Jason when they heard the door knob turning. "Skookums?!" she asked.

"Car keys, Kate!" Jason yelled at his sister. He grabbed Cody, picked him up, opened the back door and ran out, his grandmother and Kate running behind. They turned the corner of the house and went into the car port. Their old Ford Taurus waited and Jason opened the back door and threw Cody in. Kate jumped into the driver's seat and started the engine while Grandma got into the back with Cody. Jason had one foot into the passenger side when Kate saw a huge hairy hand grab him by the shoulder and lift him off the ground, then through the windshield watched her brother fly backwards through the air. Chief leaned down and looked at her through the open car door, Kate shrieked throwing the Taurus into reverse, banging the swinging car door against the monster as she backed out wildly.

"Jason!" Grandma Ellen screamed but Kate saw the beast standing there, watching her. Cody pointed and cried, "Mommy!" and they saw three dark giants walking across the front yard toward them. Kate threw the car into drive and floored it.

Lying on the ground next to the firewood pile behind the house, Jason looked around. Next to the stacked wood was a table and underneath the table he saw their chainsaw, the little one used to trim kindling. He rolled and reached under the table, grabbed the saw and thumbed the on-switch. Still lying down Jason yanked the starter chord. It sputtered. He pulled back again, it hesitated, then kicked on with a two-cycle motor scream. Turning over Jason held the chainsaw out in front of him and faced two massive, growling shadows. Jason got to his knees and saw movement to his left. Two more of the monsters stood a few feet away, now stopped, watching him. Jason stood up waving the chainsaw back and forth. Light from his grandmother's house allowed him to see it was Old Red and Chief standing directly in front of him. Chief stepped forward and reached toward Jason as he swung the chainsaw, a thick chunk of hair flew into the air, Chief screamed and jumped back. Jabbing and waving the chainsaw at the beasts Jason yelled, "aarrrggghhhh, aaarrrggghhhh!" The three Sasquatch stepped back while the wounded Chief checked his forearm, then bore his eyes hatefully. Jason locked eyes with Chief, the chainsaw in his hands out in front. Chief growled but backed away and the other Sasquatch did the same until they moved back into the trees behind the house. When they disappeared, Jason gripped the running chainsaw, sprinted around the house to the driveway not stopping until reaching the highway. Breathing hard, Jason caught a few breaths before running west down the middle of Highway 62.

# Chapter 36

## GAME OVER

**THE DUCKS SCORED** another touchdown, the running back actually disappearing from TV view in the Eugene fog and the game was now utterly decided. CP jumped from his chair and did a little jig while those clad in black and orange did their best to ignore him. Michael noticed though, it only took a minute or two before the just recently believing they could get back in the game but now broken-hearted Beaver fans were back to their beers and enjoying themselves. The Oregon Ducks were finishing off the Oregon State Beavers and the Mazama Creek locals seemed to shake off the defeat more easily than he expected, given their early bluster. After several beers and still tired from the prior night, Michael sat in the back by a pool table quietly watching the Buckhorn patrons. Considering whether hard times had resigned them too easily to a loser's fate, or whether hard times help one keep an even perspective about things like football, Michael, unlike the still dancing CP, had no desire to kick them while they were down. Soon however, the first set of Beaver fans to mention it had been a long day killed their beers and with a, "great to see you Eric, the Ducks suck," and a friendly wave toward Michael, ambled out the Buckhorn door. Wet, cold air rushed in.

"Drive safe and close the damn door," Kelly yelled after them. Before long the Buckhorn was empty save Michael, Eric, CP and Dewey playing pool while Jake and Kelly cleaned up.

Michael rose and took the pool cue resting against a chair and absently watched smeared tail lights through the rain speckled front window pull out one by one, each turning left toward town. They were nearly all big 4 x 4 trucks and jeeps. He smiled, the abuse he'd taken earlier about the wife's minivan earlier seemed funnier now. Michael had a moment of really missing Carol, feeling the inner warmth of sudden gratitude. It would be fun telling her about his weekend. He checked his cell phone; still no signal. The pool game was winding down. Eric had gotten hot and after Dewey missed, Michael was left with a tough shot to win. He shifted to the side of the eight ball until he was on a direct line to the corner pocket. The white circle and the top half of the black '8' smiled from the black underside and Michael moved behind the cue ball. He kissed the lower half of the '8' with a soft touch and the eight ball dropped gently into the corner pocket. "Atta boy, yeah, baby," exulted Eric, cue raised in triumph. Michael smiled and set his cue next to a chair.

Dewey slumped against the table. "That's it fellas, I'm done. Been fun, Eric, good to see you and take care, Mike. You stayin, Shithead?"

"Nope, I'm outta here with ya," CP answered. "Great seeing you, Mike. Hey, Eric, we're all going to the bluff tomorrow, right?"

"Yes, yes definitely," Eric answered. "The bluff tomorrow, Kell?"

"You got it, we'll party like olden days, I'll make margaritas!" she called back from the kitchen.

"I'll roll-up a little green present or two," CP added.

"And don't forget, Ducks suck," finished Dewey, as the men shook hands.

Kelly walked in from the back door. "You guys see Jake? He took the trash out, now I can't find him."

"Sure he isn't taking a whiz?" CP asked.

"He doesn't answer out back. I don't know, is his truck still in the lot?"

"I'll check the bathroom, Kell and we'll check his truck," Dewey offered. "You gotta whiz, CP?"

"Of course."

"Then let's go, jackass."

"10-4 that, shithead. I mean, loser shithead."

"Close the door behind your asses and don't forget Jake's truck," Kelly instructed as they walked out the door to go around to the restroom. As the door closed, Kelly sighed to see the headlights of a small car pull into the parking lot.

"Tell 'em you're closing," Eric said to her.

"It's not really that late, I'm just tired. We'll see what they want."

# Chapter 37

## FIGHT OR FLIGHT

**HEADLAMP FLICKERING AS** she jogged the trail, the battery finally dying, Nicole rounded a corner and stopped hand over her mouth staring down at Ian's bike, pretzel twisted at the frame, pieces scattered about. Sweeping with the dimming headlight praying not to see him similarly mangled, bravely she called out, "Ian! Ian!" Standing in the rain and wind waiting to hear him call back to her, the headlight went out. With a moaning sigh she ran down the path in the dark.

Nicole reached the trail's end at the campground running as hard as her aching legs could into the wide open parking lot and saw her car patiently sitting where she and Ian left it. For a moment she hesitated, needing to believe it was real before sprinting, sliding the back pack off her shoulder, unzipped a side pocket and found her keys. Unlocking the door breathing fast she dropped into the driver's side. As the engine started she turned the heat on, glancing over at the empty passenger seat. The pressure behind her eyes welled again and though the windshield fogged, she threw the car into gear and drove out of the campground to Highway 62, turning right to go home at last to Medford.

Driving without thinking until noticing her gradually clearing windshield, *your brights,* floated through and she reached and flipped the switch for the high beams. “No!” Nicole screamed at something big standing in the road at the edge of the head lights. She braked on the wet pavement and saw the figure was wearing clothes, but still something was not right. Her car stopped a few yards from a man holding a running chainsaw, standing on the center line of the highway. She was about to hit reverse when the man set the saw down on the road, still idling.

He turned to her and mouthed, “Help me.” Clearly dazed he walked to the passenger side. Nicole opened the door and Jason collapsed into the seat. “Go, they want me,” he said in a hoarse whisper. Nicole looked at the young man, soaked and shivering, scratches and bruises on his face. “Go!” he begged her.

“They killed Ian,” she said quietly while giving it the gas. Jason looked at her and saw she was wet, dirty and also shaking from the cold.

“They killed Hank and Sam,” he whispered back, head down. “It’s my fault, I killed their baby.” Nicole looked over at Jason. “I didn’t mean to,” his voice trailed off. They were quiet save Jason’s labored breathing until the car’s heater kicked in. “Warm, please get warm,” he croaked, holding his fingers to the vents.

“The heater works good, it just takes its time,” Nicole said, her voice also shaking.

“Can’t feel my fingers,” Jason said. They both saw the lighted Buckhorn Tavern and Grill sign. “The Buckhorn, my aunt’s there.”

“I don’t want to stop, I want to go home,” Nicole answered.

“My Aunt Kelly, please I gotta warn her, please. You can

leave me there."

Nicole said, "No," yet turned her car into the opening in the trees. She parked near the Buckhorn's door and Jason grunted painfully trying to push himself out. "I'll help you inside," Nicole offered.

Dewey and CP walked into the men's room on the back side of the Buckhorn. "No Jake in here," Dewey said while lowering his zipper. CP pissed into the toilet, Dewey into the urinal. "I think I hear Jake," Dewey said. Someone stopped by the door, then walked on. "Jake, that you? Kelly's worried about ya," Dewey yelled, then turned toward CP. "Damn, dude, if you gotta dump, can you wait till I get out of here?"

Inside, Kelly cleared the last of the pitchers and glasses while Michael put away pool cues as Eric helped wipe down tables. The front door opened and Kelly saw Jason, leaning against a girl. They were both soaked, muddy and looked beaten, but it was the same wild, state of shock look in their eyes that sent a shudder through her. "Jason, what the hell happened to you?!" Kelly asked.

Breathing in grunts he sat in a chair, looked up at her, grabbed a half full glass of water off the tray Kelly held and gulped. "Skookums want to kill me. Aunt Kelly we have to go, now! Everybody, now!" She stared at Jason in disbelief, then out over his shoulder through the rain pelted window at CP and Dewey walking, leaning forward into the storming night, almost to Jake's truck.

Walking over Eric said, "Jason, you both look like you need a doctor. Did you say skookums? What's going on?"

"It's true," Nicole started to say when Kelly screamed, pitchers and glasses flying off the tray, shattering on the floor. Her eyes were huge; mouth open. Michael ran over as he and Eric followed her stare to the window, straining to see the massive, dark shapes moving fast across the parking lot, straight toward Dewey and CP. In a moment, they were on them. Through the howling wind a screeching "Heyiiaarrgghh!" came from Dewey as his body was yanked violently upward, his feet flying out, then slammed brutally into the gravel. Through the window, they could see Dewey being lifted up again by his feet. CP screamed a muffled, "Help!" and struggled against the black thing that held him.

Eric ran to the door and pushed it open to see out, Michael and Kelly followed. Only then could they clearly see the beasts staring back at them. Kelly screamed again, in the light of the Buckhorn's sign they were gigantic; covered with long, thick fur except around their eyes, eyes that glared over flared nostrils and mouths opened just enough to show sharp canines. In those faces, in the hostile eyes Michael saw the glint of intelligence and instinctively felt the hatred there was somehow reasoned, somehow the more terrifying.

Upside down off the ground, Dewey dangled limply. Old Red raised him higher with long muscled arms and with apparent deliberation did not break eye contact with the three in the doorway. Holding Dewey by the ankles, the Bigfoot started swinging him slowly back and forth. "No," Kelly gasped. Old Red smiled at them, then grunted whipping Dewey head first into the back of Jake's truck, the nauseating thump, sharp crack and spraying blood happening so fast, so unbelievably, the three stood mute trying to comprehend what they were seeing. Still looking at the humans, the creature smiling letting go, Dewey crumpled onto the ground. They watched Old Red grin hideously at Chief before the two giants strode together across the parking lot, dragging CP by the neck toward the trees.

Michael felt the strength drain from his legs as the Sasquatch disappeared with CP into the swirling branches.

He asked himself if he were dreaming one of those bad ones where his feet refuse to move and he would have to force himself awake. He looked around at the rain in the Buckhorn lights, his van across the parking lot and then at the grotesque, lifeless pile that was Dewey just a few yards in front of him. "It's real," Michael simply said. He put his hands on Eric and Kelly's shoulders and pulled them back inside the Buckhorn. Eric clutched his knees and bent down, Kelly breathed hard and fast, making quiet, "oh, oh, oh," sounds. Michael slammed the door closed as they backed in. No one spoke until Michael recognized Kelly was beginning to hyperventilate.

"Kelly, Kelly, breathe...breathe Kelly...you need to slow down Kelly. Kelly, slow down, you have to breathe Kelly. Look at me, Kelly slow down! You can do this, that's it, just breathe slower, slow now Kelly, take breaths, try taking a deep breath, think about making a nice deep breath. Good job Kelly, good job. Atta girl Kelly, that's better, slower now, just breathe Kelly, ok that's better Kell, c'mon baby, slower, slower, breathe now, one breath at a time Kelly, you can do it, I know you can breathe for me, just breathe easy now Kelly, that's all, just breathe Kelly, good job." Michael could feel coaching Kelly helping to restore some order in his own mind and he worked to calm himself while calming her. Eric had dropped to one knee, his eyes boring into a single spot on the old wooden floor, listening to Michael talk Kelly through her breathing. Then Eric rose and watched Michael put his arms around Kelly while saying, "You did it, good job." They all turned to Jason, unable to break his eyes away from the window, transfixed by the wrecked heap that was Dewey lying in the parking lot. Nicole had backed away, sitting in a corner behind the pool table.

"I did it. They want me," Jason said, his voice distant.

Michael looked at Jason, then to Eric and Kelly. Getting

Kelly's breathing controlled did slow his own mind and he then had the realization that he'd resisted panic. Michael exhaled and a series of thoughts rolled through his mind. The monsters were Bigfoot, his encounter at the bluff, talk with Mrs. Larrsen and CP's museum exhibit, walking the tracks at the bluff with Eric came to him in fleeting, moving pictures along with their accompanying feelings. He remembered the terror in his sleeping bag followed by the self-contempt he'd felt in the museum rolling through him as a single, emotional wave. Michael exhaled once more and closed his eyes, letting go, and the words came out of his mouth, "Fight or flight, they'll kill us, fight or flight, fight or flight, this is fight or flight... weapons, Kelly, weapons. What is there, does Jake have a gun?"

"Skookums," Eric blurted. "God, they're huge."

Michael spoke looking into Eric's dazed eyes. "They'll kill us too. Fight Eric, we gotta fight. Weapons, Kelly, what is there? Eric, Kelly, we have to fight. Eric! Eric, dammit, right now! Eric stop and think, c'mon think, I need you to think! Think right now or we'll die!" Michael could see Eric struggling and yelled, "Eric, think right now about your kids, right now. Brianna and Kylie, cheerleading, playing piano, see it, see them, Eric, see them right now! Think about your babies, think about your babies. Think about holding your babies Eric, remember, you have to! Kelly, who do you love, Kell, see who you love for us Kelly. Help me get Jason out of here, we have to, I'm going home to my babies, I will see my wife and children, I will hold them again. Please, please help me, we have to do this together."

Kelly spoke first. "Jake never keeps a gun. There's an old baseball bat behind the bar."

"The rifle," Eric said. "There's a rifle in Michael's van." A piercing scream snapped their heads to the window. It was CP from behind the trees.

"I'll get the rifle, where's the key?" Jason asked.

Michael pulled the van key from his pocket saying, "No, Jason, not by yourself."

"No, you can't go by yourself. We'll go together," Eric said nodding at Jason. Kelly had gone behind the bar, found Jake's wooden baseball bat and tossed it to Eric. He gripped the bat, looked it over and said to Michael, "It's a 35 incher, not a kid bat," Eric said, giving it a practice swing.

"That's good," Michael replied, "those are long-ass arms."

They turned and scanned the room. Michael walked over to check out the baseball bat when Kelly looked up, said, "yeah," climbed onto the bar, then stepped across to the counter. She stood up and Michael and Eric saw her face to face with the great elk buck mounted on the wall. Pulling away cobwebs, Kelly carefully lifted the turn of the prior century bow and quill from the antlers, clumps of dust dropping to the floor. She jumped down and ran to them. "I've got this!" She slung the quill over her shoulder, reached back and pulled out the three arrows. They examined them. The arrows were wood, each with three faded stripes. At the ends Kelly held were feathers that interestingly still held some color, black, yellow and white. Their eyes followed her hands to the black rock arrow heads. They were hand chiseled to penetrate deer hide and looked hard, razor sharp and lethal. Kelly felt them up and down checking the sinew twine that held the head to the shaft. "They feel pretty sturdy," she said. Next, she held out the bow and tugged on the bowstring. It flexed, snapped and held tight. Kelly smiled.

"Kelly bow hunts damn good," Eric stated with grim intensity to Michael and then to her, "You kick ass at this, Kelly."

She nodded and looked at Eric, "I do, you're right. Girls kick ass."

Michael set his keys down to hold one of the arrows. "Real sharp and hard," he said, nodding.

"They want me," they heard Jason say and he was out the door running toward the van.

Kelly screamed, "No, Jason!"

Immediately Jason felt the night was warmer now, the rain and wind somehow soothing, no longer his bitter cold, relentless enemy. Running across the parking lot Jason raised his head letting the elements come full force, laughing at their futility, for he was not cold anymore. Jason squeezed the keys imagining the rifle in his hands, *C'mon, Old Red and Chief!* Avenging Hank and Sam, saving Aunt Kelly, he only needed the rifle. In his left ear he heard CP behind the trees, begging them to stop.

Eric, Kelly and Michael chased him outside as the two dark giants emerged from the trees, loping toward him with their arms outstretched. Jason never reached the van. Old Red grabbed and turned him, Chief swung claws into Jason's chest and dug down. Eric swung the bat up over his shoulder but Kelly yelled, "Move!" and shoved him hard out of her way. She set her feet and turned her shoulder, Michael could see she had an arrow set on the bowstring held by two fingers. Kelly pulled back and let fly, Michael turned to see the beast holding Jason take one full stride with the arrow sticking out of its stomach. With a groan of surprise and pain Old Red dropped hard to his knees. The other Sasquatch with its claws in Jason stopped and looked down, then flung Jason into the air. He landed a few yards from Kelly's feet as she watched the two skookums while setting another arrow on the bowstring.

Chief reached and lightly touched the wooden arrow, the eagle feathers still quivering in the belly of the old one. A circle of blood formed, soaking hair around the point of entry.

Michael saw the wounded beast look up at the other, the animal rage and fury replaced with hurt and confusion. Chief however turned and faced the three, eyes shifting from Jason lying on the ground to the two men, finally over to Kelly, eyes narrowing and from behind red stained fangs uttered a growl low and deep, worse than menacing. The three humans stepped back reflexively, expecting it to charge.

Two more Sasquatch stepped out from the trees, one smaller than the other. In the Buckhorn light, Michael could see female breasts under the hair of the larger one, looked into her face not seeing rage but fear. Michael crouched and moved in front of Kelly, then grabbed and dragged Jason back behind her, watching carefully.

The female and the smaller Bigfoot stopped at the edge of the parking lot and the female made a sound, part hooting, part bark, her urgency conveyed. She watched as the one bent down and put its arms around the wounded Sasquatch. They rose together and walked slowly to the two. Chief stopped, holding up the old nomad for the mother to put her fingers out over the arrow. Michael saw her fearful expression change as her eyes shut, then almost appearing asleep while long hairy fingers drifted down the arrow to the point of entry. Opening her eyes a grim, baleful face turned toward the old one. Putting her arm around her son she turned and the four Bigfoot went together back into the trees.

Eric closed the Buckhorn door as they backed in, all breathing fast. "Great shot, Kell, damn good shot," Eric said. Michael pulled Jason to an open area by the pool tables, sitting him up while blood streamed from deep gashes across his chest. Michael noticed the girl hiding in the corner.

"What's your name, sweetie?"

"Nicole."

"Nicole, can you help me? I need you to do a tough job for us, ok? I need you to take this sweat shirt," and Michael took off his sweat shirt, folded and held it out. "I need you to hold this sweatshirt against Jason and you need to push hard and hold him up like this. We're gonna stop that bleeding, ok?" Michael held out his hand and Nicole took it, she stood meeting his eyes and he sensed she was up to the task. She sat down on the floor behind the pool table, back against the wall and Michael dragged Jason over, leaning him back against her so she could reach around to hold the sweatshirt against his bloody chest. Jason moaned softly.

"Harder Nicole, harder, good, that's it, good job, you can do that. The little car out there is yours, Nicole? You have the keys?" She nodded. "Good job, Nicole, you're going to be the driver here real soon and get us out of here, ok?"

"I'm ready, mister."

"Good. I'm Michael, that's Kelly and Eric, this is Jason. Michael turned to his two friends. "Eric, Kelly, we have to fight smart," he said.

"Oh my God, Jason," Kelly cried coming over to her nephew.

"We need guns, some kind of better weapons," Eric said.

"Pool!" Michael yelled it and ran to the wall. He pulled a pool cue from the rack and swung it like a baseball bat. Then he grabbed three more and held the cues together in both hands, swinging like a batter warming up. "Tape, Kelly, tell me there's some tape." She went back behind the bar and retrieved a roll of duct tape from a cabinet and tossed it to Eric. "Tape 'em!" Michael yelled at Eric, holding the wooden cues out toward him. Eric started wrapping the pool cues together at the narrow end and worked his way up with Michael forcing the heads to stay together. The result was real solid. Eric ripped the tape and squeezed the base. Michael lifted the four pool cues now constructed as one and brought the end around, then swung the giant sized bat in slow motion. "Good job, a pool club," Michael said approvingly. "We ready?" Michael, Eric and Kelly looked each other in the eye as the men swung their pool club and baseball bat weapons back and forth. Kelly pulled gently back on the bowstring, one arrow hanging between her right index and middle fingers. A howling scream from outside turned their heads toward the window. It was CP again, horrible, high pitched uncontrolled screaming that somehow became worse.

"Fight and flight, both!" Kelly said. "Mike's right. We just have to get to Nicole's car. We fight 'em to her car, we get in, we go. Can you carry Jason, Nicole?"

"I can make it," Jason groaned. "Just help me, I can walk."

"We can do it," Nicole said looking up at Kelly.

"The three of us out front, Nicole and Jason behind us," Kelly instructed. "Put the keys in one hand, Nicole, make sure you unlock all the doors."

CP's screaming suddenly stopped. Michael swung the pool club with short, sharp snapping motions. "Fight smart, together," he told them. "Don't waste body shots, knees, balls or head, break their toes. Just buy time. Hit the fingers when they reach. We go after them together. You go low, I'll go high, then Kelly takes 'em out. Can't waste arrows."

"Two arrows, three skookums," Kelly said.

"One down anyway," Eric added. "I'll try to stay out of your way this time."

"Sorry about that," Kelly answered, and leaned against her friend.

"No, helluva shot Kell, a girls kick ass shot," he said holding her.

"Kelly, is there a land line? Can you call the cops or somebody?" Michael asked while staring out the front window.

"Aunt Ellen's place is closest. She set the bow and arrow on the bar and picked up the phone. Eric joined Michael, holding their clubs, watching the trees through the window.

"Not home, Kate got them away," groaned Jason from the floor. Kelly set down the phone and stared at her nephew.

"Kate got away? Kate, Grandma Ellen, Cody, what, drove away from the house?"

Jason nodded. "They'll call the cops," Kelly said. "Let's get out of here."

"We could try my folks," Eric said, "but they'd come here, why bring them here? Skookums will come after us any time now. You're right, let's go. I gotta get home to see my girls."

Kelly spoke, "Jason, I love you and I'm getting you out of here. I'm ready, Mike, you ready, Eric?"

"You do kick ass," Eric said, then added simply, "You're my best friend, Kell, you know that," then breathed out saying, "Brianna and Kylie, I need my family, God bless it, I miss my babies," Eric said while swinging the bat.

Eric and Kelly turned toward Michael. "Alright, let's get the hell out of here. Nicole, get ready, I'll help you get up," Michael said reaching with his left hand, gripping the pool club in the right.

"Maybe the damn skookums left," Kelly hoped out loud, just as the awful smell reached them, just before the goliath stepped from the shadows, its monstrous reflection filling the window. It had come in quietly through the back door. Kelly gasped as the men turned and faced it. CP's blood glistened on Chief's face as he raised his massive arms, extending gigantic hands ending in red stained claws. Kelly grabbed the bow and arrow running from behind the bar, set her feet but had Michael's tall frame directly in her line of fire. She moved, planted her right foot stepping in beer spill, her foot sliding out from under her. Kelly fell forward protecting the bow and arrow in outstretched hands, her chin smacked the floor hard, a flash of white stars filled her eyes.

"Kelly, Kelly!" Eric yelled. She did not answer. The Bigfoot stopped with arms and hands still out in front, watching Michael and Eric, growling at them.

*Its arms are too long,* thought Michael.

"Chief, you want me, you piece of shit!" Jason yelled deliriously from the floor. Chief moved over, leaning down to see Jason behind the pool table, Nicole seeing the Sasquatch smile as if pleased to find Jason still alive. The beast's eyes then fell on Nicole, its smile and eyes grew wider, the growl louder and deeper. Nicole screamed and pressed the bloody sweatshirt harder against Jason, pulling her arms tighter around him.

Michael and Eric moved forward, pool club and baseball bat held chest high, waving their weapons. "Feet apart, stay low," Michael somehow, crazy calmly said to Eric. Despite the men's approach Chief's dark eyes shifted distractedly to the bar and looked up, drawn toward the television, the football players running around taking its attention. Hearing "unngh," they turned to see Jason throwing a billiard ball like a baseball outfielder. The ball bounced hard off of Chief's forehead, Michael and Eric immediately lunged swinging low and hard together. The crack of the monster's knees was loud, it's howl louder. They swung hard and fast again smashing the knees, the beast rocked back, then violently toward Eric, but the left knee buckled and it dropped to the floor. Eric back peddled away as Michael drove the pool club hard from over his head, Chief turned but the blow struck heavily against the left knee again. Michael hopped backwards as the Sasquatch roared and struggled to rise, checking the pool club as he bounced away, feeling in his hands it had survived the blow. They swung their weapons again, this time the pool club smashed first into Chief's right knee, screeching again in pain as Michael fell with the blow's force, tumbling away. Chief reached for Michael, Eric swung the bat and the barrel smashed into the jaw, the giant's head rocking back. Michael stood in time to see its eyes roll, but then shaking its head, the Sasquatch began painfully pushing slowly up, until another pool cue crashed down hard twice across hairy toes and it sat back, howling. The men turned to see Nicole standing between them, her eyes wide, pool cue gripped in her hands.

Attacking again, the three swung together but the beast was ready, the forearms thrusting out reflexively. The pool club crunched again into a knee but Michael heard the sharp crack of something hard breaking, looked to see pieces of Nicole's cue flying across the room. She stumbled, Eric reached to push her away from the monster. The black claws stretched to Eric's lower left leg, grabbed and tore through his jeans into the calf muscle, digging down to the leg bone. Eric yelled and Michael slammed the pool club at the monster's legs but it moved and took the blow. Chief turned to Michael with a barred teeth growl. He swung again but the beast reacted swiftly, standing up and jumped back, dragging Eric up off the ground helplessly. The pool club missed and as the skookum came down it caught the thick end with its free hand and yanked it from Michael, Chief grimacing for landing on his battered legs. Nicole backed away and saw Jason and Kelly lying on the floor.

With Eric writhing upside down, Chief roared and hurled the man across the room, flying over the bar crashing into the big screen television, a brief explosion of sparks falling with him to the floor. The Sasquatch watched the smoke still hanging where the big screen had been, then broke its gaze looking down at the pool club it now held. Chief turned it over curiously before his eyes turned hatefully to Michael.

The arrow struck suddenly and deep into the chest. Michael saw Kelly on one knee, a gash on her chin, holding the bow when the Buckhorn's front door exploded. Kelly fell to her right, away from flying glass and wood shrapnel. She scrambled to her feet still clutching the bow in her left hand, turned and in front of the bar the female and smaller Sasquatch were getting up on their feet. Kelly followed their eyes to Chief, sitting on the Buckhorn floor. The giant sat with the arrow in his chest, small spurts of blood spraying at heartbeat intervals, looking up at the two moaning a wounded animal's cry. The smaller beast started at Michael, only a few feet away. Kelly yanked the final arrow from the quill, fitted it to the string and pulled back. The female Bigfoot jumped, grabbing and extending her arm holding him back, barking at the young one. He stopped with an outstretched, black haired hand inches from Michael's throat. Kelly kept the arrow pointed directly at his face and met the eyes of the female skookum, read her fear and knew she was protecting her child. Holding the mother's eyes in a steady gaze Kelly said, "Mike, get Eric. Jason, right now, get up. You and Nicole, time to go."

As Nicole talked to him, Jason nodded his head and rolled slowly over, revealing a bloody puddle. When Nicole and Jason got to their knees, the young Sasquatch saw her and yipped, "Aarrook." Nicole kept her head down and raised up with Jason in her arms. Michael used a stool to climb over the bar. His friend lay unconscious, an ugly stream of blood running from his lower leg, another red trickle coming out of an ear. Working Eric over one shoulder, Michael hoisted him and looked to Kelly. "Go, Mike, I got it." He carried Eric to the open doorway and waited for Jason and Nicole, then used his free arm to help brace Jason and led them outside.

"C'mon, Kelly," he yelled. She kept the arrow straight at the young one's head, moving toward the doorway, not breaking eye contact with the mother. She backed out and glanced at the big male skookum sitting in a spreading pool of blood, one hand around the arrow shaft, its head down. Kelly ran out the Buckhorn door, arrow pointed at the trees. Michael also watched the trees with Eric over his shoulder and the other arm around Jason, hustling to Nicole's car.

"Go, Nicole, get your car open!" Kelly yelled.

She opened the doors and Michael dropped Eric and then Jason into the back before getting in and working his way between them. Kelly ran to the other side, finally lowering the arrow and bow climbing in. Nicole dropped into the driver's seat and as she reached to pull her door closed an unearthly, howling moan came from within the Buckhorn. Kelly, Nicole and Michael glanced to one another, each knowing implicitly the mother Bigfoot's wail would haunt them. "She's keening," Nicole whispered, pulling the door closed. Gravel flew onto Dewey's corpse as Nicole ripped out of the Buckhorn Tavern parking lot.

Michael pulled off a t-shirt and pressed it against Jason's bloody chest. "Jason, you gotta hold this while I put Eric's leg up and wrap it."

"Where's Aunt Kelly?" Jason whispered, his eyes closed.

"I'm right here, Jason."

"Where's the girl?"

"She's driving, Jason, she's ok." Kelly said.

"Oh, good."

Nicole hit her high beams, Michael looked up as she and Kelly both gasped, "No!" Two big Sasquatch were crossing the highway in front of them. At the roadside the skookums stopped and for a long moment, the humans and the two

Bigfoot watched each other pass by. In the next moment they were by them and Nicole pushed her little car faster. A few minutes later, just before they reached Mazama Creek, they saw flashing lights coming toward them. Kelly turned back to Michael, “State troopers!”

# Chapter 38

## FAMILY

**MICHAEL WOKE WITH** a start. His eyes focused, and he saw Veronica sitting there.

"Hello, Michael."

"Veronica. Veronica, how's Eric?"

"Still in surgery, the nurse just came and said he'll make it. It's bad though. He should be out soon, then they're airlifting him up to Portland."

"He's ok, they're sure?"

Her voice cracked. "He has a bad concussion and skull fracture. They're trying to save his leg." Michael looked around. He was on a couch in the hospital's surgery waiting room. Eric and Veronica's daughters, Brianna and Kylie were sitting next to her. They looked very tired and he could see they had been crying.

"Your dad fought to stay alive for you," Michael told them. "He was thinking of you, all of you. I'm glad you're here, Veronica." Eric's parents were also sitting in a corner leaning against each other, Bill and Marcie looking over at Michael. "Skookums, Mr. and Mrs. Larssen," Michael said.

Veronica asked him, "Have you talked to Carol? I got called

about 12:00 and a friend flew us down. They said you were attacked by some kind of wild animal. They won't tell me anything else."

"No, no, I haven't. Cops wouldn't let me call, they questioned me for hours. The State troopers were ok but then the FBI showed up. They kept telling me we were attacked by bears or people in costumes. I finally told this federal agent what to do with himself."

"When we got here the mom of the girl you came in with was really letting the cops have it about not letting her kid go home."

"Nicole, the cops wouldn't let her go?"

"I don't know what the deal was, but they had her somewhere and her mom was going ballistic."

"The kid was great, she fought with us."

"They brought a friend of Eric's in, a Paul Thomas, he was with you? He was barely alive but the nurse said he didn't make it. We heard there are more dead people up there."

"CP, my God, we left him, oh. Veronica, have you seen Kelly?"

"Her husband just showed up. I think they're outside."

Michael shook his head. "Kelly saved us. It seems like a dream, Veronica. I have to call Carol."

Walking outside through the front of the hospital into sprinkling rain, Michael gazed at the green hills on the eastern horizon with dawn just breaking. He saw Kelly standing with a man in a Forest Service uniform. They were embraced and Michael chose not to disturb them. He would thank Kelly later. Checking pockets for his cell phone, Michael frowned as another Oregon state trooper car, lights flashing, pulled to the curb. He was done being questioned.

The police car's back door opened and Michael saw the

faces of his children. The passenger door opened and his wife looked up at him. Carol, Megan and Zach rushed out, Michael opened his arms, and the Gardner family held each other for a long time.

# Chapter 39

## COLORS

**THE FBI CONFISCATED** their van, so the Gardner's drove home in a rental. Carol drove and Michael grew tired again. After he told them everything that had happened to their dad in Mazama Creek, Megan and Zach were quiet in the back. Michael looked absently out the window, grateful to be going home. They were on I-5 near Mt. Shasta and he watched the rugged, evergreen covered mountains pass by, the countless trees a rolling green ocean broken occasionally by a leafy yellow, orange or red breaker, ripples on a verdant sea. Carol slowed on an uphill behind a string of big, plodding trucks. "Sorry," she said, "I can't get over to get around them."

"No worries, babe, thank you for driving. You look really good for no sleep, by the way." Carol reached and set her right hand on his forearm as the rental chugged the upgrade behind the trucks, and he smiled at feeling soft warmth emanating from where she touched him.

Michael resumed gazing out the window and he noticed the rolling sea of trees had slowed as well. Clouds separated just enough for sunbeams to play emeralds upon undulating, breeze rippled evergreen branches. It struck Michael that he was seeing every single tree on the mountainside with remarkable clarity, all of them at once sharing their own unique shades of green. A peaceful calm filled him, wondering in that moment if anything could possibly be more beautiful.

"Dang. Hey, Meg, mom and dad," Zach announced from the back. "Check out the purple, black and grey thunder clouds all around Mount Shasta. Crazy awesome."

# Chapter 40

## DREAMS

**NICOLE'S MOM TAPPED** on the door, entered and sat at the edge of her daughter's bed.

"Good night, baby," she whispered in the dark.

"Hi mom, I'm still awake. So, what did the lawyer lady say?"

"Mrs. Marquez said they can make you wear that ankle thing and keep you restricted to the house until they go to the grand jury to try and charge you."

"I thought they already charged me."

"That jackass US Attorney and Agent Watts will take the government's evidence to a group of people who decide if there is enough evidence against you to have a trial."

"Oh."

"You didn't already know that from following The Clan's trial?"

"Mom, I told you, that was Ian's thing. I never went on the eco-terrorist web sites."

"No, but he did. And, on your computer and you were out there to vandalize in a US National Forest, and then people got killed."

"Mom, we"

"I know, Nicole, I understand, I do, I know why you and Ian were out there. I'm just afraid of the lies they keep putting together. Everything you say the Bigfoots did they want to blame you and Ian for to get to the people he thinks you're covering for. Those fed guys seem to really need to not believe in Bigfoot."

"That guy still thinks we killed all those people and threw boulders at the logger's stuff?"

"He thinks real environmental terrorists dressed as Bigfoot killed all those people and you and Ian know who they are. They think Ian escaped with them." May stroked her daughter's hair. "I like Mrs. Marquez, she's good, baby. She says we just have to wait for the forensics evidence to match what you and everybody says happened."

"It'll be ok, mom. All of us, Kelly, Jason, Mr. Gardner and Mr. Larssen, we all know what happened, we know what we saw, what we did."

"Let's don't talk about that. Are you sleepy?"

"Kind of, you know."

"Mr. Gardner's wife e-mailed some more information for trying to help with nightmares. I'll look at it tonight. Carol also said Jason will get out of the hospital soon, and Eric might go home before Christmas."

"That's good, mom. So weird we all keep having the same freaky dreams."

"I'm not surprised you're all having freaky dreams but how could you be having the same dream?"

"I don't know how I know, mom, I just know I'm having the same dream everybody else is having."

Her mother sighed, "The one where you all get dragged off into the trees like that poor CP fella?"

"All of us, one by one. We can hear each other screaming

like him."

May picked up the smooth, oval river rock sitting on Nicole's nightstand. "Maybe you should move the healing rock the Sasquatch put on your head. Is it ok if I stay here by you for a while?"

"Thanks, mom, I love you. The rock reminds me of Ian."

"I got two more interesting messages today."

"From who?"

"From your grandmother and great grandmother, they are both coming to see you for Christmas."

"Oba-chan and Nanny here at the same time?"

"All the way from Japan and Ireland."

"Wow, I'm so glad you told them how they helped me in the forest."

"Nicole, I didn't tell you everything. They both left messages on the phone checking on you the night you were lost. They both knew you were in trouble that night, Oba-chan called right after your Nanny."

"Why didn't you tell me before?"

"Oh, I guess it scared me. You know both of your grandmothers are very wise in old, really old, Japanese and Irish traditional ways. I've told you we come from an ancient line of women being religious leaders in both Japan and Ireland, and I've known since you were a little girl you had the same feel for the power of the natural world in your spirit, just like they do. You were always my camper kid and then some, Nicole, trust me, your mom's not that surprised you were out there with Ian saving trees and that your grans were there somehow. Anyway, both your grans say they want to help with the nightmares and they're coming."

"That's great, mom, I know they were with me out there, it wasn't a dream."

"Knowing you and knowing them, it almost doesn't sound crazy, Nicole. You get to sleep now and I'll pray to Jesus for your sweet dreams tonight."

"Thanks, mom, I love you."

Nicole expected to feel the horrible pit in the bottom of her guts to open black and yawning once more, the pure fear always the first realization she walked in the Sasquatch's dream again. She prayed this one would be different, *please just a dream, not the nightmare, please,* allowing herself to hope when this one did not start the same as the others, with everyone finding each other at the Buckhorn. *Something is different, something is not the same, I'm alone, where are my friends?*

In the nightmare she did share with the others, Nicole would come out of the trees and find her car across the Buckhorn Tavern parking lot, smashed to pieces. Kelly then appears, coming out of the tavern and stands next to her. She holds the bow. "No arrows," she says quietly. They wait together in the rain, watching the trees, holding hands, feeling each other's terror. Michael and Eric walk out of the Buckhorn to join them and then Jason runs out of the trees. They always talk first that they have no weapons, the car is destroyed and then they all turn to see Dewey dead, his head and body crushed, on the ground next to his old friend CP, moaning with gruesome red bites bleeding into a red stream of his and Dewey's blood. It is always at this moment Chief, that's Jason name for the scariest Bigfoot, steps out of the trees, always walking first to Kelly.

*I'm not having that dream,* Nicole realized with growing certainty as another new feeling nibbled at her. Her fear subsided, yet Nicole noticed her heartbeat quicken with each step. *Ian is somewhere near. Oh, I like this dream.* It was then the night forest she walked transformed into iridescence. Suddenly, each plant glowed subtle greens, orange and yellows, the huge conifer branches radiating their own deep blues and greens. *Their colors, their light is inside, coming out of the plants. It's always there, isn't it? I can see it now, oh, I like this dream...*

Behind azure willow trees she stopped in front of a rocky mound, reached out feeling the stones hum and Nicole saw she was looking at hands that were not hers. Hairy, black clawed fingers opened before her and rather than terrified, Nicole giggled at the thought she dreamt of herself being a Bigfoot. Moving her hands over the rocks, seeking one with a denser pull than the others without knowing why, Nicole felt heaviness in her palm and moved toward the source, picked up that rock and walked on. The vibrating density of the stone felt good in her hand.

She came before a blackberry bramble, parted it carefully and walked through, the thorns not penetrating the fur or her hands. Stepping out of the bramble she reached a black rock mound decorated with scattered stones and boulders, some piled on top of and against each other. Climbing up between boulders she reached a narrow, black rock slit in the ground, the opening to an underground lava tube. She lowered herself into darkness.

As her eyes adjusted, the walls of a tall but narrow tunnel showed the passage way as a blacker shade of black. She walked forward until reaching a wide opening and stepped into a great, round cavern. Apparently waiting for her, as Nicole sensed their impatience, were the creatures Jason called Old Red and Young One. They sat on layered pine branches and Nicole understood they in fact waited for her. *I'm a Bigfoot, wow I'm the mother Bigfoot,* she realized. Her eyes turned to another large pile of branches on the floor, Nicole seeing the beastly hand reaching again and she felt a very different, warm humming tap tapping at her fingertips. The furry hand pulled back a bough, and Nicole looked down at Ian's face, sleeping.

Suddenly awake, Nicole sat up in her bed. The Bigfoot rock was vibrating on the night stand. She got up and threw clothes on, pulling her jeans over the ankle bracelet, grabbed and tucked the rock into a sweatshirt pocket. In a few minutes Nicole drove east on Highway 62, speeding alongside the Rogue River, quite sure she would know where to go.

Passing through Mazama Creek's Main Street she hit the accelerator harder leaving town, reentering the evergreen bordered two-lane highway, then pushed the gas again coming up on the unlit Buckhorn Tavern & Grill sign. She tried, but could not resist glancing over at the yellow tape wrapped around the surrounding trees, parking lot, and the Buckhorn. A dark wave rolled inside, she turned quickly away, *Could this be a trap? No, I'm going where I need to go,* she told herself, fighting away the fear.

Her sweatshirt pocket buzzed. Touching the gently humming river stone, Nicole turned left into a familiar campground and stopped where the paved road ended at the trail. Nicole got her flashlight, stepped out and ran, ignoring the December night air hurting her fingers, face and ears. Passing the windswept trees, the small flashlight allowed her to see enough to keep to the trail. After a time she slowed to a jog, sensing she must go deeper into the forest. This was their trail, Ian and Nicole's. Finding a comfortable pace she ran absent of thought, feeling pulled, alert to the sharp cold and any strange movements in the brush and trees. Rounding a bend she stopped suddenly. A single, flapping tail of yellow tape, one end tied to a tree, tightened her stomach. This was the place she left Ian.

Breathing hard, puffs of steam syncing her heart pounding, a dark mound just off the trail caught her attention. Shining her light, Nicole stepped forward until it became a heap of pine branches. She broke and ran, dropped to her knees and with trembling fingers reached, pulling back a bough. Ian looked up into her eyes and smiled.

# Chapter 41

## ORCHARD WORK

**THE QUIET BEAUTY** of the orchards on a windless, June afternoon was shattered by a ripping the starter chord on a chainsaw. Mrs. Larrsen waited several yards away, watching her new worker's handiwork send a sawdust blizzard and dead branches cascading together down to the base of the pear tree. When the saw was abruptly silenced she peered up into the leaves, finding the shadowy figure moving from branch to branch.

"Aren't you about due for a lunch break, Nicole?"

"Almost, Mrs. Larssen, this is the last one in this row. I just need to get that big dead branch right there."

"You be careful, sweetie."

"I am, thanks Mrs. Larssen," Nicole said while adjusting a sweaty, sawdust decorated bandana, then taking off and wiping clean her dark safety glasses. "Have you heard anything from Jason?"

"I talked to Kelly, he sent her a post card from San Diego. He wrote he likes looking at the ocean and is going to live there for a while."

"Oh, maybe the ocean will be good for him, Mrs. Larrsen, help him stop blaming himself."

"Lord I hope so, Nicole."

"Mom and I are praying for him, for all of us, actually. How's Kelly?"

"Ok, worried about Jason but she and her husband are happy he decided to stay at the Ranger station at Hood River. She says it's windy but the Columbia and the hills are pretty. Oh, and she just signed up to learn wind surfing. Is Ian doing any better?"

"He's getting stronger, but he kind of just stays inside, watching TV, playing video games. I keep trying though." Nicole noticed Mrs. Larrsen glance at the ankle bracelet and was grateful she did not ask about the case.

"How is Eric?"

"Better, his leg will never be the same, but his head is healing. He's back to work."

"That's good Mrs. Larrsen, glad to hear it."

Wedging her butt against the trunk and another thick branch, Nicole leaned back before pulling the starter rope. After the deadwood fell with a crash and as the dust cleared, Mrs. Larssen held up a brown bag and a water bottle. "Thank you for lunch, Mrs. Larssen," Nicole said while taking off the sunglasses and bandana. "You should climb up and join me."

"A little hot for me to be tree climbing, sweetie, I think our summer finally got here. Have you seen your friend?"

"I'm feeling like I'll see her today."

"I think she's been watching you for a time."

"Really, where?"

"Behind the cots on the other side of the ditch, being very still, watching you. We made eye contact and she didn't hide right away this time. I still can't get used to this. You're very brave, young lady."

"She would never hurt me, Mrs. Larssen."

"I'm heading in, please don't be out too long. Mr. Larssen will be back from town soon and he'll worry about you."

"Thank you again for my summer job, Mrs. Larrsen."

"Thank you for your good work, Nicole. The trees look great."

Climbing toward the top Nicole sat with a view across the pasture where the flowing, narrow irrigation canal separated the Larrsen's property from the wild fruit trees. Though excited for wondering what the afternoon in the forest would bring, she took her time eating the peanut butter and apricot jam sandwich and washing it down with cold water. Nicole used her lunch to prepare. Her eyes rested upon the apricot trees at the north edge of the wild orchard, standing with the taller evergreens as backdrop. *Just taste your lunch, breath, relax, stop thinking, just breath and listen. Please work through me Lord, help me respect and be grateful for this moment,* Nicole thought prayerfully while exhaling purposefully. Dropping her chin stretching her neck she felt the shoulder muscles unwind. After holding her chin at her chest for several seconds she looked up, narrowed her eyes and a sliver of luminescent purple surrounded by fuzzy sky blue appeared next to a tree trunk. *I see you!*

After enjoying her last bite and a good swig of water, Nicole ambled easily down the pear tree branches, dropped to the ground and walked across the pasture to the gate at the small wooden bridge. Stepping through the gate onto the bridge that for five generations had only been crossed by Larssen men and one old Indian medicine man, Nicole laughed to see the mother Bigfoot's toothy smile peeking out from behind the apricot tree.

# THE END

CPSIA information can be obtained
at www.ICGtesting.com
Printed in the USA
LVHW04s2057100918
589678LV00002B/35/P